A Charge of Angels

BOOKS BY L.D. CLARK

FICTION

The Dove Tree (1961)
Is This Naomi? and Other Stories (1979)
The Fifth Wind (1981)

CRITICISM

Dark Night of the Body (1964)
The Minoan Distance (1980)

A Charge of Angels

A NOVEL BY

L. D. CLARK

CONFLUENCE PRESS / 1987

Special thanks to the Idaho Commission on the Arts, whose assistance helped make this book possible.

This book is published by
Confluence Press, Inc.
Lewis Clark State College
8th Avenue & 6th Street
Lewiston, Idaho 83501

Distributed to the trade by
Kampmann & Company, Inc.
9 East 40th Street
New York, New York 90016

Library of Congress card: 86-072561
ISBN: 0-917652-49-5

Manufactured in the United States of America

9 8 7 6 5 4 3 2

FIRST EDITION

PART I

1

I don't know whe'er you'd call this a history or just what. I reckon if it was any history, it'd take in more'n just what's been happening to me this year of 1938 in two different necks of the woods. Powerful different they are too, these places. One of them's down home, and not a bad corner of the world to my way of thinking. The other one's this sorry little old pissant town I'm in now and just as soon not talk about. But I aim to jaw some about it anyhow—I have to, you might say, seeing as how I'm stuck here with nothing else to do.

I got run off from home, you see. And this two-bit burg is where I run to.

Now how did it all come about? I keep asking myself that over and over. That's why I feel like trying to set it all down in some kind of order. And besides that, if I can sort of keep myself occupied with the trouble I've done had and ain't got settled yet, maybe that'll steer me around some trouble I see coming up ahead. What's more, like I say, I've got to do something to keep from going crazy. I can't just cooter around up and down the streets of this dam place all the time, or just set here in this rented room and stare out of the window at the weatherboarding of the church-house across the street.

Still in all, I don't quite know where to commence. Up to about a hour ago I didn't have no idey of writing anything down. But something taken place then that made me more lonesome than I ever have been.

I'd been setting around studying about Ellen and home for the biggest part of the day—like I ever do anything else here lately!—and then I rushed off up to the post office to get there before the General Delivery window closed up, still hoping for that letter I guess Ellen ain't ever wrote. Not finding it I decided to walk off my misery up and down the streets. But then once when I got about a block off from the Frying Pan Cafe, making my second round of that territory, why all of a sudden a girl stepped out of the door of that place, just like she'd been waiting for that very second to show up so's to catch my eye—when as a matter of fact I'm satisfied she didn't even know I was alive.

It was about that time of the evening between sundown and good dark when you can see everthing as plain as you can in the daytime, seem like, and you don't realize at a first glance how your eyes can fool you—because, for a minute there, I could've swore that girl was Ellen.

All I done, right then, was go over to the curb and lean on a parking meter and take to watching the cars go past—the few they was out—not even looking at the girl as she walked on off in the other direction. Because of course I knowed it couldn't be Ellen—later on it turned out they didn't look anything at all alike—and I didn't want to be tricked any more'n I could help. The thing was, just seeing that girl at a distance brought back so much, and brought it back so fast, that I couldn't hardly stand it.

I reckon I must've been sort of afraid to look off after her too, just to be honest about it. Because I felt for all the world like following her, even walking right up to her and trying to get acquainted in some way or another.

But then, like I say, maybe if I stick to figuring out old trouble I won't get into any of it that's new.

Well anyhow, after I'd stood there again that parking meter for a little while, I headed out along the street the way I'd come from, not exactly knowing what I was up to, and on my way I happened to pass by a five-and-dime store where all these school tablets and pencils and crayons and stuff was piled up in the show-window, this being the time of year for school to start. And then, like I wasn't already feeling sorry enough for myself over Ellen and all that happened back home to cause me to get run out of the country, I commenced to studying about something else that only made matters worse. Here I was in the middle of my thirties, and now that it was turning fall again, with winter coming up, I thought how I was one year closer to the end of my life and how the time behind me had been so short, but still the days on ahead looked long and lonesome. On top of that the idey of getting along in years reminded me of Grandpa. I remembered how old and feeble he was when I started to school, and how he died that same year, and then how a lot later on in some of his belongings I come across a bunch of old tablets about like the ones in the show-window in front of me, old tablets all dingy and fleeking at the edges, where Grandpa had wrote and wrote, in a hand you couldn't hardly read, about what he'd done back in Civil War times. When I first laid eyes on them old tablets I made up my mind I'd puzzle them all out one of these days, and maybe have it typed up so later generations of the family could read it. Only up to now it looks like they won't be no later generations—not direct from me nohow, and

I don't know whe'er any of my brothers' kids'd ever take any interest in it or not.

But then I'm sorry to say I ain't ever done nothing about Grandpa's tablets. They're laying at the bottom of my trunk at home right this minute, I reckon. If I ever do go back there again, which don't look any too likely, that's one of the first things I mean to take care of, that bunch of tablets.

Now I wonder what made Grandpa write about hisself. Come to think of it, I believe he had to draw up a pretty long statement on his war service to go along with his pension application, and I reckon he just kep on from there. Of course, the difference between me and him is that what he wrote about was all settled and done with a long time ago. He must've been just entering on paper what he'd gone over a thousand times in his mind, repeating it for the last time, so to speak, before he died.

But that ain't my perdicament. Leastways I hope it ain't. I'm a long ways from being ready to die, lonesome as I am. And none of my problems ain't settled yet, not a single dam one of them.

But anyhow, to go on. I went right into that five-and-dime store, bought me some tablets and a little old cheap fountain pen and some ink, and then come on home.

But it wasn't no easy matter getting up to my room, at that. You see, ever since I been in this town, I been staying at Bee Coleman's rooming house. Bee runs a beauty shop here in town, besides renting rooms, and her old man, Boggs Coleman, he drives a taxicab. Now tonight I hadn't hardly got inside of the front door when here come Bee out of the kitchen and through the hall, and right in behind her, I'll swear, was that same girl I'd seen coming out of the Frying Pan Cafe: tall, dark blonde, solid, wearing a silk floweredy dress. It was the dress I knowed her by, and sure enough it was a good deal like one Ellen used to wear.

Good Godamighty! I thought. Is she staying here too?

Seeing as how I couldn't sneak past Bee, and didn't actually want to when I noticed the girl, I stopped and waited. Now Bee, once she sets in to talking she never quits. The worst of it is, she rattles on like she ain't sure of anything she says, and like if she ever could be sure she'd dry up. But she made me acquainted with the girl—her name turned out to be Dilly, if you can imagine such a ugly name for such a pretty girl—and then she went on about how windy it was during the day, and wanted to know if I'd heard about a car wreck north of town on the highway, and I don't know what all.

The girl she didn't say much, just stood off to one side like and looked from Bee over in my direction and back, smiling some, but seem like she had her mind on something else entirely.

I'll say it again: She's good-looking. I wonder what room of the house she's living in. I imagine the one the clerk from the hardware store just moved out of yesterday. Bee said she just come in today.

It sure is quiet in here. Getting late too. I reckon the girl—Dilly, if I have to say it—and Bee are both in bed. Boggs is on shift, won't be in, I don't expect, till away after midnight. Ever once in a while I stop writing and stare out of the window. You can't see nothing in the yard except what looks like the dark wrinkling up a little when the wind shakes the limbs on Bee's crape-myrtle bush. This street looks better in the dark, I must say that. The weatherboarding of the church-house across the way, that's so white in the daytime, is still light enough in the dark to catch the shadow from the leaves when that wind hits the trees overhead. Looks like the whole wall shakes, with shadows quivering over it ever which way. Two blocks down there where the nearest street lamp is, you can tell even at night how bald and dusty the yards are, with just a patch of dry grass ever here and yonder, and how narrow and rough that bridge over the creek is. You can look on down to that thick stand of live-oak trees blacker'n the rest of the night there behind the railroad station, and the hotel beyond that, with a couple of windows glaring. And nothing else can you see of the town but the lights glowing up and turning the sky kind of red above the trees and all around the hotel, like something was afire behind it. Not a soul in sight, nothing moving but the wind. While ago a car did drive along this street, with the whole town and the whole night to itself.

But I better quit just drifting along here and get down to business if I aim to. That ain't going to be easy, I see. To have any idey at all of what's going on now I've got to go back a right smart and work up slow to the present time.

So....I been here in this town about a month or such a matter, even if it does seem like a year. I don't know for sure how far off I am from home, because I ain't ever bothered to find out. When I come to a halt here I could just as well've gone on, even on to St. Louis or Chicago, away up north where some of my brothers live. But then I do know, all right, what it was that made me stop when I did. It was realizing I was futher off from home than I'd ever been before in my life, and seem like if I went on I'd soon be plumb out of the world—I mean out of the part of it that means something to me.

So I just got off the bus and called it quits.

For the time being, then, here I am. I can't go back home because that bastard Haley Blair fixed it up to where I had to leave the country. So what do I do next?

2

Well....When it all begun I was just another citizen down there around home, just plain Amon Lamb. I can remember that certain day mighty well—one Sunday at preaching it was, with me in the church-house like everbody else, right up there next to the pulpit where I ordinarily set. Brother Ike was about to wind up his sermon. But I hadn't been paying much attention to what he said. When you've heard a man preach as many times as I have Ike, he can't be saying much you ain't listened to a dozen times before.

I do remember what his text was, all right. It's one I memorized when I was little and never will forget:

For it is written, He shall give his angels charge over thee, to keep thee. And in their hands they shall bear thee up, lest at any time thou dash thy foot against a stone.

I do remember, besides, one thing Ike done. I can still see as clear as anything that big old hairy fist of his coming down hard on the pulpit. Or that is, he meant for it to hit the pulpit. But instead of that, it whammed right onto the Bible that was laying there, and kind of glanced off of it. He didn't hit it apurpose, that much I can tell you. Because you can talk about your Bible-pounding preachers all you want to, but you can't include Ike among them. He'll beat a pulpit nearly to pieces when he's in his best shape, but he'd just as soon take a whip to his grandma as lay a rough hand on the Bible. So his voice fell out of kelter when he realized what he'd done. But still it didn't faze him too much. In a second he was right back at it, in that snorting-like voice of his that works up louder and louder till I reckon it shakes the limbs on the postoaks a mile off.

And somewhere along about the time Ike made that bust, my mind wandered away back yonder to when I was a kid of a boy, twenty-five years ago, I guess. And plain in my memory stood Parson, my oldest brother, up there before the rest of us boys, behind that log pulpit we'd built down on the creek bank, Parson laying it out to us good and proper about sin and death and damnation. Of course, Parson wasn't nothing but his nickname, but once we'd tagged him with it we hardly ever called him by anything else, even after he growed up and all. Ma and Pap didn't take us to preaching much back then, but I reckon enough for Parson to get hisself initiated, as you might say. For it was all you could do to make him play anything else besides preaching. Being the biggest, he could euker us into doing whatever he taken a notion to. And we enjoyed the preaching, or the meeting, as we called it, might near as much as he did, me and the rest of my brothers.

We'd drag up some old logs and set them in a row like benches, and the one for a pulpit we'd prop up with sticks. And after that we'd all leave out in different directions and drift back in like folks coming to a regular meeting. As soon as we all got in a bunch, we'd act like we'd watched them do. You never seen the like of hand-shaking and "How're you, Brother So-and-So?" Somebody'd make out like they had a whole family of kids, camming them down and maybe giving one of them a slap. Somebody else'd fight around like they was having a hard time handling their team, hollering "Whoa!" at the top of their voice and mumbling a few cuss words about mules, eyeing around all the time to make sure the preacher wasn't in hearing distance.

Before long Parson'd stand up and call us to order, and from then on nobody couldn't say a word excepting "Amen," and Parson'd give you a cross-eyed look if you said that too much—except of course for the one of us that'd been picked out to set in the Amen Corner for that day. That was a special place Parson had right up next to the pulpit, and whoever set there was called "elder and deacon," and his job was to shower down on "Amen" ever time Parson let up for a second. Since they wasn't but four of us in the congregation, Parson wouldn't hear of letting more'n one party in the Amen Corner at a time, and that party was kep pretty busy, with no more help than Parson allowed him from the balance of the congregation....

Setting there that Sunday in the church-house with my eyes on Brother Ike, I seen ever move we used to make at them play meetings. Parson shouting, with some kind of sense when he could think of it, or just mouthing when he couldn't, working hisself up to a pitch where his face'd get all red and sweaty, and once in a while tears'd even come in his eyes, denouncing Satan's kingdom and all his works, and after us as hard as thunder to repent and be saved. When he wore hisself plumb out, he'd stand up there wiping his forehead with his shirttail and requesting Brother So-and-So to begin the song of invitation. Once that started, Parson had a hard time keeping us all from coming up and confessing at once. Or he did, that is, till he got us trained, allowing as how they wasn't no hurry about it, since we'd all have our chance before it was over with. He worked it out so the oldest one, next to him, would lead off—he said because the oldest one was the closest to the grave and didn't have as much time to spare as the rest of us....

And so, as I set there in the church-house that Sunday looking at Brother Ike, in my mind I seen Van marching up and taking Parson by the hand and looking down in the mouth, then Parson asking him to take a seat on the front row and bending over to talk real confidential-like to him for a little bit. Next come Anse's turn, and then Mac's. Me being the youngest, I always come last. I remembered us lined up there as still as fenceposts while Parson said a long prayer, and then all of us filing off down towards the creek to be baptized.

Now when I remembered the baptizings, I come might near laughing out loud. The first time we ever held a meeting Parson led us straight into the creek clothes and all and soused ever last one of us. It was summer, and Lord knows we spent enough time in the creek, but naturally without our clothes on. Parson had just got carried away with hisself and didn't think what he was up to till we all come out dripping wet, and wondering by now what Ma'd say. So we had to pull off our clothes—I was wearing a new pair of duckings that day, I recall—and run around in the sun waving them so they'd dry out a little before time come to go home for dinner.

But of course Ma found out about it anyhow, and you can bet she give us the devil.

Well, Parson was stumped by that one for a while. He wasn't about to baptize us naked, because he said that wouldn't be decent. And though he tried hard enough, he couldn't persuade Ma to give us some old clothes to use regular. But then Parson never let a problem bother him for long. He wouldn't tell us how he meant to get around it, but we soon surmised he had a way figured out. And when the next meeting time rolled around and we come to the place where we was supposed to be baptized, he headed a little ways off for a patch of tender young Johnson grass about hip-high. When the wind blowed over it, that grass made waves like the prettiest hole of water you ever seen. All the time going on with his praising and praying, Parson dipped us down in that grass and pulled us out, and he made it seem so real not a one of us cracked a smile. Oh, we got chiggers of course, and Parson called that a plague, said it was punishment for our sins. Even at the time it didn't seem right to me, that we'd be punished for our sins at the same time we was being baptized. But I didn't let on, because in such matters as that, Parson's word was the law.

And now to think, Parson's dead. That terrible winter when so many people in the community had the pneumonia, when Pap caught it and for a while there we thought he was a goner. All the boys was growed up and married by then, all but me. I was still at home, and Parson was the only one that lived close by. He was real good about setting up and helping tend to Pap, Parson was. I remember right well how red-faced and healthy-looking he was back then—let's see, he must of been twenty-two or three that year.

And then, before anybody hardly knowed how it come about, there was Pap setting up in a chair and Parson in the bed sinking faster'n you could imagine. He died less'n a week after he taken sick.

When Parson seen the river of life, I hope it made him think of the wind running green and tender over a field of young grass....

As I set there looking at Brother Ike that Sunday, I seen a world of other things too. I didn't make no effort to keep a count of them, but more'n I could write down in a week, and all of them crowding around in a matter of minutes. But two of them stood out in particular.

One had to do with swimming. Like any other bunch of boys, we used to scour the countryside. Not just me and my brothers, but a whole passel of us from the community at large. We had three or four swimming-holes scattered up and down the creeks and branches. Some of them it taken a couple of hours to walk to, of a Sunday after dinner, but I don't think a Sunday ever went by, in the summertime, but what we made it to at least one of them.

This particular time was later'n when we held the meetings. Parson, and it could be Van, was old enough by then to fly at the girls, so they didn't have much to do with us younger ones anymore. They used up their time hanging around houses where they was a girl or two. Me and Anse and Mac, though, and I don't know how many more—Cephas Bailey and Hap Carr and Ike hisself—we'd air out through the woods in a pack, pulling off elem bark to chew, climbing saplings all the way to the top and taking ahold and jumping out so they'd bend over to the ground with us. Most of them same boys, or men as they are now, was setting around me there in the church-house that Sunday, looking as pious as you please. You sure couldn't've told it by looking at Ike—beg pardon, I mean *Brother* Ike.

Anyhow, finally we'd get to one of the swimming-holes. The one I remembered right then was on the Monroe place. It was a dandy one, too, with grass and shade trees and a good-size sandbar at the shallow end, with one bank low for running into the water full-speed and the other one high for diving, the water deep all the way from a foot to over your head next to the dam. They was just one drawback. It was pretty close to old Jim Monroe's house, and it was a hard matter slipping in when he didn't want you to be there. Of course, it appeared to us like he might near always didn't want you there. Jim was friends with some folks from town, and if it so happened they meant to come out and swim that evening, Jim didn't want ever boy in the country down there muddying up his swimming-hole in advance. Then besides, Jim was accommodating enough to let two or three different denominations use that hole for baptizings, which for some reason they always set for Sunday evening about sundown, and it didn't look right to Jim for them to have to use stirred-up water.

Now Jim was deef, but you take a herd of boys swimming, even a deef man can hear them a hundred yards off, which is about how far it was up through the copse to Jim's house. Jim he had a pointed nose with a lot of little scabs on it, and one of the reddest faces I ever seen—so red, I mean to tell you, that you could just about see it blazing among the postoaks when he come faunching down from the house to run us off.

But if it was a day when we knowed Jim didn't care, we could make all the noise we felt like making. We'd work up quite a sweat walking through the woods to get there. Directly we'd come in sight of the place and stampede like a bunch of yearlings—last one in's a rotten egg, and all that cutting up. Scamper and splash and dive and rastle. Out on the bank and chase one another buck-naked till we wore ourselves out. Back to splashing and diving and thrashing around and ducking each other.

Seems to me I seen a good many of them times there in the church-house while Ike was charging on towards the finish of his sermon, but one time come out clearer'n all the rest. Right down below the dam was a thick patch of brush and vines, with enough trees sticking up to shade everthing, and a clean sandbar under them sloping down from one side, making a kind of a hidden hollow. That day we'd made it by somebody's watermelon patch, and after we'd swum around for a while we carried our watermelon down to that hollow. All of us being naked and our pocketknives back in our britches pockets, we busted the melon with our fist and got some of the meat so sandy you couldn't eat it. But they was still enough to go around, and we made out our meal with the entire gang of us squatted around gouging into the rinds with our fingers, squirting juice all over ourselves. And when they wasn't nothing left but rinds, we taken to breaking them up and throwing them at one another till the pieces got too little to even do that with, and all of us was as sticky as glue.

Then, with Ike in the lead, everbody made a dash for the swimming-hole to wash off, like a tribe of wild men gone berserk. Me, I was still looking around trying to find some pieces of rind big enough to throw at somebody, and before I knowed it they'd all done run off and left me.

I was about to tear out after them, when all of a sudden a strange thing brought me to a standstill. Naked and free, I seen how the sun broke up, in the big tree limbs overhead, glittering up there but not down here where I was, my spot being in a dim light that went green or brown according to the moving of the leaves high up in the breeze. And as I looked sharp-eyed in ever direction in that dim light, I seen rotten creepers and briar bushes and bloodweeds and mustang grapevines as big around as snakes. I seen the sand tore up where we'd scuffled, the dark stains where juice had spilled, and seeds scattered all around. Everthing showed up in that dim light just like it might at the very beginning or the very end of the world. And if you didn't either run off from it or discover some charm to make it change, just the way it looked would be enough to do away with you altogether.

So I didn't tarry. I lit out after the rest of the bunch.

But just the same, that evening before I went home I sneaked off from the other boys, went back to that hollow, collected up all the little pieces of rind I could lay eyes on, dug a hole in the sand and buried them—all except for one, a pretty good-size piece with some meat left in it, a piece that had fell in the weeds out of sight and hadn't been used up in the battle. That one I propped up again a big old elem tree heavy with grapevines.

Because whatever it was that give the hollow that certain kind of a light, I had to begin somewhere in finding out how to charm it.

I said back yonder a little that two memories stood out strong that day in the church-house. But they went together, and this is how it was. In my other memory I was in the schoolhouse, and it was a year or two after the watermelon day at the swimming-hole. I was all slouched over my desk supposed to be reading my lesson. It was away down in the evening, and the sunshine coming in at the window was ripe and swarming with dust. Right between me and the window set one of the Bradshaw twins, I didn't know which one, because I never could tell them apart. They had real black hair and faces as white and rosy as any you ever seen. The way she looked right then—Mary or Sherry—between me and the evening sun, made me feel like I'd never be able to move a muscle again.

Not long before that I'd got ahold of a book full of stories about gods and goddesses and satyrs and nymphs. The teacher we had then give it to me, because she knowed how well I liked to read stories and she said that book was better'n *Ranch Romances,* or the James Oliver Curwood books I checked out of the county library whenever I got the chance. It *was* a better book, too.

As well as I can remember, I never had till that minute seen any kind of a similarity between the stories I'd read and what went on around me. But there set Mary—or Sherry—gazing off towards the blackboard, her long black hair in spiral curls so rich and lovely thick it made your stomach sink. Ever here and there, full as her hair was, you could see little spots of her neck or cheek. The mellow sunshine run all over her curls and broke up shining here and yonder. She was gazing off the way you do when you're deep inside of yourself, when all you are or ever will be flows along through you in the blood of your veins. Her face was shining as soft as the light does when it settles down through high limbs and lays in patches on still water.

All at once, it appeared like I was seeing a nymph before my eyes, only that wasn't all. That light in the hollow below the swimming-hole dam and that light in the window poured together in my mind and lit up Mary or Sherry and also us boys deep in the thicket of that hollow.

And then it was like I was all alone on the bank of the stream and she was swimming naked through the water, and she was a nymph tolling a boy into the water to love him and drownd him....

What brought me back to the church-house, and to myself, was Ike finishing up with his sermon. First thing I noticed he'd quit talking and was spreading his handkerchief out on the floor to get down on his knees and pray.

Old Ike. I've heard this one and that one criticize him, on the sly, for making sure he don't dirty the knees of his britches when he prays. In their line of reasoning, he ought to be too concerned about what he means to say to the Lord to worry about a little dust on the floor.

And so the rustling and stirring commenced all around, men kneeling down, feet shifting and all, clothes swishing the way they will in a quiet church-house. Me, I always just drop my chin right where I am and shut my eyes. These people that make a big show out of praying ain't no different, for my money, from that Pharisee or whatever he was that done all his praying on the sidewalk.

Ike taken his time about praying when he got going on it. I finally opened my eyes and looked out from under my eyebrows.

And you know what! That Haley Blair—he was planted straight across the house from me, facing me, the way they had the benches arranged—he'd been watching me all that time. As soon as I caught him at it he looked down. So then he couldn't've been doing much praying in spite of that show-off position he was in. There he was down on one knee with the other crooked out in front of him and his elbow on that one and his face in his hand—except he'd been watching me out from under his hand. You could've swore he was just waiting there for somebody to come up and take his picture, the shitass!

But don't let me get started on him. If I do, I'll be setting here writing all night long.

3

I sure must've been tired out when I finally got to bed last night. Because I went right off to sleep without a bobble and I didn't stir till after daylight. As a usual thing the wind wakes me up along in the night, and I lay there pop-eyed for two hours at a stretch sometimes.

Oh how I hate that wind. As long as I been here it's blowed from the south. And home being south, that wind brings just enough reminder of home with it to set me off to thinking how I despise being stuck here.

God, how I wish it would come a norther!

Yep, wind and sand and dam sorry people—that's all you can make out of this town. Ratty little old place made out of shacks looking like they was throwed away from making a better place—except for the hotel and the few brick buildings around the courthouse square, and they ain't a whole lot to look at. And them red-dust plains coming right up to the town on all sides, and the wind never slowing down one bit on its way through, like it's carrying the plains in the south on north and never bringing them back.

So there you have it. I felt pretty good when I got up. But by the time I'd walked down to the Frying Pan and eat some of that slop old Bick cooks up, and then back by the post office and still didn't find no letter from Ellen, I come on to this room in about as bad a humor as ever.

One thing I better explain before I go any futher. I see I been making it sound like I'm cut aloose from home altogether. And of course really I am. What I mean is, though, a day or two after I hit here, I put in a long-distance phone call to W. D. Clagg, the lawyer in Milcourt that's always handled the little bit of legal business I ever had. I told him to let Ma and Pap know where I was, and—dam her hide—Ellen. Ma does write now and again, and mails her letters in town, but I don't answer, for I wouldn't put it past that mail carrier to blab to Haley Blair about where I am.

Hold on a minute....

That was Dilly leaving the house. She come out of the front door and headed down the street. I set here and watched her out of sight. She was wearing that same floweredy dress she had on last night, with big petals of a grape-purple color that wrap ever whichaway around her curves. She sure made a pleasing sight, and for once the wind come in handy, pushing the cloth against her body. Nobody else on the street but her stepping out slow and graceful, real tall, in front of the white weatherboarding of that little church-house across the way, past that rusty lamp post and the windows of the houses futher on, past the scraggly lawns and dusty flowerbeds and scrawny hedges. The flowers on her dress looked fresher'n the real ones she was walking along next to....

But then let me get back to what I'm supposed to be doing.

To pick up where I left off that Sunday, I come out of the church-house with the rest of them and santered over to my car. Being as how I nearly always stood around and talked for a while, it might've looked funny I didn't that day. But I was all caught up again in the memories I'd been having, and I didn't want to take no chance on losing them. They floated around me and ahead of me like I had to follow them, so I climbed in my car and drove straight on home.

When I got there, Ma and Pap was setting on the front porch waiting dinner on me. Ma stood up the minute she seen the car spinning up the lane. It felt good to see the two of them setting there, even if they are getting so old, and Ma's practically blind with the cataracks. But then her bad eyes don't keep her from finding her way around the house and cooking a good meal's vittles. She knows everthing by touch, anyhow, and she can see as well as hear a whole lot better than she makes you think she can. Like you can take a pan out from among the cook-vessels and say, 'Ma, what's this?' and she'll touch it and say right off, 'That's the aluminum stewer your Pap give me for Christmas the year it snowed all day.'

"Step on it, son. You're just in time for dinner," Pap sung out as I was climbing out of the car. And then he set there chuckling, which is one of

Pap's favorite pastimes. Pap don't like to go nowhere much. He never did. He'd just as soon set in his rocking chair on the front porch and puff his pipe and devil Ma and chuckle about it till they carry him off to the graveyard. And I'm satisfied if they's a place to set still in the hereafter, Pap'll find it. I've heard him say to Ma I don't know how many times, whenever she's pestering him to take her to some community gathering, 'Next time you marry a man, you better inquire into his going qualities.' Then Ma'll rare back her head like she's fixing to snort and say, 'What do you mean, next time I marry a man?' And that sets off another one of their quarrels that don't never seem to end but in the long run don't amount to much.

"I swear, Pap, you ain't budged a inch since I left!" I said as I walked up on the porch.

"Nor don't aim to neither, son. Take a seat."

"Better wash, I reckon."

Ma was stirring around the kitchen and dining room, pretty fast for a woman her age with bad eyes. The pots and pans was sure jumping when I come through on my way to the washstand on the back porch.

"Well, if it ain't Ma!" I said, like I was surprised, and patted her on the shoulder.

"Get out yonder and wash your face and hands and don't tromp around in here under my feet."

Anybody that ventures into Ma's kitchen can expect to be treated like a kid, no matter how big nor how old they are. I agg her on just to hear her, because all that snapping sure sounds funny coming from somebody that ain't as big as a minute.

Oh me, Lord alone knows when I'll ever see Ma and Pap again.

So I finished washing and all of us went in and set down to the table. Pap mumbled a little grace. You can't never hear nothing in it but 'Lord' and 'amen,' he says it so fast and it's so short anyhow.

And then we dipped in.

I sure did put it away, let me tell you. You take when it's spring like that—Lord, it was just this last spring, too—when everthing you touch or see or even smell makes you think of crops growing and life abounding, you can eat like the very devil, especially when you're sinking your teeth into Ma's fried chicken and fresh tomatoes and okra and black-eyed peas and green onions, not to mention chocolate pie and pound cake.

But if that makes me hungry, the thought of my next meal in this town only makes me sick, having to gnaw on a tough old chicken-fried steak and bolt down some old pasty mashed potatoes and pale-looking canned peas.

Christ! That Frying Pan Cafe turns my stomach!

We hadn't been eating but a minute when Pap spoke up, "How was the bunch at preaching today?"

I swallowed a mouthful and said, "All right, I reckon. I didn't hang around long."

"What made you skin out so fast?" Ma asked, and then she was up and struck out for the kitchen before I could give her any answer. She'll do it ever time, grab a bite or two and run off to the kitchen to take up some more vittles.

I sort of hollered after her, "I was too durned hungry, that's why."

Which really wasn't so, but I knowed she'd like that for a comeback.

"I don't see what anybody gets out of standing around yapping, anyhow," Pap put in. "I don't object to talking my head off in my own house, or at a neighbor's once in a great while, but I'd about as soon take a licking as hang around a church-house all starched up and jabber about the weather. I guess old Kiss-my-foot Blair was present."

"What do you reckon? Of course he was."

Pap made some growling remark about Haley Blair, but I didn't halfway listen. For I didn't want to get started on *him.* I don't want to dwell on him now neither, because I'll have plenty to say about him when the time comes. But I guess I at least ought to set down one or two things. The Lambs and the Blairs, you see, have kind of had it in for one another for a long time. Grandpa Lamb and Old Man Jim Blair served together for a while in the Civil War, and they was regular cronies. Then later on they had a falling-out over some cattle or something—I even heard over a dog, but I don't know just what. Anyway, ever since then, the Lambs and the Blairs have sort of stayed out of one another's way.

To my mind, though, Haley Blair is the only hateful one of the bunch. He's a right smart older'n I am, ten years at least, so when I was a little kid he was a young fellow like. I'll always remember the first run-in I ever had with him. At the time he was keeping company with Lissie, the first woman he married. One Sunday when he was over there at her folks' house sparking, Ma and Pap and the whole bunch of us happened to stop in for a visit. Lissie she always thought I was just about *it,* and I thought the same of her. She was along in her late teens and fixing to get married, and I was eight or nine. She never passed up a chance to grab and hug me, or to give me some little something, or comb my hair, or just talk and talk to me. If they wasn't any other boys around to devil me about it, I hung out after her ever minute I could.

That Sunday her and Haley had one room of the house to theirselves, though it was right next to the one where all the rest of her folks and ours was. Him and her was looking through some old picture albums. I'd sneak in there like I wanted to see the albums too, when all I really wanted to do was stand as close as I could to Lissie's chair. When Ma'd discover I was gone she'd call out sharp-like, "Amon, get yourself back in here!" And

I'd mind her, yes, but just as soon as I seen another opportunity I'd head right back in there. The last time I went in that room, just before Ma got enough of it and called me off and threatened to wear me out if I didn't mind her, Haley he threatened me in a way that scared me a whole lot more'n Ma had. Catching Lissie not looking, he took ahold of my arm and commenced to squeezing it, not enough so I'd yell out and give him away, butenough to hurt. Worst of all, though, was the look he give me. It was cold and despisable, like he'd just as soon as not keep on gripping my arm till he cut off the circulation and caused me to get blood poisoning and die. Thinking of that in the wild way a kid will, I want you to know I stayed out of his reach for the rest of the day....

Pap hadn't much more'n got out his remark about Haley there at the dinner table when Ma chimed in: "Listen here, Mr. Lamb," coming down hard on the "mister," which she don't ever call Pap unless she's about to sail into him, "if I didn't have no more consideration about me than to wallow around home ever Sunday morning when they's other people in the family that'd like to go to preaching, I wouldn't criticize them that did go, Haley Blair or no matter who!"

"I reckon them that wants to go can, and them that don't can stay home." Pap said it like he hoped that was the end of the matter but knowed it wouldn't be.

Ma bridled up. "That'd be a pretty out, now wouldn't it? Me running off to church of a Sunday morning and leaving my old man at home!"

Ma's got set ideys about a woman not going places without her husband, and she won't hardly ever break them, even to go to preaching and Sunday school.

Well, they went at it from there. We finished up our dinner, and just as I was about to get up from the table, Ma interrupted her spat with Pap long enough to throw out her usual Sunday evening question: "I expect you're heading out to see Miss Ellen."

I swear, Ma can ask the same question in the same words, at regular times, like she ain't already asked it a thousand times before. With that particular question she always comes down hard on the "miss." I'm satisfied if you counted them, you'd find out Ma uses "mister" and "miss" more times hateful than she does respectful.

But that time I fooled her. "Who?" I said, and looked at her hard, even if I was grinning. She shut her mouth tight and clapped them eyes on me for a second, like they'd bore a hole right through me, then she got up without saying another word and begun to clear off the table. Me, I got out of there while the getting was good. And durned if she wasn't back to jowering with Pap before I'd made it to the front porch.

I set down in Pap's old cowhide rocker, meaning to get up and give it to him as soon as he come out and wanted it. He didn't come, though, and from the way they sounded, it appeared to me like him and Ma would be at it for some time to come. I couldn't make out what they was saying, nor I didn't try. Like it was with Ike's sermon, it couldn't've been something I hadn't heard before.

Ma'd been right, of course. I was supposed to go over to Ellen's. But the fact was, I didn't feel much like it, and that was strange in itself. The thing I always done, the first chance I got, was make a beeline for Ellen's house. But now after about ten minutes of thinking about going, and telling myself I better get ready, all I done was creep over to the front-porch cot and flop down on it. But I wasn't fixing to take no nap, because I wasn't sleepy, just sort of lax in my arms and legs, with my heart thumping slow and powerful.

That day the woods was hazy, the fields laid stretched out thinking about the plants growing in them. It must've been a Sabbath like the one when Christ and his disciples walked through the grain and stripped off handsful of it to eat. The sun itself looked lazy. Grasshoppers flew up out of the weeds and come down a little futher on, ticking their wings as they went. Katydids, mockingbirds, even once in a while a frog down on the branch—you could listen to all of them, didn't have to pick out one at a time. When the world's like that, you get the feeling it's a part of you, like your blood could circulate away out as far as you can notice anything and bring it all back to where your heart keeps thumping strong.

A full hour passed, I'm satisfied, before I come out of it. And when I did, it was all at once. I set up so quick it made my head swim. I must've been asleep, after all, but I wouldn't swear to that. I concluded I'd had a dream, all right, or more like several dreams. I just couldn't remember a thing about them. Only I did have, in the strongest way imaginable, a feeling that something big and maybe terrible and maybe wonderful was about to happen, something I dreaded and still wanted to see in the worst way. It seemed like a whole crowd of mighty dreams had come in close to me, so many I couldn't bring them all to life nor even count them. If my blood circulated as far away as that world, the dreams might drink it. All I could do, for the time being, was run away from these many dreams by waking up, or at least setting up, as fast as I could.

Ma and Pap's voices had quietened down some. Pap must've been back in the kitchen helping her wash the dishes.

No matter whe'er I wanted to or not, I was going to make myself dress up and go over to Ellen's.

In the few minutes while I was in my room sprucing up, Ma and Pap planted theirselves on the front porch, and when I come out Pap was firing up his pipe and Ma was stitching on something. They was still quarreling, but they hadn't got no piece from where they'd started out. Ma was saying, "If I didn't get in after you once in a while, you'd never so much as set foot off of the place."

And Pap's comeback was, "A man's got something else to do besides gad around all over the country."

Going past in a hurry, I said, "I'll see y'all sometime tonight."

"You watch out," said Ma, like I never had been gone from home before.

It's a good little ways from our house down to the county road, and the ruts of the lane're deep sand, so you have to watch your business herding a car down it or you're liable to get stuck. Driving along the lane and not studying about anything in particular but steering, all of a sudden a thought struck me that I didn't know where it come from at first. It was about that big old monument in the graveyard close to our place. It was the kind of a thought you can't talk back to, and so I thought Ellen would have to wait a little: I just had to drive by that graveyard.

It didn't take me but a minute to figure out, neither, why it was I wanted to see that monument: it had to do with Ike's sermon about jumping off of the temple.

To get to the graveyard you have to turn north off of the county road about a half a mile down east of our house and follow a rough lane down across a branch where the ruts are all full of chugholes, then you climb a hill over some bad sideling places and end up on a knoll all thick with trees and brush except for a couple of rocky acres where the graves are, and that's usually growed up in sprouts and weeds. Because nobody buries there nor takes care of the place anymore. None of the Lambs is buried there—we always bury at New Canaan—and I hadn't been around there in a year or two. The only reason I ever had for going was that big old tombstone, which I taken a big attraction to when I was right little. I used to think it was like the Rock of Ages when I was too young to know what that meant except from the song, or to know how the tombstone got there.

It's a great big block of granite around seven foot tall and I don't know how big asquare, four foot or so at least. I recollect I was pretty good-size before I could reach from one corner to another. It's flat and polished on all four sides, with a rounded-out pillar at each corner like they was needed to hold the roof up. It's got a regular roof like on it too, done up in the shape of a pyramid with a right steep pitch, except the peak of it's been chipped away, leaving a rough flat place on top. In later years, after I'd read the stories that turned Mary or Sherry into a nymph, I realized that tombstone was supposed to be shaped like the Greek temples I seen pictures of in that book about the gods and goddesses. Naturally I knowed any temple on the order of this one couldn't be like the one in Jerusalem the Devil had tempted Christ to jump off of—I knowed it, but that didn't make no difference, because that verse kep drifting around in my head.

Around the bottom of that monument they's a ledge in two or three banks, like steps only narrow. I used to walk around and around on them, trying to keep my balance so I wouldn't have to step off on the ground when I come to one of the pillars. I'd flatten out again that shiny wall of granite like they was a thousand-foot drop below me. Later on I finally got to where I could climb that monument too, grunting and straining around till I made it to the top. The first time I done that, I had to stay all evening because I was scared to come down. Pap come and got me about dark and give me a whipping for laying out from home and worrying them all to death.

At one time or another, I've heard all about that stone. It was put there more'n twenty years before my time. Some Blair, I forget who exactly, had his wife to die in childbirth, and the baby along with her. Him and her both being young and that their first baby, it hit him pretty hard. I've heard tell he went crazy for a few days—Pap says he did—wandering around in the woods and calling out her name like he believed she was just lost and not dead. Pap said the nights was awful quiet while the man was out there, like the whole country was listening. I thought it must've seemed like the man in the Bible crying out in the tombs and cutting his flesh with stones. Pap said the man's voice would squall out once, and then you couldn't do nothing but set and listen for it again. Pap said he heard a panther scream one time that sounded as human as that man did. Only the man's voice was scarier because you *knowed* it was supposed to be human.

Now that man was well off, had lots of land and plenty of money. And he was so young it looked to him like he never would get over losing his wife. And so he sent all the way to Georgia for the right kind of granite for a tombstone, had a slab of it shipped over on a flatcar all by itself. Then he hired a stoneworker that chiseled on it for a long time. It was a curiosity, Pap said, like a sideshow come to town. For people would go down to the railroad siding there in Milcourt and stand around and look on while the stoneworker chipped away. And they'd all speculate, too, on how Blair meant to get that monstrous big thing out to the graveyard, which was a long ways off from the railroad, and in them days they wasn't no trucks nor even any very good roads.

He hired a whole lot of men for several days to do the moving. They slid the monument off of the flatcar onto some kind of a platform, and worked that along on log rollers with three or four teams of mules atugging at it for all they was worth. The men cleared off a big swath of timber in some places, so they wouldn't have to go around the road, which really wasn't wide enough anyhow, and I reckon they cut off several miles thataway. Finally they had to call in a steam engine to finish the job. Pap said it was the first one he'd ever seen like that, a kind of an old tractor-like outfit that looked bunglesome to handle. Said they set it out in the pasture down there below the graveyard and hooked a cable to the stone and drug it across the last branch, then had to fuddle around for a day or two clearing off timber before they could snake the monument up to the top of the knoll and set it in place.

But that wasn't the end of the matter. Blair got it in his head he still hadn't done enough for his dead wife. He wanted to have a statue carved of her, but his stoneworker quit on him, and he went and hired another one that wasn't much account. Only seem like they couldn't get no more of that special granite, or Blair was in too big a hurry, one. And so this second stoneworker talked him into using sandstone. When he'd finished carving out a figure of her about natural size, nothing would do but Blair had to have it mounted on top of the monument. That's how come the peak of it to be flattened out.

That statue I never did see. Pap said it didn't last no time after it was stuck up there. Said it was the sorriest rock he ever seen. The moss taken right to it, and inside of a few years the rain had ruined the face of it. It wasn't long in falling down neither, not being put up with nothing but a little cement, and the fall of course broke it all to pieces.

But the worst part of it was, by that time they wasn't nobody around to see after it. For Blair had already done what nobody would've thought he'd do a few years earlier. He sold out and moved off to another state, married another woman and set up housekeeping all over again.

Well, then I reckon somebody got tired of seeing the pieces of statue laying around and gathered them up and hauled them off. Or I guess it could be they all sunk in the ground. The only sign the statue had ever been there, when I come along, was some little scraps of concrete on top of the monument that I used to fleek off and throw just to see how fur I could send them.

But I'd been told so much about it I had a picture of that statue in my mind. I seen it all toppled and broke with the head about half buried in the dirt. Sometimes I seen it just settling in the ground, and sometimes just being dug up, like when you find a wore-out doll's head or a piece of a china girl around some old house-place....

I hadn't much more'n got to the graveyard, that Sunday, before I was ready to leave. For I knowed now I'd gone over there to find some way to fit together the memories I'd had in the morning, and them with that text of Ike's sermon, and not finding a way to do all that made me plumb gloomy. So I left out right straight, made it back to the main road, and started on towards Ellen's.

Now I just don't know when I decided to do it, but what I done next was not to go to Ellen's yet but to turn off on a different road and go three or four miles out of the way so I could drop by that old Monroe swimming-hole without having to drive past Ellen's to get there. The way I circled around, I come in from the east.

They's a long lane running between barbwire fences that you have to take to get down close to the swimming-hole. The only house in sight from where you pick up the lane is Brother Ike's, up a slope like and about a quarter of a mile or so away. I didn't have nothing to hide, but I did wish that house wasn't there.

I say Ike's was the only house. I'm not counting that old Mt. Zion church that's been standing vacant for years. It's right where the lane starts, inside of a wire gate now, because the grounds of it has been fenced into the pasture. A terrible big congregation of Holy Rollers used to have it, and when they'd hold a meeting in the summertime out under the trees, you could hear them singing and shouting all over the country.

But it was awful quiet now, and the roof was caved in. I was about as glad to move on past it as I had been to leave the graveyard.

The lane hadn't been drove over in some time, so the sand was deep in the ruts. Along the center hump the sprouts was growed up high enough to scrape on the running gear. More'n once I was sure I'd get stuck in that old crawly sand and have to stay there till Ike come down with his tractor and pulled me out. Lucky for me that gate at the fur end of the lane was down. If I'd had to stop and open it, like as not I wouldn't've been able to start up again.

I come out in some open woods, parked my car under the first handy postoak, and stepped down to look around. Being as they wasn't no underbrush at that place, I could see all the way over to the old Monroe house on my left hand, and all the way down to the swimming-hole on the right. Nobody lived in that house anymore. Jim had been dead for several years, and his old lady was staying in Milcourt with one of the boys and his family. Still it was a curious thing seeing everthing so silent when I'd imagined it so noisy, with us boys hollering and Jim hollering at us. I didn't even see no signs that anybody'd been around the place at all. The land was rented out for pasture, all right, but I reckon the man didn't come down to see about his stock much during the warm time of the year. A little ways down among the trees, I did see an old feed trough and a real white and shiny salt rock about half licked up.

I thought about Lot's wife and a chill run down my back.

For a long time I just stood there. Till directly I said to myself, out loud, "I'll walk up and look around the old house-place." And off I went. But not far. Because I watched the windows and walls inching up to meet me, like they was pushing back the trees on either side of them. Then I seen the porch was leaning and most of the window lights was busted out. Windows make you think of eyes, anyhow, even when the people that live in the house are just gone from home for a little while. But they sure do when a house is altogether unlived in, with nothing inside to look out but what used to be there years ago.

So I whirled right around and headed out for the swimming-hole.

The dam was broke, had been for I don't know how long. It was about all you could do to make out where the pond part of the hole had been. One bank was all eat out by flood waters, and the other one was filled in heavy with sand. The only thing left was a kind of a gash with the water running narrow and clean through it, over some gravel.

I was a little bit scared to go on to the hollow and the thicket. But anyway I did go. You might say I creeped up on it, walking leery and my heart beating like anything.

Since the old days the branch had changed course considerable, leaving the thicket futher off to one side. The brush and trees was if anything thicker than ever, and all covered with a regular mat of rattan and mustang vines. The kerkle burrs and ironweeds and bloodweeds growed thicker, had turned the place into a jungle sure enough. It wasn't too easy picking a way in, but I pushed and tromped on the vegetation, keeping a eye out for crawfish holes and water moccasins. Once I got inside, I seen the thicket still left one open space in under a big elem—I think the same one where I set the watermelon rind. With the undergrowth hemming me in all around, and that same brown and green light filling the space from the sand to the treetops, I got so faint and dizzy I had to set down on a log, snakes or no snakes.

I stayed real still for a long time. My dizzy spell passed off and instead I begun to sweat. But directly that quit too, and I wasn't nothing but limp and drowsy, couldn't've moved nomore than if I'd've been paralyzed.

The old days was still there, and to see them plain I didn't have to make no attempt to remember—the boys freed out of their clothes and rampaging up and down the branch, the watermelon rind, the big well of green and brown light. And with all that come Mary or Sherry in the schoolhouse sun, the broke-up statue I'd never seen, the baptizings in the creek and the green grass rippling like water. All these memories spun slow and crowded in together, stronger'n the dreams I'd fought off when I drowsed on the porch. And I rested, under the thick shadow they made, half uneasy and half glad, in the wellshaft of brown and green light.

Then something moved. It could've been a rabbit, or even a snake, but it didn't sound like neither one. The fact is, I don't remember hearing anything. Just a sort of a vibration touched the air and slipped over to me where I set. I had my arms folded on my knees and my head my arms. The back of my neck, bared up to the sky, commenced to tingling like something or somebody was breathing on it.

It's a wonder to me, now, that I didn't jump up and bolt out of there. But it never occurred to me to do that right then. It could be I passed out for a minute, but no use asking myself questions in terms of time. All I can call to mind is being far away in a funny kind of a half-sleep, and that soft breathing on the nape of my neck, and that sinking like when you're falling, close to the end of a dream.

When I finally did stand up and put my legs to work, I went like a sleepwalker, not hardly daring to draw a breath of my own till I was away from that hollow and that thicket and back out in the open....

Well, here it is I've put in the morning and the biggest part of the evening at writing this, didn't even stop to eat dinner. And now then I'm as hungry as the dickens. Even what old Bick dishes out might taste good.

I'm kind of wondering, too, what happened to Dilly. She ain't come back home yet. Reckon she's got a job? Or could it be she just likes to hang out someplace uptown?

I wonder where.

4

Well, I found Dilly all right. I run on to her at the cabstand—which don't look to me like much of a place for her to hang out, though it ain't none of my business, of course.

Now I don't aim to spend a whole lot of time, in this history or what you may call it, with writing about her. The main thing is to stay with matters that taken place back home. But I think I will just kind of mull over what happened last night. That might help me forget about it.

Right after I quit writing yesterday evening, I went to the Frying Pan and eat, even halfway enjoyed it. Bick's old french fries wasn't quite as soggy as usual, and the fried shrimp didn't taste like they'd been away from the ocean for more'n a year or two. It was just about sundown when I got done eating and stepped out of the place. As I was passing in front of the post office, the street lamps up and down the main stem ever one come on at once, two rows of real pale globes all of a sudden lining out ahead of me towards the west and fading out again the dusty sky that still burned so fierce up above where the sun had just gone out of sight. Some cars had their headlamps on, the neon had set in to jumping and playing whichever way you looked. Being as it was the night for the first football game at the high school, the main street was livelier'n usual. Two or three carloads of boys and girls rolled by, whooping and hollering. I met maybe a half a dozen people walking, between the time I left the Frying Pan and the time I come to the northeast corner of the courthouse square.

At the corner of the square I stopped, wondering which way to turn. I was looking for Dilly without exactly admitting to myself I was. What I finally done was make the trip all the way around the square. Wasn't nothing open, now, but the town's other cafe, a drugstore and the picture show. She wasn't in neither one of the first two, and I was stopped in front of the signs at the show trying to decide whe'er the picture playing there would be of any interest to her or not, when it hit me that I was a pretty foolish kind of a character if that was all the clue I could rake up. So I left the square, then, and went on around to the cabstand. I thought I might as well drop in and see Mrs. Armbruster, but I sure didn't expect to find Dilly there.

But anyhow she was there, setting and talking to Mrs. Armbruster, the lady that does the dispatching. I didn't see Dilly at all till I was already inside of the door, and I'm satisfied the look on my face give me away to Mrs. A., hard as she is to fool.

"Good evening, good evening," I said, as feisty as I could make it. Then I flopped down in an old chair next to Mrs. A.'s desk, like I was used to making myself at home, which in a way I am, because Mrs. A. is one of the few people I talk to regular around here. Her boy drives a cab, a boy that's awful young—around seventeen, I guess—for her to be as old as she is. She looks to be close on to seventy, and she works at the cabstand, she tells me, just so she can keep a eye on her boy and help him steer clear of trouble with women. But that's a good one, because the boy don't never listen to her, and she can't seem to make him. He's already mixed up with two or three women, as it is, and Mrs. A. she'll complain to me about it, but as for anything else she ever does or can do, I don't know what that would be.

Dilly didn't say nothing. She did look at me and smile, though, friendly enough. Mrs. A. said to me, "Say, where you been the last day or two? I ain't seen you."

"Not much of any place. Home most of the time."

Just saying that word made a pang run through me.

"Home?" She perked up and looked expectant. You see, I've told her a little bit about my situation, and she's always willing to find out some more.

"I just mean the rooming house."

"Oh? And you've got to where you call that home, have you?"

"Might as well. Seems to be the only one I've got."

She kind of snorted. "That's a windy if I ever heard one."

Me, I was trying to give her warning looks to hush her mouth. No telling what kind of a notion Dilly was forming of me.

"You two know one another?" blurts out Mrs. A. all of a sudden.

"Yes, we got acquainted yesterday," says Dilly, bright-like.

"Why, that's right," says Mrs. A., like she'd just come up on some hellacious big discovery, "both of you are staying at Bee's, ain't you?"

I got kind of irritated at the sly way she said it, though I don't know what I cared for. I sure ain't on the lookout for another woman, even if me and Ellen have broke up—I reckon you'd call it broke up.

Hell, I don't know! But I do know she could write me a letter—if she just wanted to.

Dilly! God, I wish she had another name—any kind of an old nickname would do.

Anyway, there she set in that junky old cabstand, on a broke-down sofa under a bare lightbulb that made too many shadows and throwed her face and the front of her body in too strong of a light. I never seen a face that give the appearance of being any wider and calmer, nor any prettier dark blonde hair—the way it kind of swept to the sides above her forehead and fell smooth nearly to her shoulders. Her eyes are big, gray-green, I believe, although they looked some darker in that light. They meet you more than halfway, and that look of hers is a wonder, when it strikes you. They just ain't no way to describe it. And, in spite of her being as big as she is, everthing's the right size and in the right place next to everthing else.

I didn't want to just set there and stare at her like a idiot, but I couldn't think of nothing to say right then that wouldn't sound plumb ridiculous. Mrs. A. is generally good and ready to pipe up with something, but she went back on me that time, and I'll swear she done it apurpose.

Only about then that boy of Mrs. A.'s drove up. When he come inside he didn't pay no attention to her at all, nor to nobody else. He stationed hisself in a chair over in one corner and squinched up his eyes and looked at the floor. I felt like slapping the little bastard, the way he treated his Ma.

And then another cab wheeled in, and this hulk of a looking character driving it got out and barged in on us. And be dammed if Dilly didn't come out with a smile that filled up the whole place and say, "Hello, Wert." The only consolation was—or did I just imagine it?—that while she looked glad enough to see him, seemed to me like she was a little bit afraid of him too.

He just sort of grunted and got this smirk on his face as he went right over and set down beside of her.

So Wert Fleming was who she'd been waiting for! Not that I know him very well. I've just seen him driving his cab around town and heard a little bit about him, never done more'n speak to him at the cabstand. But they tell me they ain't nothing to him, and from his looks I'd say they're right. Some say he bootlegs, and does some pimping on the side.

For Christ sake! You don't reckon she's one of his string? No, I don't believe that. Ain't no whore looks like that!

Still, what's she doing fooling around in his company, then? Because, I want you to know, they left out right at once and drove off in Wert's cab.

I stayed around the stand for a while after that, but even talking to Mrs. A., which I've always kind of enjoyed, got plumb boresome. So I just come on home and went to bed and right off to sleep.

It's real early in the morning now, and I'll just see if I can't set down some more of this before I go to breakfast....

Let's refer back to when I left that hollow below the swimming-hole that Sunday when all this business got started.

It taken me around fifteen minutes to make it back to the car and drive on over to Ellen's house. All that time I kep thinking about how peculiar everthing was turning and wondering what was the matter with me, and wondering too if I ought to mention any of this to Ellen, her being the only person in the world I could ever dream of talking to about it. Only the more I studied about it the more I decided it couldn't be done: I couldn't tell nobody.

And that's where I was still hung up when I come to Ellen's house.

I guess mine and Ellen's situation would look funny to might near anybody besides ourselves. It sure does to her folks and mine. Ellen's right around thirty years old, five or so years younger'n me. We been sweethearts for six years or such a matter, and for a long time now her Ma and Pa have been mad at us for not marrying or quitting one another altogether. That was the cause of Ellen moving out to herself in a little house in their backyard.

Here I am talking about it like it was still going on.

The thing is, not counting the ceremony and occupying the same house all of the time, me and Ellen was married and everbody in the community knowed it. That's how we always preferred it to be—both of us, I mean, and not just me—and both of us being so headstrong, if we want a certain thing a certain way, why that's how we'll have it, and other people can like it or lump it. Most everbody got used to our ways eventually, and they let us alone. Ma and Pap and Old Man and Old Lady Gray, they let us alone too, but you can't say they ever got used to the situation.

Ellen's folks, Old Man Gray and Mrs. Gray, they've lived over there where they still do for as long as I know anything about it, and Ellen growed up there. Her being so much younger when we was kids, I never paid no attention to her back then. So she made it all the way through her teens without me ever knowing much about it. She boarded in town and went to high school after she finished the eighth grade in the country. Later on, she went futher off from home, down yonder to Garsville to normal school. She stayed there, I think, just one or two years, enough so she could get her a school and teach, which she done. It was up here in this state where she commenced her teaching, some ways on futher north. She married up here too, some yap in the community where she taught, and one that wasn't no count, I take it. He went to drinking or something. Ellen stuck it out for several years though, till she finally just had to give up and quit him for good and come on back home. They never had no kids, which in their case was a blessing.

One day I'll never forget is the first time I seen Ellen after she come home. It was in Milcourt one Saturday evening. I was standing around on Kress's Corner joshing with Hap Carr. It was a clear day, getting on towards crop-gathering time. The weather was breezy, cool enough so you knowed summer was about over. The breeze slid down the streets and filled up the town with crop-gathering air from the country—nothing like the wind that blows through this God-forsaken place. The sidewalks was busy with country people walking slow from one bunch of neighbors to another, turning their heads ever now and then to take notice of the wind, getting ready to follow it to the fields but not in any hurry about it. I happened to step back and look off for a minute, for that red nose of Hap Carr's had come in a little too close over whatever yarn he was telling. Right then I seen a woman stepping off the curb on the corner by the main moving-picture show.

The first thing that struck me about her was her hair. It was brown with a touch or two of gold when the fall wind lifted it up in the sunshine. She was slender, you might say lean, with a brown kind of thinness about her that was more female than the whitest fleshiness would've been.

I wished I hadn't been talking to Hap Carr right then. He seen and he knowed about as soon as I did how the sight of her took ahold of me. I can't never hide nothing, seem like, not from Mrs. Armbruster nor even from Hap Carr.

But as soon as I could get away from him that day, and all the rest of them, I did. And I spent the rest of the evening santering around up and down the streets, all the time keeping a eye out for Ellen—for I'd heard about Ellen Gray coming home, and by now I'd remembered enough what she looked like to know that was her. Milcourt ain't a very big place, and so you're liable to see the same person over and over, of a Saturday evening, especially if that person moves around as much as Ellen did that day. I'd catch a glimpse of her here and there, or I'd stand and watch her while she walked a block or two. It appeared to me like she was inspecting ever corner of the main part of town. Her face, when I got close enough to see it—though she didn't recognize me—had a sort of a anxious look about it, but a soft one too, like when you set to looking at old things out of a trunk, things you played with a long time back, and can't get over nor can't really get back to neither.

The next day I made certain I went to preaching, and she was there all right. That Sunday evening along after dinner I made up a big excuse to drive over to Old Man Gray's and borrow some implement I didn't have no need for. When I clumb out of my car and hollered hello at the yard gate, Old Man Gray poked his head out of the door and asked me real friendly like to step in. As a usual thing, I wouldn't've done it. I'd've told him what my business was and gone on down to meet him at the barn. But that day I didn't hold off, I marched right on into the house.

And that was one of the last few times Old Man Gray, or his wife either, ever spoke to me civil. Things got out of hand right off as far as they was concerned. Me and Ellen looked at one another too strong, I guess, and Ellen wasn't even divorced as yet. In less than a week's time, I was over there to see her nearly ever day from right after supper till away on up in the night.

It must've looked to her folks like it would've been the easiest matter in the world for us to get married as soon as Ellen's divorce come through. But we had different notions about that, me and Ellen did, and the funny thing is, we never laid down no agreements, it just all come about by happenstance.

Now then, it's a big old house the Grays live in, two stories and a railed porch plumb across the front of both the top and the bottom. Ellen sort of fell heir to the second floor when she come home. Most of the rooms up there hadn't been full of nothing but junk, I reckon, for years. What they'd all three done was clear out a fine big room on the west side of the house and fix it up for her benefit, the old folks tickled to death to have her back home again, her being the only child and all. But now, with me around, everthing taken on a new light. It got to where I'd barge right in and, without hardly saying hello to the old man and the old lady, go straight upstairs to where Ellen was. We drawed the line at me staying all night there, but the old folks could tell easy enough we was carrying on like man and wife.

At first I didn't think much about it. I just taken it for granted we'd marry right after Ellen's divorce was made final, and that'd be all they was to it. But when I brought the matter up she let me know right off she wasn't in no hurry about it. I was surprised, but that kind of arrangement was mighty fine with me. I did sort of want to do something to pacify the old man and old lady, but Ellen said it was her place to do that, so I just let matters stand. She might near waited too long, though. Till I judge she had some pretty hard words with them. For one night she just asked me what I thought about her moving into the renter's house, and of course I said if it suited her it suited me.

The renter's house was a little old four-room affair set off about halfway between the big house and the barn. It hadn't been lived in for some time, but before you know it Ellen had the place in good shape, without hardly any help at all from me. So now when I come to see her, all I had to do was drive over a cattleguard and into the lane that runs next to the big house, and on around to her front door. The hard thing about it was to keep myself from looking in the direction of the old folks, who was bound to be taking in everthing from somewhere in the house or the yard. The big front porch upstairs, though, that was their favorite perch to watch from.

Ellen was as happy as she could be, and so was I. She'd knit and crochet and quilt—she does the finest needlework imaginable—or she'd jump up and tend to her flowerbeds. Or she'd saddle up her pony and ride around the country visiting folks. Or she'd head out for town in that little old Chevrolet of hers. Me, I'd be at home farming, and I never enjoyed it more. I'd come over to see her three or four times a week after we kind of got settled down, and it was all love and tenderness and happiness.

Oh me, I wish I had them days back again.

So anyhow, the Sunday I been talking about I drove in pretty fast over the cattleguard, like I was in the habit of doing, like I had ten miles futher to go and was in a devil of a hurry to get there. But I seen the old man and old lady, all right. There they was, planted in their cane-bottom rockers on the downstairs porch, I reckon mouthing about nothing, like I'd left Ma and Pap adoing. And I knowed before I'd be with Ellen ten minutes, they'd carry out their usual project, which was to head for the porch upstairs and two more cane-bottom rockers, and there they'd set till after night, or till I left, one. Because, you understand, from the upstairs porch, leaving the door open into the hallway, and that running right straight back to a big window in the rear of the house, they could turn around in their chairs ever once in a while and glance through towards Ellen's house and kind of check up on what was going on.

As I drove up, Ellen was cootering around in her flowerbed in front of the house, wearing overalls and a workshirt and scratching in the ground for all she was worth, like she hadn't been expecting to see nobody, and me least of all. She stood up the minute she seen me, big eyes and happy face and dirty hands and all, slim as a kid in her man's clothes but more woman than I've ever seen brought out by a silk dress, even a floweredy one like Dilly wears.

"Amon! Oh my goodness, hold on a minute, and I'll go in and change my clothes. Is it that time already?"

But I just laughed and followed her on into the house. She really did seem a little flustered about being caught in her everday clothes, though not that I hadn't seen her thataway plenty of times before. If I know Ellen, she just likes to go to extremes in matters of that kind. She'd've headed straight in and dolled up in her fanciest, if I give her a half a chance, just to show me how sudden she could change her looks. Once we was in the front room, though, I stepped in between her and the bedroom door and grabbed her.

"You're a good one," I said. "You can't even say howdy without tearing off to put on your Sunday clothes."

"But listen, Amon. If I'd knowed it was getting so late in the day, I'd've been ready."

She didn't try to get aloose, though. Like she was surprised she'd been caught but glad of it. Ever minute's a new thing with Ellen. Like there I was gripping her close, and her looking like it never had come about before.

Matters taken their course after that. Before you know it we was on the bed making love hot and heavy, and we stayed there for a good while.

Directly we got up, and Ellen started putting on her Sunday clothes. All of a sudden, I thought of something, so I went into the front room, still naked, and stood at a place where I could peep out from under the window shade towards the big house. When the sun was just right, as it was then, you could see all the way through the back window up there, and along the hall and out onto the upper verandah through the front doorway, which was a whole lot like a picture frame you'd hold up to the light. Along the right side of that frame I seen a rocking chair moving slow, one arm, one rocker, and about half of the ladder back, with Old Man Gray in his Sunday shirt giving it this and that, back and forth, slow and sleepy. But I knowed if I just stood there long enough, he'd make another move, and pretty soon sure enough he did. I seen his white head turn around cautious-like and his eyes under his lifted-up spectacles peering back down in our direction. I don't reckon anybody could've seen me through the crack between the shade and the window frame. Still, I didn't move a muscle, for if I drawed back, he might catch a glimpse of motion and know somebody was there.

He looked off in another direction. Ellen come into the room. Without thinking I stepped back from the window and said, "You ready to go?"

"I am. But you don't look like you are, with that thing swinging around. Besides, go where?"

I made a run at her, and she squealed and jumped behind a rocking chair. I kep agoing right on past her and into the bedroom where my clothes was. As I grabbed up my drawers I hollered back, "For a ride."

Course that answer wouldn't satisfy her long. I wished I hadn't've blurted out "You ready to go?" with her all unprepared. You see, I'd made up my mind, but I don't know exactly when, that if I wasn't going to talk over my strange feelings with Ellen, to at least take her around to some of the places where I'd been that day, and see what her attitude might be. Then maybe later on I could talk to her. We wouldn't go to the swimming-hole, I'd concluded. You can't tell nobody, especially your woman, about a ghost, or whatever you want to call it, hanging around a certain waterhole—not in so many words you can't. But at a graveyard—and that's what I had the most in mind—you can say a little and hint at a good deal more.

It had to be kep in mind, though, that Ellen hated to go around a graveyard. I had to work it slow. But still, while I was in there dressing and trying to think of how to smooth things over, I got that kind of a thick-headed feeling you have when you need to study hard about a thing and can't. All I could manage to do was repeat, "Just ride around a little."

"All right. But let me comb my hair."

Like she hadn't been standing at the front-room dresser combing it ever since I went into the bedroom. One time Ellen won't worry about her hair at all, and another time she'll wear you out waiting for her to fix it up just so.

We finally got out of the house and into the car. As we drove by the big house, Ellen leaned out and waved to her Ma and Pa, like they was neighbors, and I swear she wasn't trying to be funny or nothing. But they never let on like they seen her. They just kep on arocking.

Dam it all anyhow! Ever now and then when I'm on the subject of Ellen, it just hits me right square in the heart. I feel like turning over this old beat-up table I'm writing on. But all I do instead is stand up and walk the floor. And then next thing you know I'm recalling Haley Blair, too, and how he had me run off from home. And all of it together just about drives me crazy....

Haley Blair, you sonofabitch! Sometimes I feel like coming home and taking a gun and shooting you. You've got a fine woman for a wife now, and a big bunch of kids. I'm satisfied you think it's no more'n you deserve. But look how you treated Lissie before she died. Of course, I'll admit I'm going by hearsay on that, but they tell me you never said a kind word to her. What I do know is, you used to slip off in the woods, after Lissie died, and meet that crazy girl—or they called her crazy anyhow—I can't think of her name right now. And your son Duncan accidently shot and killed her, didn't he? Just when you was so mixed up with her you couldn't've got out of it no other way. Pap says he always will believe you put that boy up to shooting her, in some way he never realized. Sure, he was supposed to be guarding the Old Blair home-place again people sneaking in to dig for the gold they used to say was buried there. The girl's brothers done some of that digging. That come out in court, all right. But what I want to know is, how come the girl happened to be over at the Blair place by herself the night Duncan shot her? It sure worked out nice for you, didn't it? You married the school-teacher and turned pious and mealy-mouthed and now you've got the whole community thinking you're a regular piss-cutter.

Oh, well, no use going on about it. No use making wild accusations again him like the ones he made again me. Though one of these days, Haley Blair, I'll find out a way to get even with you for what you done to me, and to get back what you taken away from me. Preaching ain't over till they sing, and don't you forget it....

Like I say, me and Ellen was driving out past the big house. It sure was a pretty day—sun and spring and green leaves. No trees I know of are so much the color of spring as the postoaks and blackjacks along the fence-rows of the lane from the Gray place to the county road, trees with leaves so dark and rich and holding them out in big sheaves to make a shade so thick it's might near black next to the sunshine around it.

I drove pretty slow, and we didn't talk much. More'n anything else, I was giving myself time to get Ellen ready for where I wanted to go. Circling back like I'd come, I made it a five or six-mile trip to the graveyard. But dammed if I could think of anything to say to lead up to the subject.

Directly I come right out and asked, as we drove along, "Would you do something for me if I asked you to right nice?"

"Why yes, of course I would."

"You won't care much about doing it."

"What is it?"

"I wanted to run over to the graveyard for a little."

"What for?"

"Now you see there! You said you'd do it."

"I will too, but I didn't say I wouldn't ask questions."

"Well, I'll let you know when we get there."

But that was too definite, and I knowed it. Like I could've told her in so many words what I wanted her to know. But I'd already opened my mouth, and I'd worry later on about sticking by what I said or hedging around it.

Before you know it, we was there. And when I seen that big old monument shining in the sun I begun to get scared. I don't know why exactly, but the idey of bringing together Ellen alive and all these people dead was like violating the law somehow. So I talked fast, once we left the car, to try and cover up how uneasy I was.

I said, "Did you ever stop and think, now, how that old monument's a pretty unusual sight even if it don't seem like it to us, because we're used to it? Don't you reckon when it sinks down in the ground and somebody digs it up several hundred or a thousand years from now, they'll make a big to-do over it? You know how it got here, don't you?"

She did, of course, and I was well aware she did. However though, she fooled me. I guess she seen I was trying to work up to something important. She said, "I used to know, but I've forgot most of it."

I was right thankful. You take when somebody you think a whole lot of will let you repeat a story they already know by heart, you appreciate it. So I opened up and started in and kep agoing. Told her that story about like I'd remembered it a hour or two before. At first we was walking around through the gravestones, but directly we come to the far west side of the cemetery where it was too rocky for the weeds to take ahold, and we set down on two big rocks and Ellen listened like what I was saying was all new to her.

Everthing went along just fine till I come to the statue. When I was about to begin on that, I happened to notice a bee flying past—first just one bee, and then another one, and pretty soon another one yet. And them bees, I want you to know, seemed just as important as everthing else did that day.

Now I been coursing bees all my life, and might near any other time I'd've settled right from the jump-go exactly what direction they was flying in. But now I didn't. Without letting up on my story, I taken to watching them. Easy to see where they was coming from: a big stand of wild flowers across the north fence of the graveyard. They was travelling back and forth, naturally, between that patch of flowers and their tree. But you couldn't tell where they originated at all. They'd whiz toward the flowers and light, then they'd zip back, quick-moving specks you couldn't keep in sight long enough to tell where they went into the woods.

Anyhow, somewhere over to the south they was a bee tree, and I could always come back to look for it later on.

But then the bees got mixed up with my story. I'd done made it through the steam engine and all the trouble they had working that big tombstone up the hill. Seems to me like I remember comparing how easy it was for a bee to cover the same territory with *his* load, and Ellen looked at me kind of funny, because she hadn't seen the bees like I had.

That was just the beginning of letting myself get out of hand. I begun to tell Ellen how they set up the statue, and how it fell off and broke, and how it looked while it laid there sinking down into the dirt. I wish I could call to mind my exact words, but for the life of me I can't. I do know I was talking pretty wild, because what finally pulled me up was the way Ellen was staring a hole through me, like I'd gone batty or something. All of a sudden I felt guilty, and I changed my tune right at once.

"Well no," I said, "now that I stop and think about it, what I'm telling you I'm just adding to what Pap told me. The truth is, I never seen the statue."

If I hadn't played it, I'll quit! But I don't know what I expected, making a bare-faced admission I was lying without no preparation.

Ellen bristled up. "What! You mean to tell me, Amon Lamb, that you been setting there making up this story as you went along?"

"Nomore of it than some things concerning the statue."

"I'll swear, you're the limit!" And up she got and off she went towards the car, leaving me to follow her if I wanted to. I got kind of scared the minute she left, thinking, it's a good thing I put a stop to myself in that direction. In a minute I'd've been telling her about the swimming-hole and Mary or Sherry and I don't know what all.

So then I got up and followed her, bound and determined I wasn't going to mention anything else like what I'd been talking about. It was too dangerous. I felt like everthing was going out of kelter. And all of a sudden I was as ready as Ellen was to leave that graveyard.

But even so I kind of lost track of things, till I heard Ellen snap out, "You better be careful how you drive. You'll turn us over."

There I was heading down the lane a little livelier than I ought to been. So I slowed down.

Ellen was riled. I wished I knowed some way to get her out of it before she got any worse. But I was afraid to open my mouth, afraid I'd put my foot in it one time too many that day.

About the time we struck the main road again, without any warning, she rapped out, "I suppose you got it in the trunk."

For a minute there the craziest thing yet took ahold of me. It was like she meant the statue, like I had that in the trunk. Just a fool notion, that's all.

Soon enough, though, I woke up to what she was getting at. And when I did, a kind of freezing started up away down in my innards, and in a wink it spread all over me.

What I'd done was this: on Thursday Ellen had give me a little sample of yard goods and told me to buy her a length of the same stuff when I went to town a Saturday. Two days I was supposed to remember that. Christamighty! I could've stopped the car right then and there and got out and kicked myself up and down the road. Because I don't reckon I'd even thought about buying that cloth since Friday. In town a Saturday, I know, it never so much as crossed my mind.

Ellen must've seen what had happened, from the look on my face. As a usual thing, knowing me to be forgetful, she don't raise much of a stink about it. I judge she was looking for an excuse to get mad, though, and she'd found it, and she didn't waste no time taking advantage of it. Foolish as it may sound, I suspicion she was jealous over the way I'd been talking about that statue. You know how little it takes to make a woman jealous anyhow. And I mean to tell you, she give me down the country over that length of yard goods, and they didn't seem to be much I could do except take it. All I done was keep on moaning inside and saying to myself, 'Here it is I brought her off out here to see if I could tell her something important, confide in her, and we just end up having a racket.'

Well no, we hadn't had no racket yet. Leastways so far she was doing all the fussing, about how I couldn't be relied on to remember nothing for five minutes and the like. But I knowed I couldn't hold on to myself for very long, if she didn't quit. And she didn't seem to have no intention of doing that. She lowered her voice when we drove past the old folks' house, and once we got inside of her place she raised it again, hollered out for about the fiftieth time, "I'd like to know what you've got on your mind half the time, anyhow. A person can't ask you to do something for them and expect you to remember it till you're out of sight."

And it must've been as plain to her as it was to me that she wasn't nomore talking about that piece of yard goods than if they wasn't such a thing.

Bickering. If they's anything I hate it's bickering. Even when I'm doing it myself and know I'm partly in the right, I hate it. I followed her into the bedroom—me still doing the tagging along behind. She'd just throwed her purse on the dresser and whirled around, still chattering, when all at once I couldn't stand it nomore.

I didn't say nothing. I grabbed her. I don't know whe'er I meant to kill her or kiss her. I forced her again the wall with her fighting like a sack of cats. She managed to make me give a little and leaped out so both of us weaved around and fell on the bed. I got my legs around hers and stiffened out. I had her by the wrists and her forearms trapped in next to my breast under my own arms. So she couldn't move much. But that didn't discourage her from fighting. She heaved and swelled and strained like some fury that if you give it long enough it'll bust through anything. I laid real still and taut and let her struggle, figuring she'd stop when she got enough of it. I got to feeling real tender towards her. I could've kissed her sure enough now. I could've cried even.

She calmed down all at once, seeing she wasn't making no headway. Then she said real level-like, "If you don't turn me aloose and get yourself out of this house, I'll tear you and me both to pieces."

I was about to say, 'Don't look to me like you're in much of a shape to do anything of the kind.'

But I didn't. I let go of her quick and jumped up.

"All right," I hollered. "I will leave this house, and I won't be back anyways soon neither."

"Make certain you don't," she yelled out after me.

When I drove out past the big house, trying to look unconcerned, Old Man and Old Lady Gray was still perched up there in their rockers. In fact, Old Man Gray hadn't much more'n got settled again after looking back through the window to see me start up and drive off from Ellen's. I tried to make it look like I didn't even know they was up there.

It was getting on towards sundown when I come in sight of home. Ma and Pap, too, was still on the porch, but not placed like I'd left them. Pap was away over on the east end rared back in his rocker with one leg propped up stiff again a porch post. Ma was plumb over on the west side next to the door of my room, looking kind of shrunk up, sewing like the dickens, and not paying no more attention to Pap than if he hadn't been on the place.

"Been a fuss going on around here or something?" I grumbled out at them as I went past. And when I'd made it into my room and shut the door, I thought to myself, "Quarrels going on everwhere. And here I am losing my temper and roughhandling my woman and all. I swear, if I don't look out I'll come to the point where I'll have to start calling myself Haley Blair and be done with it."

5

I sure did put in a day at this yesterday. I wrote some before breakfast, picked right up and went on afterwards. So as a result I felt kind of loggy-headed when I woke up this morning.

You know what though? A weak norther blowed in here sometime during the night and put a stop to that south wind and brought enough rain to lay the dust. As soon as it was daylight enough for me to see what the weather'd done, I begun to feel livelier than I had in a long time and to see clearer into some things back home. I've got to turn my hand to it right now and put it all down or some of it's liable to get clean away from me.

Now the next day after that strange Sunday it happened so I was going to fly into planting cotton on a piece of ground down east of the house that Pap had taken lately to calling the Shin Patch—because earlier in the spring, when he was digging out simmon sprouts down there, he busted his shin with a grubbing hoe.

I went to work down there a little bit after sunup. I had me a new planter attachment for my tractor, and up till nearly the middle of the morning I was enjoying myself about as much as a man could, so much that it even put the day before out of my mind for a good long while. Because they's always something satisfying about a shiny plow cutting a furrow, throwing moist dirt out on dry. And out of the planter funnel behind, a trail of seed falling. Then the sweeps mixing the moist dirt and the dry while they're lifting it and throwing it back over the seed. You can look back over the field behind you and see the straight mounded rows that you know will soon be bringing up something new to look at the sun and grow.

But I must've had the bees somewhere in my mind too, for right in the middle of planting a row I said out loud, to myself, "I've got to go over there and see about that." The idey was so pressing once I'd put it into words, I pulled up at the end of that very row and left my tractor setting there. I was in too much of a hurry now to see about the bees to let anything stand in my way.

I struck out for the graveyard, which wasn't but a little piece off through the woods and across the line fence of my place. Maybe I was afraid if I taken time to stop and study about it, I'd back out on going.

I come to the west side of the graveyard, to the rocks where me and Ellen'd been setting yesterday. From there I angled off a little to the south and traipsed around through the weeds and sprouts. I didn't see no bees in the air today, so I figured I'd wait a while. And to give me something to do in the meantime—I was so impatient—I looked around for old graves.

You know, in all the years I'd lived around there, I never had really noticed how many graves they was in that graveyard. You'd think, just to look, they wasn't no more'n a few in the neighborhood of the big monument and several scattered ones with their headstones planted here and there in all the weeds and sprouts. I'm satisfied the main reason why I thought the graves was sparse was because it never had been a very popular burying ground during my lifetime. But at one time it must've been, for when you got to looking close you found graves everwhere. Some you couldn't tell at all except by what was left of the mound, no headstone nor nothing to mark them. Others you come on had an old sandstone no different from the natural rocks around it, excepting the name and date scratched on it one time and about wore off by the weather. The regular tombstones—and some of them wasn't high enough to show above the vegetation—was coated might near all over with some kind of a pale green, crinklety moss that didn't grow nowhere else around, moss covering the suns with rays and the flying doves and clasped hands and verses. Ever once in a while, as I walked around, I'd stub my toe on something and look down, and there I'd see a tombstone plumb over on its side and half swallowed up by the ground.

Around and around and in and out I went. But I didn't forget, all that time, I was waiting for the bees. I'd glance off ever minute or so towards the patch of flowers, and seemed like ever time I did, there'd be that big monument standing between me and the flowers. The glassy sides of the granite was might near blinding if the sun caught them just right, and I couldn't get over how solid it looked, like it was put there to hold this hill in place and keep it from sliding down into the creek. Of course, when you got nobody to keep you company but the dead and the hope of some bees that never show up, your mind runs in funny ways, thoughts like: It's a fool thing to set up so much cut rock for people who see enough stone underground. If they want for anything we can furnish them, it might be a little sunshine piped down there. Or if you could fix a tunnel through down there for the bees to fly in and out of, maybe the bones of the dead would tingle when the wings buzzed by. Thoughts like: what if all these people stood up this minute and gathered around to look at me, come to life like the memories I had yesterday and the dreams on the porch, only more so.

If I was the kind of a man I ought to be, I'd be able to go around and shake hands and welcome each one back to this upper world. And without turning a hair I'd set down with them and tell them about all that's happened since they left the earth, and they'd tell me about life on the other side of the grave.

For a minute there, I come might near seeing all of them collected in next to the big monument, and instead of the statue I myself stood up on the peak of the monument and spoke to the dead.

But I soon had to put a stop to thoughts such as that, remembering it was just yesterday that I'd felt a breath from somewhere on the nape of my neck in that thicket full of twilight. So I broke off the circle I'd been making around and around the graveyard and went over to the east fence and commenced doing the first thing I could think of, which wasn't nothing but throwing rocks at a tree.

And still I hadn't forgot about the bees, or didn't think I had. But I must of for a little while, because when I happened to look close, the place was alive with them. The flowers—wild pinks, if I'm not mistaken—was right at the peak of their blooming, so much at the full of their color and so thick in their growing it looked like they couldn't last in that condition for another minute. And now they was literally firing bees off into the air, little bitty bullets shooting, it looked like, right towards me, missing me by a few foot and whizzing on. I could follow them good with my eyes now, too, so I jumped in to coursing them.

Some chase they led me on too. Four or five times, before I left the graveyard, I sighted on a bee and lined up on a treetop a good ways off to the south. But it always turned out the treetop was crowded in so close to the rest of them in the woods that I knowed I wouldn't be able to tell which trunk it belonged to when I got there. The woods was just too close to me, and too thick, and still that stand of flowers was firing bees at the woods like bullets. But then directly I picked out the futherest tree I could see the trunk of in that direction and headed for it. Arriving there, I stood with my arms out spreadeagle fashion from that tree back towards the patch of flowers, sighting on ahead till I'd picked out another tree trunk. Then I went to it, and so on, till I come to the spot where I figured I could commence hunting for the bee tree itself.

You can't tell, of course, just how far a swarm of bees'll go after flowers. It may be a mile or more. So I kep on searching and getting deeper and deeper in my job till I forgot how fur I'd come, and when I finally realized my whereabouts, I seen I was a way over a mile from the graveyard, futher off than any bees was likely to go. Another thing, I was on some of Haley Blair's land, a whole lot closer to his house than I wanted to be, because I sure didn't feel like running into him.

Being hot and tired, though, I concluded the best way to work it was to set down under some tree where I wasn't likely to be seen if somebody was to come by, and after I'd rested a while, get up and head out of there as fast as I could scoot. Happened I'd just crossed a wide moody-grass pasture and the branch that run through it, and come up to some woods that reached out pretty thick down a slope to join the pasture. I set down on the dead leaves under an old blackjack and scrooched in close to the trunk.

Right at once I commenced to feeling snug. That's a funny word, I know, to use for out of doors, but the situation was this: I was settled down again a tree, as good a backrest as the world can provide, just sweaty and tired enough to enjoy being both. The limbs of the tree was low and straight out in front of me. They filled up all of the top part of my vision with thick green, shading not just me but the way my eyes seen the country, like they formed a big green hand over my forehead. Now even the bees didn't seem important anymore. But I done a lot of watching: that huge old cottonwood down on the branch, a simmon thicket so green it was black, a little bit of wind rippling the grass, the clouds sliding west over a smooth blue sky. And, as well as watching, it was like I was being watched right back by all of it. Most of the time you know for sure the wind and the clouds and the trees don't care much about you. Then again, generally when you're a long ways from anybody else, these things move up closer to you, and if you don't do something to scare them off, they'll might near tell you who they are.

Directly something did happen to scare them off, the wind and the clouds and the trees, for I noticed signs that this pasture had at one time been lived in, and the thought of humans begun to take charge. I noticed what had been humps and gouged-out places on the ground before the grass and several years' time had smoothed them over. Next I seen a rough square of ground enclosing all that. So it must've been an old house-place, I thought.

Then it come back to me all of a sudden. So sudden, for a matter of fact, that I jumped nearly out of my skin. And when I did, I hit my head again a knot on the trunk of that blackjack and might near knocked myself silly.

That sure was an old house-place, all right, I remembered. A good-size family of folks lived there at one time, a many and a many a year ago, a family massacred by Indians long before Pap's time.

As well as I could remember—I couldn't think of their name right then, but it wasn't any of the Blair bunch—they homesteaded the land, the man and his wife and several kids, and hadn't been on it no time before the Civil War come along. Everthing being in a stir the way it was, the Indians taken to raiding more'n they had in a long time. Mostly they never got this far east, but one time anyway they did. They caught all of this family off their guard and killed ever last one of them. Burnt the place to the ground too, of course. The littlest kid, just a baby, they was taking away with them. But somebody said when a bunch of men went after them and caught up with them and the fighting started, the Indians killed that baby to keep from leaving it for the whites. They picked it up by the heels and knocked its brains out again a tree like you would a rabbit.

Seem like I seen it all at once: Indians screaming and hollering, coals spilling out of the fireplace with a brave about as big as a tree strowing them around, corpses all lined up for scalping, and away off out yonder another brave, naked and red-painted, knocking out the baby's brains.

In a second or two I got over being dizzy from bumping my head, and stood up and walked around a little. Not wanting to show myself too much, it taken quite a while for my curiosity to get the best of me and send me out in the open to poke around. I couldn't help from feeling I was sneaking around on Haley Blair's land. Of course, I knowed he wouldn't run me off if he was to find me there. More'n likely he'd just pass off a few remarks in that cold, suspicioning way of his, and both of us would go on about our business. But it ain't the facts that makes you uneasy in a case like that. It's the feeling. So I walked as wary around that old house-place as if I'd been trying to steal something.

They wasn't much left to see, just the mounds and sunk-in places I mentioned before. The moody grass was thick but right short, so it covered and showed up in green all the humps and grooves. I remember thinking, they's probably an old well around here someplace, so I better watch out for it. I gazed at this little bump and that little notch, kicked and gouged around with the toe of my shoe, turning up first one thing and another: one old nail so near rusted in two I picked it up and snapped it like a straw, a few chips of crockery, what looked at first to be a artificial egg but turned out to be a door knob. As a person will, I started looking for bigger objects, hunkering down and digging with my pocketknife.

Right about what I judged had been the middle of the house I come upon a good-size rock, maybe part of the underpinning at one time, barely covered with a skim of dirt and grass. Scratching out around one corner and hefting that rock up was as exciting as coursing bees. Kind of disappointing underneath, though, because I didn't see nothing but yellow grubs, one end of a red earthworm disappearing, and some ants with lower bodies like drops of black ink.

Then I noticed a rough edge of something hard and gray, and I begun to use my pocketknife to flirt the dirt out from around it. Pretty soon I seen it was a rock of some kind, a cylinder-like with a rounded top. A little more and I made out a notch gouged in one side, and below the shoulder of that the whole business commenced to taper off to a edge. I got so excited my hands set in to shaking, and I had to stop and wipe the sweat off of my face. Then real careful I went back to digging, and in a minute or two I had all of it out of the ground.

Sure enough, it was the head of a tomahawk.

That's all the time I had, though, to think about it right then. For I looked up, and it's a good thing I did. Haley Blair was coming. Lucky for me, he was still a good ways off, walking slow up the branch bank, looking for cows or something maybe. All in a flash, I thought how foolish I'd appear knelt down there on the ground holding that tomahawk. Worse yet, this being Haley's land, it was in a manner of speaking his tomahawk. For all I knowed, he might try to take it away from me, and when I thought of that I knowed I wouldn't let him have it without a fight. It was plumb unreasonable, I know, but right then it seemed like the most important thing in the world to keep that tomahawk out of the hands of Haley Blair.

It was about twenty yards, I'd say, from where I was to the timber. As yet he hadn't caught sight of me, I didn't think. If I stood up too sudden, he was sure to see me, but if I crawled it'd take too long, so what I done was to raise up real slow, with the tomahawk held next to my leg on the opposite side from him, and walk regular pace to the woods. Like that I wouldn't look suspicious, and if he seen me and hollered, I'd just keep right on walking till I come to that blackjack I'd rested under, lay the tomahawk down, come back down to meet him with whatever story I could think up, and go back for the tomahawk later.

I made it, though. It was like a narrow escape from some big disaster or another to walk off scotfree with that tomahawk. And hiding behind the blackjack, I watched and waited.

It taken Haley ten minutes or more to walk up one side of the branch as far as where a stock tank was and back down the other side. And just about the time I calculated he was leaving for good, danged if he didn't turn right around and come up the slope towards where I was.

I want you to know, I started scratching out dead leaves and dirt worse'n any dog after a gopher, covered up that tomahawk and stood up flat behind the blackjack. I'd've been in a pretty fix if he'd taken a notion to head for my tree. And it was just luck he didn't. He picked out another tree about a hundred yards down along the edge of the timber and set down under it to cool off from his walk.

Seemed to me like he stayed forever. It was getting on towards dinnertime, and I was hungry as the devil. But then I figured sooner or later he'd have to go home to dinner hisself.

Finally he did. He left out after I was about as stiff as a statue from hugging that tree to keep all of me behind it.

I lit out too, just as soon as I could without running any risk of him seeing me. I scratched out my tomahawk, of course, and taken it with me.

And I clutched onto it like I was walking off with the most valuable thing in the world, that still by rights belonged to me. On the long jant home I commenced to feeling real secretive about it, didn't want nobody at all to see it, not even Ma or Pap.

Or maybe I'm exaggerating some. Maybe I'm taking into account before I ought to what come about later on, so much of it having to do with that tomahawk. But one thing I do know. Ever since I'd begun to daydreaming in the church-house the day before, ever little thing that happened seemed to fit together in some mysterious way, one thing leading to another but never stopping at anything real definite: the swimming-hole, Mary or Sherry, the tombstone, the bees, my racket with Ellen. The bees, yes. For the day when I went out coursing them, I was led to the tomahawk, so everthing in some way or another was connected to it.

Which don't make no sense, but anyhow there it was.

Still, I couldn't figure out what to do with the tomahawk. It had been in the ground so long, it didn't seem right to bury it again so soon. But I had to hide it somewheres, because Ma would be on the lookout for me and waiting dinner and all, and so I'd never be able to sneak into my room with it. Ma may be half-blind, but she'll see what you don't want her to ever time without fail.

The spot I settled on at last was an old hill about a half a mile over northeast of the house, might near on the border of our place. After walking so much, I really didn't feel up to climbing no hill, but anyhow I did, and a hard go it was, with brush everwhere and rocks so thick you had to scramble over them. Right on to the top I went, sweating like anything, to where they's a big old rock and a lot of busted-up little ones laying all around it. On one side of the big rock was a long crack full of twigs and dead leaves and trash. I tore out some of it, wedged the tomahawk in the crack and put everthing back as near as I could like I found it.

Then I went on home.

And from that day on, no two ways about it, matters taken on a different light. Not that they wasn't strange enough before, but up till I come in possession of that tomahawk I didn't realize how serious they actually was. I knowed right then that even stranger things was liable to happen. I didn't know where they'd lead me, but I knowed they wasn't any turning away from them. And I knowed they wasn't a living soul, outside of maybe Ellen if I could ever catch her in the right mood, that I could confide in in any way whatsoever.

Looking back on it now, I wonder if I didn't go sort of crazy there for a while, as many up and downs as I had. Some people thought I did, all right. But I'll just have to decide on that after I've wrote all about it. But if I did lose my mind for a while, I know I begun to get it back the night

I run away from home. So I reckon I ought to thank Haley Blair for at least that much, him being the direct cause of me leaving—only, of course, he thought he was doing me the worst turn possible, not helping me....

This is skipping ahead some, and I won't come to the real matter of it for a right smart while, but I never will forget how Haley Blair looked that night later on, standing there in the lantern light inside of the church-house, with practically all of the men in the community assembled there. Nor his voice when he told them how dangerous I was, and how I wasn't fit to live, no matter if the law did say I was innocent. How the only thing for a God-fearing and self-respecting community to do was to see to it I left the country and never be allowed to come back.

And all the time I was scrooched up next to the windowsill outside, seeing and hearing everthing, when nobody in there had the slightest idey I was anywhere in two miles of the place.

Well, so with that much of a warning, I had a headstart, and I didn't tarry none in getting out of the country. Because Haley Blair had that bunch so worked up, I'm telling you, if they'd got their hands on me they might've done more than just run me off.

I remember when I crossed the state line that night I felt like I was on some big adventure sure enough, exploring or going off to fight in a war or something. I crossed on that old low-water bridge that hardly anybody ever uses anymore, and I slept in the woods till sunup. I recollect how warm and comforting it was in the woods, with black treetops overhead and little rags of sky not quite so black. And stars burning hot and thick up yonder in cold space. For the whole night long I'd sleep a while in my bed of leaves, then I'd wake up feeling happy and excited, like all the strange things behind me had been a heavy load on my shoulders that had dropped off as I crossed the river. There would be strange things ahead, too, things as black as the sky or as bright as the stars, but between this time and that time, I was free. And I knowed for certain I never had been more sane in my life.

And while I'm about it, I've got to try and make some sense out of what Ike's Bible text had to do with my situation. Because it still keeps coming back to me:

> For it is written, He shall give his angels charge over thee,
> to keep thee. And in their hands they shall bear thee up,
> lest at any time thou dash thy foot against a stone.

Ever since I was a little kid, I used to picture Bible happenings taking place around home. Like Jesus spent his forty days in some old hills and canyons four or five miles south of us, setting on a stump in a little clearing. Satan drifted up in black, like smoke from a woods fire, on that fortieth day just before dinnertime, and pointing to a rockpile he said:

"If Thou be the Son of God, command that these stones be made bread."

And Jesus wouldn't do it.

And then all at once they stood on Limestone Hill, where on a clear day you can see the courthouse clock in Milcourt, and in the other direction the business houses around the square in Harper's Knob. And between you and either town you look at, the ridges lay in lines again the hills, the creek bottoms are heavy with trees, the green against green of rich crops spreads out in field next to field:

"All these things will I give thee, if thou wilt fall down and worship me."

And again Jesus wouldn't do it.

Next thing you know, there they was on what looked like the courthouse dome in Milcourt. Only it was really the pinnacle of the temple. It was a long ways down past the sandstone walls, the eagles carved with spread-out wings on the cornices, the columns set in next to the many windows, the broad steps running down on four sides, down to the streets busy with Saturday evening crowds. Ever now and then somebody would look up, and you could tell from the size of their face, no bigger'n your fingertip, how awful far down it was. The stone down there was the concrete sidewalks, the spaces of it standing out among the people passing. When you made ready to jump, you knowed you'd smash into a pulp when you hit.

But then again, no. It looked like the people and the sidewalks didn't really exist at all, but was just reflections from some place. And if you did leap off, you'd fall right on through all that reflection and keep agoing to no telling where. Somewhere away on below you might strike hell itself, a desert of sharp rocks and burning sand.

And the jar of landing wouldn't kill you. No, but it would break ever bone in your body. So you'd have to crawl around for ages hunting water and a shade to get well in before you started climbing out....

"Jump!" said Satan.

> He shall give his angels charge over thee, to keep thee. And in their hands they shall bear thee up, lest at any time thou dash thy foot against a stone.

"Jump!"

And still Jesus wouldn't do it....

But you know, sometimes I sort of wish he had, even if it was the Devil that told him to. His answer was, you're not supposed to tempt God. Yet, to my way of thinking, you never would get nowhere if you didn't tempt God. If you set around waiting for God to tell you a thing's right before you start in to it, you're liable to find yourself waiting till doomsday. It's safe enough up there on the pinnacle if you never make a move. But you have to hold so still you might as well be dead.

So I say jump. God may catch you and he may not. You may splatter on the sidewalk or you may fall on through to perdition. But sooner or later, if you want to bad enough, you can come back to life and climb up to the temple again.

Not long after I got ahold of the tomahawk, I begun to imagine that's what I'd done—jumped. Sometimes I was horrible afraid, and another time, like the night in the woods by the river, I was free. And I'm still falling. I don't know if God'll break my fall. But a whole lot of the time, even when I'm feeling low, I'm glad I made the leap. They's one life behind me, and another one in front of me, and we'll just have to see how it all turns out.

6

Here it is Monday, and I ain't wrote a word since Saturday morning. I thought I had some things pretty well understood when I quit then, but now seem like in a way I'm futher off from knowing where I am than I ever have been. I have made up my mind about some things though, and the writing's helped me do it, I think.

But I better take all this latest stuff in order, I reckon.

To start with, things just about got completely out of hand over this weekend, and this is how it all come about. Saturday about dinnertime I laid my tablet aside and went up to Bick's and made out my dinner as best I could on some old sloppy hash. Then after I et I went out in the streets and done a lot of ambling around. Most of the time, and I've said it aplenty, this is a awful windy and dusty place. But Saturday the weather was pretty. During the night it had come that weak norther I mentioned back yonder. So it was cool with just a touch of breeze, and the sky was deep blue, and the sunshine was real sharp on everthing. It being Saturday, people was thick on the streets, tromping up and down, most of the women still in summer clothes, print dresses and such, and the men that wasn't in overalls still in ice-cream britches and broadcloth shirts. Sometimes, though, you'd see men in dark suits of clothes, and women in fall get-ups like jersey dresses and bright sateen.

Guess I'll have to admit this country ain't quite as sorry as I thought it was. Some of the people, at least, are nice enough looking folks.

So anyway, I fiddled around town all evening long, and along about night I ended up at the cabstand. All of the drivers was out on runs, and Mrs. Armbruster was setting there looking glum as ever I seen her, wouldn't hardly speak to me when I said hello, just mumbled. But then as I was taking a seat, she popped out with, "Do you know where they went the other night?"

I might near got into it that time, for at first I thought she meant Dilly and Wert. I come in a inch of blurting out, 'No, and I don't give a dam neither.'

But she wouldn't let me say nothing. She was charging on ahead: "The very idey! A woman her age dragging a boy around by the nose, and him without enough gumption to stay away from her!"

Then I seen, of course, she was referring to that boy of hers and one of his women—as I ought to've knowed she would be in the first place. And I knowed how that subject went with her. All I could do was leave or let her talk, and I decided to let her, because I might ease the conversation around to where I could prise something out of her about Dilly.

"A boy of mine wallowing around in dirt like that!" she was growling, a whole lot coarser'n she usually talks. "That bitch ought to have a horsewhip taken to her."

I didn't say nothing.

"I went to see a lawyer though. Did I tell you about that? I mean, he is a minor, and she ain't, not by a long shot!"

I couldn't tell a flat lie and say yes she had told me. But if I'd said no, no telling how long she'd've bent my ear about it. I seen what looked like my chance, so I said, "Not to change the subject, but speaking of lawyers reminds me, ain't they one here in town by the name of Gorman? Seems to me like I seen his shingle."

That drawed her up short. They may be a way to ease people out of one subject and into another without them hardly knowing it, but I ain't never found out yet what it is. I tried to look as innocent as I could.

Finally she said, "Why yes, sure they's a lawyer here named Gorman. His office is right down the street."

"Is Miss Gorman any kin to him?"

You see, I'd found out that was Dilly's last name, I mean her maiden name. But I said 'Miss Gorman' so awkward I might as well've said 'Dilly' and been done with it.

You never seen anybody get so foxy-looking as Mrs. A. did then: "What do you want to know so much about her for?"

"Just wondered."

She wasn't a bit fooled, of course, and we both knowed she wasn't. I wasn't worried, though. You can trust Mrs. A. I mean if she likes you, you can, and I can tell she likes me. If she's got a grudge again you, she'll tell everbody everthing she knows on you—and of course she's in a position to know a whole lot, sending cabs all over town. But if it's somebody she likes, they can be the worst rounder in the world and she won't say a word again them.

But then she didn't have no objection to talking about Dilly, for she wanted to brag on her. And you could follow ever little move she made towards getting me and Dilly paired off.

According to Mrs. A., Dilly was a local girl that about ten years ago moved out to California with her Mammy and Daddy, married some man who had moved out there from here too, and lived with him till a few months back. From what Mrs. A. said, he always was the next thing to a fool, and mean besides. They had split up—and that was quite a story in itself, Mrs. A. said—and Dilly had been living out in the country here with her Grandma till right lately.

But that's as far as Mrs. A. went, because who should walk up out of nowheres right then but Dilly herself, looking taller in the dusk than she actually was, and that thick head of hair turning to sudden gold in the glaring light when she come inside the cabstand.

I'd just about had time to get up and offer her a chair, when what do you know but Wert's cab come wheeling in from another direction. And then to top it all off, before he could walk from his cab to the building, some stranger, a grizzly old-like man carrying a checkered suitcase, beat him to the door and pushed on in ahead of him. It all happened so fast, I was left kind of puzzled. For where before, me and Mrs. A. had just been setting there by ourselves with her talking and me listening, in no time now, that little room was crowded full of people.

Wert was sort of leering at Dilly, but she was gazing back at him so calm and steady—and still, I thought, with something scared about her she didn't quite hide—that it was purt near impossible to draw any conclusion about what was between them.

That bristly stranger was resting his suitcase slantways on the edge of Mrs. A.'s desk and looking around bug-eyed like he'd busted in on a squabble and didn't know how to act but anyway meant to be bold about it. Me, I was just about to step into a corner out of everbody's way when I realized it might look like I was giving in to Wert Fleming, and I didn't want nobody to get that idey, for sure. So I just stood there shifted onto one foot in front of the chair I'd got up from.

Mrs. A. taken charge of the situation, chirping out in her business-hours voice, "Did you wish a cab, sir?"

"Uh huh."

"Wert, here's a run for you."

Wert give her a dirty look, and me one too, like I had something to do with it. Then he walked out of the door to his car without saying a word to nobody.

"Just follow him, sir," Mrs. A. went on. "He'll take you wherever you'd like to go."

Well, the man went out there, yes, but you could see him and Wert having some discussion by the cab fender. Looked like Wert was trying to put him off, and in a little bit you could see the man was commencing to get mad. Mrs. A. seen it too, for she went to the door, stuck out her head, and called out, "Yes, what is it?"

The bristly man turned around but didn't say nothing. Wert kind of shrugged his shoulders and said to Mrs. A., "He wants me to go to Pawnee. Don't you reckon I better wait and take him later on tonight when we're not so busy with local runs?"

It was plain enough he wanted her to say yes, but then she didn't: "We ain't been so very busy, and it don't look like we aim to be. No, I reckon you can go ahead."

While the truth of the matter was, they had been busy, with most of the cars out most of the time.

Wert shrugged his shoulders again, and went to his cab, mad as fury, motioning for the man to climb in. Then they tore out of the driveway.

Mrs. A. taken her seat again and said to Dilly, "But let's see, you was figuring on him taking you out to your Grandma's, wasn't you?"

"I was. But then it's not all that important for me to go right now."

Mrs. A. filled in on her dispatcher's sheet where Wert had gone to, making the remark, "Well, he won't be back for over a hour at least, or more like two."

I had set down again by now, in another chair, next to the door where I could have a good view of Dilly—that wide smooth face of hers, and the eyes and hair with so much glowing light in them. And her tall body easy on the chair, the way her breasts give a slight move when she breathed and her legs curving up in stockings to the hem of her dress right above her knees and turning to full thighs that plumped out in that same floweredy dress that still looked as neat as you please.

Mrs. A. spoke up all of a sudden, moving little items around on her desk like she wasn't really paying no attention to what she said, "Amon, why don't you run her out there in my car. I guess that's the only chance she'll have to go, and I hate for her to miss seeing her Grandma."

"Why, that's not necessary, Mrs. Armbruster," says Dilly. "It's too much trouble for Amon, and I don't just have to see Grandma tonight."

My name sure sounded good in her mouth the first time I heard it.

I didn't need no begging of course. Anyway, I was sure Dilly was ready and willing to go. From the way they talked, the place must be a pretty good ways out in the country, and on the trip there we'd have plenty of time to get acquainted.

"But the thing is," Dilly was saying, "I didn't aim to stay all night. I just wanted to visit her for a while and then come on back."

"All right, then," said Mrs. A. "Go on. Take off. Just as long as you're back by midnight, so I can get off shift and have a way home."

And she shooed us out of the door.

Now, not having the least idey where we was going, nor what I was doing neither, as far as that goes, I expect I acted pretty dumb for a while there. I was might near afraid to open my mouth. We just got in Mrs. A.'s old Pontiac and drove off without saying a word to one another. For you see, I ain't what you'd call talked to another woman besides Ellen for a long time, and you might know she was on my mind and kep me from talking as I rode along there beside Dilly, right down through the big middle of town where it had just turned dark, and where the sidewalks looked fuller of people than they actually was, and where all the store lights and street lamps and stop lights stood out clear and bright in the fresh air. Fall weather had creeped into the evening, with a coolness to tingle your skin and a mustiness in the air for you to breathe.

And whenever I had a pang of shame about Ellen, riding along there with Dilly, I always had a answer for myself, like 'Yaow, but she could at least write me a letter!'

I finally got my tongue back. Then I said to Dilly, "You better tell me whichaway to go, or we'll be fooling around here all night."

She laughed like she really had forgot I didn't know the way. "Why of course. Excuse me. Here, you head on out the street we're on, and right up the highway to the creek and across. It's a few miles on the other side of the creek, I'll show you where."

We talked some then, both of us still pretty cagey. Like she asked me if I'd ever been out this road before, and when I said no, she added yes, that was right, because I hadn't been living around here for very long. From a few things like that I surmised she'd found out as much about me as the rest of the town knowed, from Bee and Mrs. A., of course. Then I said to her I heard she hadn't been back from California long, and she was as careful answering as I was.

And so, with that kind of stuff and some odds and ends throwed in, we scooted along the highway. Now, as you head for the creek that divides this county from the next one north, you right away find the red-dust plains breaking up for the creek, which I'd call big enough to be named a river. You go over a lot of smooth ridges in prairie pasture that this time of the year has turned shaggy-looking and pale. Fields in the glades under the ridges have done turned dark with matured cotton or else they've got ragged after the corn's been gathered. Deeper down in the draws, you come on thick strips of bowdark and hackberry, and a ways on north the country's all cut up by ditches with buff-colored banks, and the knolls stand out heavy with timber.

Seem like I noticed ever little change as the night inched along. The air was so clear it looked like even the darkness wouldn't be able to shut out your view of the country altogether, because when it ought to've been plumb black outside, the knobs and ditches close to the creek still glimmered.

Then I realized the moon must be coming up over on the right and a little behind us. And when I cut my eyes in that direction I seen it flaring big and red right on the east rim of the sky and casting a bar of light onto the dashboard. Dilly's knee curved up into that light, with the tiniest sheen of it on her stocking.

With my mind trying to be everwhere at once, it's a wonder to me I didn't say some fool things, like I sometimes do when I get worked up. But I don't guess I did, because everthing was as easy-going as you please between us when we finally drove up to Dilly's Grandma's.

It's a big old two-story house with I don't know how many vacant rooms in it. For the old lady lives there by herself in two or three rooms where it looks like she's tried to crowd everthing into them that she's become attached to in seventy years or so. Old pictures stuck around on mantelpieces and dressers, three or four tall clocks, vases and bowls and little boxes painted ever color imaginable. Little rag rugs and a deerhide spread out on a floor that's already carpeted. Two sofas, armchairs, straight chairs, a bunch of endtables and a library table and magazine racks. She's a big reader of these old Western story magazines, and the place is stacked plumb full of them.

She won't have no electricity on the place, neither, mind you. She walks around from one room to another, pretty pert for her age, carrying an old coaloil lamp. I never will forget how it all looks, her showing me around the rooms, insisting on it, with Dilly tagging kind of embarrassed behind us, with the lamplight and the shadows turning and sliding along with the old lady at the center of them, dim lamplight falling on the jumbled-up things that all her life's been put into since her old man died a few years back.

Her and Dilly argued a while over what I can see is a regular thing with them—her trying to talk Dilly into moving back out there and staying with her, and Dilly on the other hand trying to persuade her to move into town where she could kind of see after her. Both of them appear to be pretty stubborn. Later on, Dilly told me she was right worried about something I'd already thought about but wouldn't've mentioned—that one of these times the old lady might trip and fall with that lamp, and that would be all they was to it, her and the house and Western stories and all gone up in smoke.

We stayed about a hour or two, and then we struck out for home.

On the far side of the creek over there is a bunch of beer joints all clustered up together like a little town, this county being dry and that one wet. Some of them joints have got a pretty bad name. I know Wert Fleming, for one, hangs out there a right smart. I kep a close eye on Dilly as we drove back past, to see if she'd let on like it was familiar territory to her. She didn't though, and that made me feel better.

On a hill right at the south end of the creek bridge, standing to itself, is a big cafe that's more respectable than the ones on the other side. So I pulled into it, saying, "Listen here, I expect you're hungry. I know I am." For although it was around suppertime when we got to Dilly's Grandma's, and the old lady told us she'd done had hers but she'd fix us some, we told her, no, we wasn't all that hungry. Dilly, that is, said it, and I didn't say nothing.

Dilly answered now, kind of offhand, "Well, I wouldn't mind a cup of coffee."

That cafe, the Trotline as they call it, is one of these places where if you want to you can take a net and dip your own catfish out of a big trough and have them cook it up for you. But we didn't fool with that. We had us some steaks. Cup of coffee, nothing! You ought to seen Dilly fly into that teebone. I bet if the truth was known, that poor girl don't get half enough to eat.

We stayed on at the Trotline for a long time, till the place was about ready to close up, before we headed out for town. The moon was away up, sharp in the sky and gleaming misty white on the knolls and ridges. A mile or so down the highway from the cafe I seen a road, even whiter, winding off up a hill, and I taken it. Dilly didn't ask where we was going, and I was sure glad she didn't. We clumb to the top of the first hill and crossed a draw and come out on another hill from where you could see a black stretch of timber and the creek shining on the other side of that.

I pulled up by the side of the road and stopped.

The moon was on my side of the car, making the world smoky white. Her face was soft, framed over there in the car window. I said, "You can see the creek from here."

She turned around slow, to look at the creek over her shoulder, making a profile and then swinging her head on futher till you could just see the curve of her cheek. I looked at that, but being afraid to study about her right out, I thought how the moonlight made so many different kinds of smokiness and mist around us, some lighter and some darker, some thicker and some thinner. It made a sheen-like over ever band of trees and ever slope, and even the deepest draws heading down to the creek had a mist film over them. What wasn't so far off looked a long ways, like you could've walked a hundred yards from the car and been in plumb new country as wild and unsettled as it was a hundred years ago. Instead of thicker woods down closer to the creek, what you seen there might've been a crack that run clear through the world, silvered over with just enough moonlight to hide how awful it was. I remembered the tomahawk, I thought how terrible it was to be lost in the living dark, and sudden and strong it come back to me that I'd jumped from the pinnacle of the temple and was still falling.

I said, "Mrs. Armbruster tells me you been living in California for some time."

She said, "Yes, I moved out there with my folks several years ago. Have you always lived down there where you come from?"

Guess she thought one question deserved another one.

"Yes, I have. Did you move back here to stay, or are you just visiting for a while?"

"I don't know for sure yet. Well, yes I do. I'm just visiting. Do you have any notion how long you'll be here?"

"No, I don't know for sure neither. It's hard to tell. Do you still have folks in California?"

And on and on like that it went, her letting out just as little about herself as possible, then asking some question, and me taking my turn at doing the same thing. What you ought to do at a time like that is either shut up altogether or else be the first one to get bold and ask real blunt questions.

But danged if she didn't beat me to it: "Did you have some trouble with your family before you left?"

I commenced to deny: "It wasn't my family, it was other people."

"Not even your wife?"

"They ain't no such a person. Who told you they was?"

"We just speculated a little, that's all. I mean, me and Mrs. Armbruster did."

"And you and Bee didn't?"

"Well, yes, we did a little bit too."

So I said, I reckon more emphatic than I needed to, "Well, you can just stop speculating. I absolutely ain't married."

But I want you to know a mighty strong memory of Ellen cut in to dispute my word, Ellen the way she is when she's naked in my arms. And I never felt more like a liar in my life than I did right then.

It wasn't but a second, though, till I remembered how wrong she was doing me by not writing, and I turned right around from being ashamed to being mad. Which riled me up enough to look matters square in the face myself:

"Mrs. Armbruster tells me you and your old man are separated."

That kind of got off with her. For a minute there she didn't say nothing, then she laughed and her voice come out soft: "Seems like we've been finding out a lot about one another."

"What made you leave him?"

Of course I expected her to say he left her, but then she didn't.

"I'll tell you sometime."

So there we set, nobody wanting to go any futher. Finally Dilly mentioned Mrs. Armbruster's boy Jimmy, and we commenced to talking about them. That turned out to be a subject that kep us agoing for some time, because we could go over the ins and outs of that boy's woman-chasing and his acting despisable to his Ma, and work on from there to some things we really wanted to talk about. After we'd reported to each other on what we'd seen of this latest Jimmy affair, she brought into it another name that I didn't care nothing about hearing:

"Wert claims Mrs. Armbruster got Jimmy started with that Stores woman herself, because he was about to marry a girl she didn't like."

"He ain't old enough to get married. And besides, I doubt if Wert Fleming knows everthing he claims to."

"Why no, Wert's truthful enough, seems to me. Why do you say that? What have you got against him?"

"Nothing in particular. I guess you know him awful well and can speak where I can't."

She let the bait drop though. She just said, "No, not so terrible well. He used to be good friends with Orville though, and Orville talked quite a bit about him."

"Orville? Who's that?"

I had a pretty good idey, of course, who it was. I just wanted to see if she'd say 'my husband' or what.

"That's the man I was married to."

"You thinking about going back to him when your visit's over?"

"No, I'm not."

"Did he take to running around with other women?"

If she didn't feel like stomping me, she ought to. She spoke up pretty sharp, all right:

"Listen here, tell me something about yourself. You mean to say a man of your age and looks and not married just set around home by hisself all the time. I bet you've give some women their share of trouble."

As you might imagine, I squirmed quite a little bit, but I managed to be fairly cool:

"Well, sure, of course I had a girl friend or two, but just one I was serious about, and that's kind of blowed over."

"Was that why you left home?"

"Now wait a minute. If you think I run off and left some poor girl pregnant, you got another think acoming. And what's more, you never did answer my question. Why was it you didn't get along with your old man, anyway?"

"You tell me and I'll tell you," she said, like it was a dare.

You know, it never had till that second occurred to me how I'd go about answering a point blank question on why I left home. It was all too dam mixed-up to explain, even if I'd wanted to, so what I said, just letting the words fall where they might, was, "All right. It wasn't no woman trouble. Me and a neighbor of mine named Haley Blair got into it over...oh, a bunch of things. I mean, we always did despise one another, and they was some question about an old tomahawk, and about a accident that taken place. It didn't amount to much, really. It wouldn't of, I mean, if Haley Blair hadn't stirred up the whole country again me. I don't even know for sure whe'er any harm would've come of staying there if I had. But I just thought it might be the best thing for me to leave home for a while and let things settle down some. And that's all they was to it. So why don't you and Mrs. Armbruster and Bee quit making a big thing out of it?"

Boy, a man sure can beat around the bush to keep from outright lying, whenever he has to. Dilly wasn't plumb satisfied with what I'd told her, I could see, and I felt pretty sneaking about making light of what had happened back home, but I justified myself by thinking about how I was writing the truth in these tablets, and how I'd tell her the whole thing if we ever got so well acquainted I needed to.

And anyway, in a minute or two, she was talking about herself so hard she didn't have time to ask no more questions. She was so frank it surprised me, us not knowing one another no better'n we did. First off, I thought she was busting to tell somebody her troubles and just hadn't run into nobody that would listen till I come along. But it wasn't that simple a matter. I reckon she'd talked to her Grandma, and probably to Mrs. Armbruster. It begun to seem to me, then, that she was putting a whole lot of confidence in how well I could listen and sympathize, and naturally I appreciated that.

No use in repeating everthing she said. She rambled around a right smart in telling me. But I tried to picture them as she went along, her and this Orville, him a great big black-headed man as thick as a postoak tree, with hands like blocks. When they first got married he always spoke in a soft voice. He picked her up and carried her around a whole lot, as big a woman as she is, and called her "doll" and "littleun" and "child baby." They spent a good deal of time at this Holy Roller church, where he'd get so serious he sometimes looked scary. I pictured him as a man that hated the iniquities of the world so much his hate might turn into iniquity itself any minute.

And still she talked on:

At home he kep some iron rods behind the heating stove. Ever now and then he'd pick up one and bend it. He'd read about Samson so much he knowed that part of the Bible by heart.

One day when things wasn't going to suit him he—she said he give her a spank—but what he done was whach her on the butt so hard she might near fell again the heating stove. But she managed to fall to one side, and so she landed right on his iron rods. He jerked her up and out of the way, and grabbed up two rods and tried to bend them both at once. When he couldn't, he throwed them down and stomped out of the house.

Seeing as how he was a Holy Roller, he never allowed her to wear no powder nor lipstick. Pretty soon he even forbid her to curl her hair and to wear anything but the plainest cotton dress and lowheel shoes. He taken to watching ever move she made, wouldn't hardly let her out of the house by herself. And when he come home at night from the fruit ranch where he worked, he'd look all up and down the lane for strange tiremarks, and around the house for foot-tracks. Then ever few days he'd pin her down and spank her—she said—till she couldn't hardly move.

She was afraid to stay and she was afraid to run off both. She just didn't know where to turn. One day, though, she mentioned giving him a haircut, a thing she'd always done, but this time it set him off. She realized how far gone he was when she come back from going after the comb and scissors and found him standing by the heating stove with two of his iron rods in his hand.

"Put down your shears, woman. You've touched my hair for the last time. Behold the strength of the Lord in my arms."

She stopped still and stared at him while he leant back again the wall, raised one knee, put the rods across it. He strained ever muscle trying to bend them, which he still couldn't do. She made out like she was going to throw the scissors at him, but when he ducked, she run for the front porch with him right in after her. As luck would have it, she done the right thing. She throwed the scissors out in the yard as fur as she could send them. He tore out after them, and while he was busy with that she made a dash back through the house and out of the back door and kep agoing till she come to a neighbor's house and called the law.

Turned out Orville had been so busy tearing around the house with the scissors cutting up ever picture of her he could find, he hadn't tried to chase her at all.

The tears was running down her cheeks as she talked, but she went on anyhow. They sent Orville to the asylum right away, and as soon as that was all fixed up she left the country and come here. I take it she got a divorce on the grounds of insanity, because she goes by her maiden name again. While she was telling her story I did wonder some, and I still am, if she was quite as innocent as she made out. She might've contributed something, after all, to running him crazy. Maybe he did find some unfamiliar tiremarks and some strange foot-tracks around his house.

In between listening to her, I heard the breeze getting up down in the creek bottom and watched the trees stir, while closer by, the bushes rustled and the grass by the road rippled. The sound of the wind, it seemed to me, was softer because it was blowing through the white and musky moonlight. She was leaning back firm again the car door, her head and shoulders in clear outline in front of the doorglass, no tears in her eyes anymore. I had ahold of her hand, had had for some time. I scooted over close, put my arms around her, and stopped right there. Her eyes gazed at me straight, wide and shining. Then for no reason she said, "You've got the whitest teeth."

Godamighty! I guess my mouth must've been open a little. I kind of shivered, because you know, I had a sudden suspicion that maybe she'd like to be bit by white teeth, or mistreated in some other way. And then she laughed—uneasy, I thought—and tried to pass it off: "I don't know why I said that. They just are. The moonlight makes them that way."

We didn't talk anymore then, for a while. I put my cheek again her hair, and directly I kissed her. But when I did, as you might know, I remembered how long it had been since I'd kissed any other woman besides Ellen. My arms didn't seem to fit right around Dilly, and with my eyes shut I seen Ellen's dark complexion in the place of Dilly's light one. And I couldn't make my lips understand it was Dilly's full lips I was kissing and not the smaller ones of Ellen.

She didn't seem to be any more anxious to go on with the kissing right then than I did, so I just quit. We both set there then like we didn't hardly know what to do next. Afterwhile the subject of Bee Coleman come up, and we gabbed about her and Boggs for a time, more or less just to have something to do.

And then directly I drove us back to town.

Try as I will, though, I don't know for sure if I'm telling this right. It could've been I lost interest in Dilly right after I kissed her. But then by the time I got back to my room, I know, I was interested again and no doubt about it. For I laid awake studying about her, and the more I studied the more appealing she got. Ellen just wouldn't stay out of it though, neither, and between the two biggest worries I had in mind about them, it looked like I wasn't going to get any sleep that night at all. I'd wonder for a while if Ellen would ever write me and why she hadn't. Then I'd wonder how much involved Dilly really was with that Wert, and why she ever went with him at all.

Sometime along in the night I realized the wind was blowing strong again, and when I raised up to look out of the west window, I could see it had changed back to the south. Scrawny tree limbs was thrashing around in the light from the streetlamp down by the bridge, and the dust was fogging in.

I thought, 'You're allowed one good day around this place, and then it don't even last the night out.'

When I did go off to sleep, I tossed around and dreamed a whole lot, went off sound about dawn, I guess it was, and when I come out of it, a little past sunup, Dilly popped right into my mind. I remembered how she felt in my arms, I wished I'd gone on kissing her. But it wasn't no time till Ellen pushed in again, and I was just confused in ever direction. To kind of ease that, I jumped up and put on my clothes and tromped down to the post office, was just about there when I recalled it was Sunday, and the General Delivery window wouldn't be open.

But I et while I was at it, and when I was home again I set by the window and wondered if it would look all right for me to go down and knock on Dilly's door. It was close on to nine o'clock by now, which I didn't think was too early.

As you might know, I tarried too long. Dilly, all diked out in a black-and-white-figured dress, come out on the street and, never looking back, off she went towards town. Not having no hat on, she couldn't be on her way to church, I didn't figure. I just knowed, of course, she was going off to meet that Wert someplace.

I fretted and fumed. I glared out of the window. I laid down and glared at the ceiling. A little later in the day, when she didn't come back, I lit out for downtown and traipsed up and down ever street except the one the cab-stand was on. Along late in the evening I walked all the way down to the city park on the west side of town and struck up a conversation with a couple of old nesters I found setting on a bench down there. The highway, you see, run right by there, and I figured if Dilly was driving around with Wert, sooner or later they'd drive by.

Only they never done anything of the kind. I'd made it back to the room, after supper, and set myself down at the window again, when finally her and Wert drove up and she got out by the front door. For a little bit there, I had a real boost. They didn't kiss goodbye nor nothing. She just stepped out of the car simple as could be. Pretty soon, though, I seen what was the reason for that. She wasn't gone inside no time till here she come back out again, and this time, mind you, she was carrying a suitcase.

A suitcase! I thought to myself. What in the hell is she up to now?

She hopped right in and off they drove.

Well, I'll be dammed! I thought. Of all the sonofabitching luck!

I set in to cussing, hard, and I rared and I pitched for I don't know how long. The longer I stayed at it the madder I got. I might near started to tearing up things. Picked up the tablets I'd been writing on and one time was about to rip them in a million pieces, thinking, 'You set around here on your dead ass scribbling and let Wert Fleming drive off with the girl, without so much as a bye-you-bye!'

After I'd raved on till I quietened myself down some, I wondered more and more just what it was all about. Was they going off to get married? Was he just going to put her up someplace? Was she leaving the country for some reason?

The best way to find out, or at least find out what kind of a story she'd put out, was to go down and ask Mrs. Armbruster.

So I headed out for the cabstand.

And what do you think Mrs. A. told me? Dilly had gone out to spend a week with her Grandma! To hear Mrs. A. tell it, the old lady had taken sick that day, but they can't convince me of that. In my opinion, she's off shacking up somewhere with that Wert Fleming.

Well, that meant another night without much sleep. And this morning when I finally decided to roll out and face the world, they wasn't much of me left to face it.

And then, after breakfast, I set down and read all I'd wrote up through Saturday morning, and the futher I read the better I felt. When I come to the end of it, to the part about leaping off of the temple into a new life before me, I got ashamed of myself and I made a resolution then and there to get a new hold on things, to let Dilly go her own way with Wert or whoever she pleases, to stay pretty close around this room and finish up writing all that happened down home, with the same hope I started out with: that writing it will help me understand it. And then, when I'm through, I'll see. I don't mean I'll see about Dilly, neither. If by that time I still ain't heard from Ellen, I don't know exactly what I'll do. But I do know that I've paid my last bit of attention to Dilly. As far as I'm concerned, she can go straight to hell.

7

And so, to pick up where I left off back home, I found that tomahawk over there on Haley Blair's land close to where the Indian massacre taken place, and after I'd sneaked off and hid it in that crack of rock not far from the graveyard, I come on in home for dinner.

Now then that evening, a little while after noontime, I got to studying, not so much about that tomahawk as about the family that was massacred, wishing I could find out more about them. I could've asked Pap, I guess.

He'd've knowed something about it. But I decided to wait a while on that, because I didn't want him to know yet just how interested I really was.

Now Pap he was lighted down in his usual spot on the east end of the porch in his hide-bottom rocker, one leg propped up again the porch post. Me, I was setting on the floor dangling my feet off of the edge of the porch and swinging them so my heels would thump the planks, gazing off towards where I'd been that morning and letting myself drift along in wondering curiosity.

It must've looked funny to Pap I hadn't jumped right up from the dinner table and taken off for the field the way I nearly always done. Pap was puzzling about it, I could tell, even if my back was turned towards him.

Directly he spoke up and said, "Boy, you going to plant cotton this evening?"

"No," I said, short-like, just to get Pap's goat. Being too old to do much, he likes to call hisself bossing as frequent as he can get away with it, and I cut him off sometimes just for devilment.

"Looks like a good day for it to me," was all he had to say.

All at once I hit on something and spoke up like that was what I'd been thinking about:

"Ain't Yas Bailey got a planter attachment something like that one of mine?"

"Think so. Yaow, seems to me like he does."

"Believe I'll run over there and see if the feeder gear on his'n works like mine does."

"Is it giving you trouble, boy?"

As a general rule I don't tell bald lies, but at the time they didn't seem to be no way out of it.

"A little bit," I said.

I jumped up to go, and glad I was the tractor was still down in the field fur enough from the house to discourage Pap from going down there and fuddling around with it and finding out they wasn't nothing wrong. Or I mean to say, he'd've had that feeder gear out of there in no time, and before he got done with it, they *would've* been something wrong with it. Machinery's one thing Pap ain't never understood any too well. He lived too much of his life before most of it come along. I like to never learned him how to drive a car. But now that I'm so far from home and he ain't got me to depend on, I'm sure glad I kep at it till I did.

Wherever you are, in the house or fifty yards from it, you can't do nor say nothing Ma don't notice. Because right then her voice come out strong from the kitchen, "I bet it's some north of Cephas's he going to."

Meaning Ellen's, naturally. Ma never did pass up the opportunity, back then, to let herself be known on that subject. And like I usually done, I just ignored it.

Old Yas Bailey—or Cephas, his real name is. I sure enough did want to see him, but not about no planter attachment. I'd recollected how that massacred family was some akin to him, or maybe to his wife's folks, and I just used the first excuse I could get ahold of to go over there.

Now I reckon they oughtn't to done it, but people around home had always kind of made fun of Yas. For one thing, it was the way he talked. A whole lot of what he said come out flat and long, like a calf blating. That was how he come by his nickname. Ever time he opened his mouth to say 'Yes' it sounded like 'Yas.' Which was just vulgar-sounding enough to make everbody die laughing the minute his back was turned. And then Yas was so excitable, too. You could get him all stirred up about might near anything in the world without halfway trying. Then I reckon what capped it all off, Yas never had made a dime at nothing. Not because he didn't work, neither. He kep at it as hard as anybody. But seem like they was so much waste motion in the way he went about it the outcome was always pretty small.

To reach Yas's place you had to drive down like you meant to go to Haley or Gil Blair's, turn off east before you got there along a branch into some woods, then snake around over a rough road for some little bit before you come out in the open where Yas's house was. I say his. Yas just rented his land and house, and a pretty run-down old place it was, nub-rock fields and the pasture full of ditches. I couldn't see how Yas and his wife and four or five kids ever made a living off of it.

I come in sight of the place, old house leaning on a weak foundation and the shingles ruffled up the way a hen'll do her feathers, looking like they'd blow away in the first good wind that come along. The woman stuck her head out of the door when I drove past, with a kid or two behind her. I waved and drove on. I run on to Yas out by the log barn, tinkering with his old beat-up tractor. But sure enough they was a new planter attachment on it. And there was Yas as busy as I ever seen a man, hovering around over his work, checking everthing he could reach on that tractor, tightening one thing and loosening up another, rubbing the new attachment off with the palm of his hand here and there, bending and squatting, his big old fleshy body in a awkward hurry like always. Like as not he'd fool away half the evening getting ready before he ever made it to the field to plant cotton.

When he looked up and seen me, he hollered, "Get out and stay a while." And bent back over his work.

"No, I ain't got much time, Cephas. Just wondered how you like that planter attachment. You know, I got one quite a bit like it."

But I did climb out of the car and walk over to where he was, and he commenced to telling me all about his new attachment. I let him explain how much he paid for it—I'm satisfied he bought it on the credit—and how it worked and where to put so much oil and the rest of it, just like I wouldn't know all about that if I had one like it myself. I couldn't halfway keep up with what he was saying, though, because I had my mind on what I wanted to get to, and that was the massacre.

Finally, when I seen we'd be on the subject of that planter till next week if I didn't put a stop to it, I said, "Say, Cephas, while I'm thinking about it, I want to ask you a question. The other day somebody, I forget who, brought up that old house-place over there on Haley Blair's land, and that put me to studying about it. Wasn't some of your folks killed there by Indians around eighty or ninety years ago?"

Well, I never expected to see my words have such a strong effect as they did. Yas stopped right where he stood. "They was," he said. Like he wanted to be awful careful and not say too much. But a round red face like Yas's can be depended on to give a man away right at once.

The way I look at it now, it was that minute when things slipped another notch. I wanted awful strong, I guess, to involve somebody else in all these curious happenings. I'd already halfway tried with Ellen and seen that wouldn't work. Now I'd reached a point where I wanted to make light of it, because it was all so serious it was scary, and picking Yas as the next choice for a person to involve was a good way of doing that. If I'd give myself time to think it over, I'd've seen the likelihood of some pretty bad consequences. I just didn't take no time to consider, and of course on the spur of the moment like that you're liable to do anything. Not that I was anyways close to confiding in Yas as I would of in a more sensible person. What come to my mind was how good a prank it would be to play on Yas to tell him some wild tale about the old house-place just to see what he'd do. And a many a time, later on, I sure wished I hadn't done it. What I thought of as a joke never was a joke. It spread over the whole community and got me into this terrible mess I'm still in. And the consequences didn't stop with me neither.

Right then I happened to recall a good example of how superstitious Yas was. One moonlight summer night some time back, when the whole family was asleep on pallets with the doors and windows wide open and no screens on any of them, Yas'd had a mighty bad fright. Him and his old lady was on a pallet by the door, and to hear him tell it, he woke up and seen a tall shape the color of the moonlight standing on the steps next to his head, ready to come in the house.

Yas doubled up his fist and hit at it while he was still lying down, but all he hit was the door facing, for Yas said his fist went right through the thing and he didn't feel nothing when it did but a kind of a tingling. By the time the old lady woke up, a second later, the thing was gone and Yas was setting there with some busted knuckles. Since that night, if he wasn't before, Yas had been a great believer in ghosts.

That incident was on my mind when I said to Yas, "You reckon a place has to have a house to be hanted?"

"I don't see why it would." He was getting uneasier by the minute.

"What do you know about that family? Did your Pa remember any of them?"

"Just barely. They was some relation to my Ma's people, but she didn't remember much about them neither."

But that wasn't so, I reckon, for he went on and told me a good bit about them: "Their name was Tandrum—funny name. The man was a sort of a preacher, I been told, and a weather prophet and somebody that could handle a water witch. Grandpa used to say Tandrum could foretell the weather for you might near anytime he felt like it, or find water when nobody else couldn't, and had some powers besides that he could put to use for bad purposes. Said several people Tandrum didn't like taken sick, and a few of them died. Some people said Tandrum got no more than what was coming to him when the Indians killed and scalped him. Course they got his family too, and they I reckon was innocent."

Then after sighing heavy, he added on, "Yas, that's sure been a long time ago, and most folks seem to've forgot about it."

He kep on staring at the ground, his face becoming thoughtfuller and thoughtfuller, and I could read in it how scared he must've been the first time his Pa or Grandpa told him that story away back yonder. I could see that jackleg preacher turning into the thing that stood on Yas's doorstep one summer night and tempted him into busting his fist on the door facing.

But here it was my joke hadn't hardly got started, and I was feeling sorry for Yas and fixing to back out already on fooling him. I imagine what made me go on, right then, was because I begun to get a little mad at him, thinking, 'Anybody that'd let a thing like that get the best of them!'

Out loud I said, "I happened to be over there around that old place looking for a cow the other night. Found the fence tore down and had to go over on Haley Blair's land. And you know what? I seen a funny glow down towards that branch. It could've been marsh gas, of course, but it didn't look that natural."

That done it. Yas turned around towards me with his eyes bugged out and his face redder'n ever. I swear you could've started a fire with it.

"You reckon!" He kind of gasped, in such a way so I didn't know whe'er I was supposed to reckon it could've been marsh gas or a ghost.

We just had to talk about it for some time after that. I must've repeated the story to Yas a dozen times, adding a few things as I went, but making sure I didn't contradict myself. Though it wouldn't've mattered much if I had. Yas wasn't on the lookout to catch me in any lie. Towards the last there, I got to where I tried to soften things down some, saying, "Come to think about it, it must've been marsh gas."

But Yas wouldn't do nothing but shake his head and mutter, "I doubt it, I doubt it." Whereas you could see he didn't have no doubts at all: to him it was a ghost.

So, what's done is done. Looking back on it now, the thing I regret the most is the part I agged Yas on to playing in this whole affair. I've wished a thousand times I'd kep my mouth shut, and then he wouldn't've put hisself in such danger to find out if I was telling the truth. What I done wasn't only just dumb. In a manner of speaking it was shifting the responsibility of my strange experiences by making them into a joke, so-called, at somebody else's expense, namely Yas's. I couldn't make light of myself, but I could of him. I see that now, but then I didn't.

After a while I went on back home and about my business. Nothing out of the ordinary happened for a few days. I figured, though, I'd hear from Yas sooner or later, and sure enough, one evening about three o'clock here he come out to the field where I was, had parked his car on the road and started towards me before I noticed him. I was right at the end of a row, so I pulled up in the shade of a pecan tree and waited. He come up and we set down on the ground. For a little while we talked about the prospects for crops, but it wasn't no time till Yas got around to what he'd come for.

"Listen here," he said, "I been doing some tall studying about what you told me, and I can't seem to get it off of my mind. So I'll make you a proposition if you got time to listen to it."

Looked like he was ashamed of being so serious but just couldn't help hisself.

"Fire away," I said.

"Well now, the other morning I had my mind all made up to go over there that night and see this thing for myself. But when the time come to go, I said, 'No, Amon's the one to see to this. You go and talk to him. He'll know right where to go and right where to look and so on.' I said to myself, 'You might go over there and lay out all night at the wrong spot, and what would that get you?' I said, 'Hit Amon up about it, ask him if he won't go with you.' But then I said, 'Yas, but Amon's sure to take it you're afraid to go by yourself.' And that put me in a quandry for a little bit. But when I thought it over I knowed you wouldn't think bad of me. You wouldn't, of course, because any fool'd know I wasn't afraid. Ain't that right?"

I believe he'd've jumped on me right then and there if I hadn't answered, "Well, of course you ain't afraid. Who'd ever dream of a thing like that?"

"All right, that much is understood. Then what do you say about going along with me over there tonight, or the first time you can get off, and let's have a look at this hant."

"Well, Cephas, you know what I said the last time I seen you. I've pretty well got myself convinced it wasn't nothing but marsh gas, a jack-o-lantern, you know. Fact of business, I'm so sure about it, I don't see no necessity for checking up on it."

Of course I was just leading him on. And you ought to seen how touchy he got.

"You listen to me, Amon Lamb," he busted out, "if you think you can start a thing like this and then just go and let it drop, you got another think acoming!"

You see there? I couldn't've pulled back if I'd wanted to. Yas was bound and determined to be fooled. Nothing'd do but I had to go over there to that old place with him, and really I was glad enough to oblige him.

So we made it up to go that very night, and he went home satisfied, I reckon.

Right after dark, then, I went down and picked up Yas in my car, and we struck out on our project. Since you can't make it to that old place in a car without passing in sight of Haley Blair's house, and we sure didn't want to do that, we drove down the county road to where a lane turns in on my side of the line fence, followed that into the woods for about a hundred yards or so, stopped the car and got out. Thataway the car was off of the road a piece, enough so nobody wouldn't see it and wonder what we was up to around there.

I had a flashlight with me, and I carried it, but I made out like using it might scare off what we'd come to hunt for. I told Yas we better not switch it on unless we got in trouble and just had to. So we made a stab at it in the dark, floundering around quite a lot, Yas more'n me, because I knowed the territory better'n he did, and because he's so big and clumsy anyhow. They wasn't no moon this early, and in the woods it was about as dark as night can be. I tried to make Yas see that he ought to walk behind me, but he wouldn't hear of it, still afraid of being cowardly, I reckon. And right off, of course, he run headon into a brushpile and fell down and laid there crashing and thrashing around making more noise than a herd of cattle stampeding through a dry thicket. I had to turn on the light then, to get him out, and from then on he was satisfied to walk behind me. Even at that he just barely missed blundering into a rick of firewood.

It wasn't but a little piece to the edge of the woods, even if it did seem like a long ways, having Yas to fool with. We made it there finally, and on down through some heavy grass and weeds to a simmon thicket fairly well out into Haley's pasture. You could hide just inside of that thicket and look down the slope towards the whole bottom and on past to the opposite slope where that old house-place was. Naturally, you couldn't see much. The gray-looking pasture disappeared in the dark maybe twenty yards ahead of your eyes. You could just make out, by the slight deepening of the night away down ahead, the place where the thin stand of trees along the branch was. But you couldn't draw no line between that and the opposite slope. Even the horizon of the hill futher up didn't have no shape to it. A few clouds, it looked like, come and went across it, making the dark solid from the hill to the sky, and even when the clouds moved on, the horizon wasn't nothing but where the stars quit.

We just stood there in the edge of the simmon thicket, shifting from one foot to another. About that time I started wishing we'd brought something to set on, for I wasn't about to set on the ground and run the risk of having a snake crawl up. And I wondered, too, how long it would take Yas to get enough of this and decide it was time to go home. But I didn't care, I wasn't going to be the one to suggest leaving, if I had to stand there all night.

Yas was awful cautious, at first, about asking questions. When he finally did get around to it, though, he had aplenty. What time of the night had I seen it? Where was it along the branch? How big was it? How bright was it? Did it have any shape? How fast did it move? And so on.

When he first commenced to questioning me, I got ashamed one more time of deceiving him so bad, I think because of the picture I had of him scrambling around in that brushpile. You couldn't help feeling sorry a little for somebody so easy taken in. As well as I could, I got around his questions. But seeing me hesitate must've made him think I knowed a lot I wasn't willing to tell, so he pressed me more'n ever. Till I got annoyed and let go, and what I told him then sure made him take notice.

I said the thing was pretty good size, and it looked at first like a shiny ball, like a balloon lit up from the inside and floating along through the air. It moved real slow, I said, right down the course of the branch.

Now at the start that was as far as I intended to go. But Yas said, "You mean that's all? Just like any other old jack-o-lantern? You made it sound like more'n that the other day."

So then I allowed myself a little more leeway, not quite remembering what I'd told him before: enough leeway, so it turned out, to send me off into some whopping big yarns and Yas off into believing ever word I uttered.

I said, "No, one time while I was watching it, I seen the thing drift towards a big cottonwood and strike the trunk. But it didn't bust. It just spread out and went on, and once on the other side it rolled up into a ball again. And right there was when it looked like a change come over the thing, like it might've been nothing but a jack-o-lantern before, and then all of a sudden something got into it. It bounced and jumped. It puffed out and shrunk up and dived and leaped. And when it wanted to it flattened out and slid around trees and bushes.

"Did it take on any shape?" Yas wanted to know, and his voice was dead quiet.

"I done told you. Sometimes it was round and sometimes it was flat."

"That ain't what I mean. You know what I mean. Did it get to looking like anything alive?"

He was just too scared to ask right out if it looked human.

"No," I said, real slow like, "not as I recall, not as far as shape's concerned."

While I was making up that pack of windies and spieling them off to Yas as quick as I thought of them, I felt the strangest kind of relief and happiness just to hear them slide off of my tongue. I never had been one to take pleasure in lying just for lying's sake. But in the dark there it was like I wasn't really lying at all, but had just found a way to put into words what had been happening to me for the past few days, stories I had to make up myself, yes, but all of them out of feelings and experiences they wasn't no other way to explain and ones that plumb demanded to be told in some way or another.

Yas had set right down on the ground without thinking, so I said, "Looky here, you better not do that. They might be snakes crawling around."

But he never even let on like he heard me. "You reckon it comes out ever night?"

"Well, I don't know, of course. I just seen it that one time."

"Well, I'm staying here till it does."

Which was all right with me. Still, I didn't want to be responsible for a man getting snake bit, so I talked Yas into letting us use the light long enough—now it was him that wouldn't allow it to be turned on—to find us some seats. We went back to the rick of firewood and carried down two big chunks and made ourselves as comfortable in the edge of that thicket as we could.

There we was, set for the night, it appeared like. We talked for some little bit in a low voice, then Yas got to studying so hard he wouldn't answer me half of the time. Directly I commenced to getting drowsy, and a couple of times I purt near dozed and fell off of my perch. Yas, I reckon, was awake the whole time, and looking a hole through the country down towards the creek.

All of a sudden he punched me and hissed out, "Looky yonder!"

"What is it?"

"There it goes. See it?"

"Where?"

"Right there. Right over the branch and square in front of us."

I looked hard, still I couldn't make out a thing, but I sure did start to feeling creepy, and I guess my voice wasn't any too strong when I said, "No, I don't see nothing."

Yas busted out, "Dam it all, man! what's the matter with your eyes?"

You know how it is when you strain your eyes to see in the dark. If you dart them around pretty often you see different kinds of blurs, but ones that don't tell you nothing. If you hold your eyes real still, the dark in front of you gets thicker instead of thinner, and in a minute's time it's like somebody drawed a heavy cloth over them. I looked and I looked, and the more I looked the more I felt like I couldn't keep shut up no longer. I'd just have to confess the whole prank to him. I wanted to do that, but instead I told another barefaced lie, shaking all over as I done it. I said, "Yaow, I think I do see it."

"Of course you do. See there, it's acting just like you said it would."

As we kep on looking, Yas went to describing what he seen. Might near ever word was what I'd told him no more'n two hours ago, but arranged some different and made wilder in some places. And while I set there getting more and more interested in what he was saying, either my joke turned on me or something happened. I couldn't make myself stop trembling, and it was like I was about to realize something important and dreaded to know it, a feeling akin to the ones I'd had when I walked into the thicket by the swimming-hole, and when I'd coursed the bees through the woods and found the tomahawk right over there where I was now looking. I shook more and more. My ears rung. My breath got hard to draw. I was so weak I had to brace my feet to keep from tumbling off of that stick of wood I was setting on.

And then I did see it! I swear I did! I seen a kind of a glow about the size of a washtub moving along close to the ground. It didn't have none of the qualities I'd described and it wasn't real shiny, but it was there all right, to my eyes, and it wasn't no marsh gas. You've seen low clouds when you stood a long ways off from bright street lights and watched the clouds drift along through the glow overhead. That's how this was, only they wasn't any lights around, and they was just this one cloud-of-a-thing brushing along the ground.

Quite a bit of time went by before I noticed that Yas wasn't talking anymore. Both of us set there in a kind of a trance staring. I finally spoke up:

"Well!"

Yas jumped up like he'd been shot at. "What's the matter?"

"Nothing at all," I said, matter-of-fact-like.

I stood up too. Being stiff from setting, we stomped around a little. I guess we was afraid to say anything.

In a few minutes we headed out for the car, using the flashlight this time. I don't believe we said over six words all the way.

Godamighty! To think I ever looked on any of that as a joke!

8

All right. Now I have to watch out here and not miss any important details. Because the first terrible thing come about on account of mine and Yas's adventure.

He didn't waste no time in spreading the news around. Inside of a few days looked like everbody in the county knowed about it. And, as you might expect, the thing got twisted and blowed up and made into different versions. One of them had it me and Yas was chased by a strange thing and fell in the creek. Another one had a ghost rising out of the old house-place and screaming up and down the pasture like a cougar. The newspaper in Milcourt got ahold of the story, and when I read their account I couldn't keep from laughing. It said a man had been hung out there one time and the place was 'reputed to be a gathering place for ghosts from a nearby graveyard.' I knowed right away they had it mixed up with another old tale or two I'd heard. To hear them tell it, me and Yas dared one another to spend the night there, halfway as a joke. Along about midnight we seen the ghost of the hung man come out of the ground and climb the tree he'd died on. Then he sailed out of it and headed towards us, and we lit out as fast as our legs could carry us, nearly run ourselves to death before we got home.

Godamighty! And to think I used to believe what I'd read in the paper!

The upshot was, the incident got to be notorious in no time. Everbody I run onto asked me about it. People from all over the country started going over there and wanting to see the spot, driving out from town and even over from the next county. They kep old Haley pretty busy, I reckon. The majority of them asked his permission to drive into his place, but some just went on in anyhow, and left gates down so his stock got out. He put locks on all the gates, so I was told, and signs pointing down to the cattleguard that was the closest way over there anyhow. It must've been a lot of trouble for him, and I was sorry about that. If it had just've been a matter of a prank and no more, I'd've made some effort to put a stop to it. But things had already moved on past the prank stage, and even if I'd wanted to, I don't reckon I could've done much to put a quietus to it by that time, no matter how hard I tried. A time or two I thought about going over to see Haley and trying to make some kind of amends, but any way I could think of to approach him wouldn't come to nothing but admitting I'd deliberately done him a bad turn, which wasn't by any means so. And before I offered any apologies to Haley Blair, I'd've had to know for sure I was in the wrong, and no two ways about it.

But now then let me bring in Ellen, because no matter if she didn't have much to do with it at first, her effect on everthing is in the long run the most important one to me.

We'd made up after that little spat we had from visiting the graveyard. Actually they wasn't much making up to it. We had our falling-outs like that one regular enough, and sometimes they ended up with me tearing out home. But then the next time we seen one another we'd be right back in a good humor again, and that was the wind-up of it.

I told Ellen about my prank: another substitute, you see, for not confiding in her about the rest of it. I ought to've knowed, though, that Ellen ain't so easy fooled. She seen right away they was more to it than I let on, I guess from the way I talked. We was in my car on our way to town, one Saturday evening, at the time. She turned on me—I catch a glimpse of her now, all of a sudden, face turned towards me, brown and firm, hair pulled back behind her ears—and I can just hear her saying, "Amon, what're you up to?" Like she wasn't quite worried, yet, about the answer she might get, but just making sure they was as much to be curious about as she thought they was.

Well, it sort of jolted me, that question, hit me so quick I couldn't think of no answer right at once. So I tried to pass the whole thing off: "What do you mean, what am I up to? I told you all about it. I wondered what Yas would do if I told him such a tale, and now you know the outcome."

"Amon, cut it out!" she snaps back. "You know as well as I do you're up to something. But anyhow, let's don't quarrel about it. You can tell me whenever you get ready, and it's up to you when."

So all I'd gained was to convince Ellen they was something important I wasn't telling her, and hurting her feelings because I wouldn't. But Godamighty! I don't see how I could've told her anything, by that time, that wouldn't've sounded plumb insane.

Me and Ellen don't go to town much together. As a general thing she goes by herself, and so do I. But I'd offered to lay off work and take her in that day to kind of make up for the yard-goods episode.

After I'd parked out close to the Market Square and Ellen had gone off to buy some nicknacks or other, I done all I needed to do: went over to the implement store and bought a new set of sweeps. Then I put them in the car and santered around killing time.

God! I'm telling you! Sometimes as I set here writing, that town of Milcourt gets under my skin and starts me to wishing I was back there so hard I don't know what to do. From time to time I wonder if it really is the way I see it, or ever was. I expect it must be tumbledown in spots and stained-up and wore-out here and there. But I know for a fact it would be heaven compared to the burg I'm in now. Like I'm standing on the corner of the Market Square in Milcourt, seeing the shacks on wheels the peddlers use. And they's an old red mule tied to a post twitching his ears to throw off flies. Or I'm walking up Industry Street where the crowd has thinned out, and ever place of business I pass I want to stop for a second and think about. I can see inside of them better than if I was actually standing there. My eyes run around Mellon's Cafe or Owens' Grocery or the Snow White Laundry or Worthington's Secondhand Store. There's Old Man Mellon in his apron spotted from frying hamburgers. There's Old Man Worthington pulling out a banjo from under a big pile of old clothes to try to sell it, in his dry way, to some kid. There's the boss of the laundry—I can't never think of his name—setting in his office that looks like a cage. Then I step down the street a ways and look over the fence into the backyard of Stafford's Hotel and there's the parrot that looks like the manager of the laundry, in a cage that looks like his office.

That Saturday in town nothing out of the ordinary occurred till I happened to see old pebble-headed Haley Blair eyeing me kind of funny from across the street. I was just fixing to go over there and speak to him, say something, no matter how little, by way of an explanation. But he turned around and disappeared in the crowd before I could get to him, and I didn't see nothing more of him that evening.

Now it wasn't till I seen Brother Ike, and Old Man Gray, that I found out just how far and in what way the thing had spread. It happened so I remembered out of nowhere the color of thread Ellen was using on some embroidery I'd seen laying out on her dresser at home. Maybe she needed some extra thread, and maybe she didn't, but I still felt some twinges about that piece of yard-goods, so I thought I'd get rid of them once and for all by doing something I hadn't been asked to do. So off I went to Kress's and picked up the thread, and just about the time I finished, who come along but Ike. He'd just been to the candy counter and bought hisself some chocolate peanuts.

He come on outside with me, acting like they was something he just couldn't wait to tell or ask me. He looked around to make sure nobody wasn't listening, then said to me in a low voice, "Would you mind coming over to the car with me, Brother Amon. They's something I'd like to talk to you about."

Now Ike takes his job of being the preacher serious. When the two of us was settled in the front seat of his car and eating his chocolate peanuts, he said, "Well now, Brother Amon, you're liable to think I'm butting in where I ain't got no business. But just hear me out on one or two items, and then you can judge to suit yourself. Then if you say so, I'll shut up and say no more. Ain't that a fair way to handle it?"

"Reckon so," I said.

Ike went at it right logical, saying, "Number one, I've heard a good deal about yours and Cephas's scrape. Number two, I want to offer you a suggestion from what happened to me."

The two things didn't quite seem to me to fit the way he put them, but I let that pass. What I wanted to do the most was to steer him so I wouldn't have to tell him just what happened in that scrape, as he called it.

So my answer was, "From what happened to you, you say?"

He bobbed his head strong for 'Yes,' and offered me some chocolate peanuts, which I taken. Then he busted aloose like he never did mean to stop:

"When I was little, my Ma told me I don't know how many times to stay away from that old house-place. According to her, the booger man lived there. That scared me at first, but later on, when I got a little bigger and...you take...well, bolder, I got to fooling around there sometimes. Never did see nothing out of the way neither. No, I expect I better put it thisaway. It'll be easier to understand, as far as that's concerned."

That last bunch of words showed that Ike was working up to his preaching self. He's picked up a few expressions he throws into his sermons here and there, not because they always go where he puts them, but because they make him sound educated, he thinks, and because they help him to keep on talking while he's trying to think up something to say. He'll pronounce each word slow and clear: "As far as that's concerned," or "In point of fact," or "If we can hold our attention on the problem for a moment."

He went on: "In point of fact, one day me and a bunch more boys was playing all up and down that branch. I expect they was eight or ten of us. They was grapevines to swing on and trees to climb and all like that, a dandy place for us to play, as far as that's concerned. Yes, and we begun to play catch out there in the edge of the pasture, with a baseball we had with us, and we kep moving our game around, without hardly knowing where we was at, till we happened to drift into that old house-place. Now, if you'll bear with me," (which is another one of his expressions), "one of the boys throwed the ball as hard as he could send it, and I was the one supposed to catch it. But instead of it coming at me direct, it curved off to one side, and in running over to catch it I stubbed my toe on a rock or something and fell down. Just as I hit the ground I remember seeing that ball roll out of sight into the woods. I got right up, of course, and lit out after the ball, not hurt any. I didn't have to chase it more'n a few yards. Into the woods I run, and there I seen the ball laying half-buried in the dead leaves under a thick stand of trees. I made a dive for it like it might've tried to get away or something.

"Well sir, just as I hit the ground and grabbed the ball, I happened to glance up a draw towards the top of the hill. They wasn't much underbrush there, so the ground, from where I was seeing it, run up in two slopes like this"—he held out his hands in a flat vee-like shape—"smooth and all dead-leaf color, only for the straight black trunks of the trees. This draw come to a point near the top of the hill in a spot where it was might near too dark for a person to see. Somebody—and it was *somebody,* though it was more'n that too—was just standing there, right where the two slopes met and it was dark, looking a lot futher off than he was, straight as any of the trees and as tall as some of them. Dressed up, he was, in Sunday clothes, in a real dark suit and white shirt, had his hat on with the brim pulled down in front so everthing was shaded out of sight but his chin. That chin had a red streak on it like he'd been eating dewberries, only they must've had awful bright juice.

"I got up and run, I don't mind telling you. I come busting out of the woods as hard as I could tear and hollered out to the rest of them before I thought: 'Old Mr. Tandrum's up yonder on the hill!'

"They all stopped playing like they was froze. Then one of them spoke up in a screechy voice, 'Who did you say?'

"I reckon I must've been white as a sheet, but I had gumption enough to say, 'Oh, I mean Mr. Jim Blair, of course. It's his land and he might not like for us to be fooling around on it.'

"They all laughed out real loud, and one of them said, 'Why, what would he care? Let's all go up there and tell him we're just playing.'

"And I couldn't keep them from going, though I hung back among the last. But of course we didn't find nobody. And after that when I'd think about it, I tried to make out like it really was Old Man Jim Blair. Guess I finally got myself to believing it—for a while.

"Now then, I have to go on and tell you something I ain't never told nobody, and I wouldn't tell you only for this reason....As far as that's concerned. And Brother Amon, don't you scoff. And don't say you ain't inclined to scoff, because I've noticed you doing it to yourself a many a time.

"What I seen in the woods that day, it ain't everbody can see. Me and you can, and Cephas in a way, and I expect Haley Blair. Yes, but...now looky here, this is what I mean. The day come when I was to be called to preach, the night when I heard a voice from down in the pasture. But when I first woke up that night, before I heard the voice, I had a full recollection of that man in the woods, as clear as if I'd been there once more in the flesh. All the little particulars come back to me: chasing the ball, falling down on the leaves, looking up the draw. But something turned clear that never had been before. They was enough light there now to see under the brim of the hat, and it was a horrible mask of a thing I seen there, twisted and wrinkled and bloody. And right then I heard the voice. And I got up out of my bed and I went to the door and I walked right out into the night, fearing no evil. Down in the pasture as far as the tank I went, and as I stood on the bank looking at the black water, I didn't see nor hear nothing more. But I felt as peaceful as I ever had in all of my life, because I knowed I'd faced up to my call and walked in the right direction. Maybe I did see one and just hear the other one calling my name, but I knowed the voice of the Lord from the beckoning of the Devil."

It's hard to describe how I felt when Ike got through talking. Embarrassed, for one thing. Because he'd admitted more about hisself than I really wanted to hear or he would've told me most any other time. Sorry for him, too, for Ike thinking he was a sort of a prophet like the ones he'd read about in the Bible. I wonder if he ever thought about how he looked, setting there in his old dingy black suit, in that white shirt that wasn't ironed smooth and that old purple necktie drawed up in such a tight knot it looked like it would choke him to death, and his old long skinny neck with wrinkles running like white grooves across it, and a whopping big Adam's apple.

We must've looked pretty comical, both of us, setting there, for one thing the way me and him got rid of that sack of chocolate peanuts. All the time he was telling his story, that little old white sack kep passing back and forth between us. About the time Ike finished up his tale, I was chewing up the last of my share of that candy, and Ike's Adam's apple was jumping up after the last of his'n like a fish after bait.

But as funny as it was, it wasn't no laughing matter. Up to then I never had taken Ike what you'd call serious, and he knowed it. Really, I never had seen him talk and act more ridiculous than I did now, but underneath all of that, I seen a man that was a whole lot akin to me.

The only other thing he had to say was in the way of advice. How I better just stay clear of that old house-place. And I appreciated the length he'd gone to to give me a warning.

So then how could I tell him the whole thing started off as a joke? And even if I'd had the spunk to do that, how would I've gone about telling him the rest of the truth, about the tomahawk and all, and the cloud of light I'd seen. I didn't see no way to make even as much sense out of it as he'd made out of his story.

One thing I had seen for sure by now, and that was how folks hadn't anyways near forgot about the strange happenings that had gone on at that old Tandrum place, and who could tell now where all of it was likely to end?

So I didn't admit nothing to Ike, just left him by saying how glad I was I'd had a chance to talk to him. My excuse for leaving was I had to get back and meet Ellen at a certain time and place.

I headed out down Industry Street, appearing to be in a terrible hurry till I was out of sight of Ike. Not watching where I was going, I come pretty close to getting myself into it again before I was clear out of the last scrape. I come in a inch of running head on into Old Man Gray before I seen him. As luck'd have it, though, I was right at the corner of Industry and Walnut and could duck around the corner making straight for the Market Square, and disappear before he could get to the corner I'd just left and might see me by looking the way I'd gone.

But my idey didn't work out. Because he was hunting for me and I reckon turned back when he seen me turn, come around on the other side of the block and out on the Square to head me off. And this time he was right on me before I knowed anything about it.

"Amon, I want to talk to you."

Dam it! Was everbody in town looking for me? It was all I could do to keep from jumping. When somebody's been avoiding you for years, the way Old Man Gray has me, and then comes boguing right up to you out in public with a greeting like that, you don't know what to think. And the tone he taken sure had me puzzled. It wasn't mad, nor it wasn't friendly neither. It was sort of like you'd talk to a kid, letting him know you was on to his tricks and telling him he'd better open his ears and listen if he knowed what was good for him.

"Well, Mr. Gray! How're you?" I done my best to act surprised and glad in just the right mixture.

"None of your business, since you don't care one way or another anyhow. What I got to say to you concerns Ellen, boy, and if you got any man about you, you won't run off till I get through telling you."

The way him and Pap still call me 'boy' is the beatingest thing! Hell, I ain't been a boy for years!

But the thing that really made me nervous was the subject I just knowed he was about to face me with. I'd always been scared that one of these days he'd step up to me no telling where and jump on me about Ellen in no uncertain terms. And they ain't no way, I'd already decided, to make preparations for a thing like that. So I was even relieved, figuring I'd drawed the bad instead of the worse, when he commenced on the same thing I'd just been talking to Ike about.

He said, "They tell me you and Yas Bailey run on to something over there on Haley Blair's place. I don't know if you did or not, and as far's you're concerned, I don't care. If something carried you off to Guinea it'd suit me just as well. But then it might make some difference to Ellen, so that's why I'm warning you. What you probably don't know is, they's an old well down there that ain't covered over any too good, and if you take to fooling around there at night you're liable to fall in it."

Not quite knowing what to make out of that, I said, "It's a pasture, of course, and don't you think Haley Blair would have the well fixed so his stock won't fall in?"

Now that come out before I thought. I wish I hadn't made light of what the old fellow said. He was just using that well for an excuse. I'm satisfied he had as many qualms about that spot as Ike did, and about the same kind, only he'd've thought it was foolish to put them in words. So he used this roundabout way to warn me, and I ought to've appreciated it more than I did at the time.

He said, "I just thought I better tell you, that's all."

He seen, of course, what a fool he'd look like if he let everthing go at that—him not speaking to me for years and then buttonholing me with no more to say than he'd just said. Like I didn't have sense enough not to fall in a well. But he didn't know what to say next, and he had me to where I didn't neither. So we just kind of stood there, and it was about the most uncomfortable wait I've been through in a long time.

After a while he taken up again, "How much you know about that old place, boy? For instance, you ever heard about what occurred there about, oh I judge fifty years ago?"

"You wouldn't be referring to the massacre?"

"Hell no! That was a lot longer'n fifty years back. No, what I'm alluding to is what happened to one of the Bailey boys back then, Cephas's uncle, I believe it was. To start out with, he taken to poking around there looking for Indian spikes, and he picked up some too. But when his daddy found out about it, he made him throw them away. Said people had been killed with them things, and who knowed what'd happen to the person that kep them around. Now then, he told his daddy he got shut of them, but he didn't do it. Fact is, he hunted around and found some more. When his daddy learned about it the second time, he give the boy a devil of a whipping, and the boy, who was a great big hulk of a kid, stood up to him. Kicked out at him is what he done, and some harder, I guess, than he meant to. Hit him right between the legs, and didn't aim to do that neither, I reckon.

They say his daddy fell over like he was dead, and the boy run off, too scared to do anything else.

"Well, his daddy never got over that exactly. It might near ruined the rest of his life. Him and his boy never made it up neither. What happened to the boy I don't remember for sure, but I've heard tell he come to a bad end off in some other state."

And he switched right there, hummed and hawed, asked me if I'd seen his wife around town, said he'd been looking everwhere for her.

I said no, I hadn't. But I was mighty busy thinking, What's all this, anyhow? All my life around here I've been seeing people in a certain way that don't include any of this. What did I do? I just told a kind of a half-joking lie to a fellow that's easy fooled. And it backfired right away. First I begun to believe my own story. Then Yas he run all over the country with it, like I knowed he would. But what's all this ruckus growing so fast for? Tales everwhere, one man telling me the history of his life and his calling, another one warning me about a crime. What have I started, anyhow?

Old Man Gray happened to glance off, about then, towards one corner of the Market Square. I noticed his eyes done a kind of a quick roll back in my direction, then he muttered, "You better heed my warning," and lit out for another part of town like he didn't have no time to tarry.

I guessed what was the matter before I looked. He'd seen Ellen coming and he didn't want her to catch him talking to me. Sure enough, there she was, circling around among a whole throng of people and cars, cool as anything, and the sweet dark of her face clear and soft even that far away. And because of the way her dad'd been talking to me, for a minute there I felt towards her, and myself too, like I'd felt just a few times, and couldn't hold on to for long. It was like having all that delicious pain of the first time you're in love—when you hovered around outside a door with a present you hadn't even wrapped, when you watched a girl from far off like she was a comet you'd see just once in a lifetime. It was like having all that carried over as fresh as ever to your grown-up days, after you've won all the freedom of love they is. And if I'd ever wanted for a minute to say to Ellen, 'Let's get married right now and grow up,' a time like then would've changed my mind for good.

Dam it all to hell anyway! Why am I setting up here in a state I never wanted to come to, writing all this down? Why ain't I doing something to bring back her and all of my old life?

But I guess for the time being I'm up again a blank wall. I see a door a ways down, yes, maybe, but till I've set everthing straight behind me, I can't decide whe'er to force it open or pass on.

The big question is, Could I just up and go back home and to hell with the whole bunch of them down there? What could Haley Blair and the likes of him do about it? Well, they could get dangerous, I reckon. I don't believe they could get the law after me, because they've already failed at that one time. But I know for a fact, because I heard them, that they'd just as soon've hung me that night as not. They may've settled down some since then, but they may not've too. Still, that ain't the main point. The main point is, What does Ellen think? They wasn't no time to find out before I left, nor even to say goodbye. But she knows where I am. She knows I'm waiting to hear from her. Why in the hell don't she write me? I reckon she's just got me down as a sorry bastard, and don't want nothing more to do with me. And if that's the way she feels, and I can't win her back no way in the world, do you think I'd go back home just to give that sonofabitch Haley Blair a good opportunity to lead a mob to tar and feather me? Or maybe string me up? In a pig's ass I would!

But let's get back to where we was, that Saturday in town. Ellen come up to me on the square, and we got in the car and started out home. It's not much I can remember of the next few hours after that, in any kind of a regular order. It's like the rest of that day was too full of joy to see any minute of it plain next to any other minute. Ellen had lots of flowers out by that time of the year, and I can see her over and over in the middle of them. We caught up two horses and done some riding around down along the branches. I stayed for supper, I know, and after supper....I remember the lamplight on the table, the shadow of Ellen as well as her body itself, and that brown glowing face the lamplight couldn't get enough of. I remember the starched cleanness of the house, the smell and taste of the bread Ellen made. I remember the kind of a smooth tingle that run over my skin ever few minutes like a new charge and made me say inside myself, I'm alive, I'm here, I love her. Then the charge would strike my heart and cause it to blaze up for a second before it settled back to its steady glow. I remember laying in bed with her till away along in the night, and the love we felt spreading deep peace through the whole night and absorbing the moonlight, from that moon so bright that when I got up to go home I felt like talking to it.

I didn't quite talk to it, but I come the next thing to doing it, as I was driving home real slow early in the morning. Different voices put up a clamor inside of me and rose close to the surface, my own voice answering the voice of Ellen, of Ike, of Old Man Gray, answering even what Haley Blair would've said if he hadn't stepped out of sight in the crowd before I could reach him .

And it seemed like to me they was some deep truth in that day that I'd never be capable of seeing all at once. I'd recollect how my prank had turned on me, and I'd become fearful. I'd recollect what Old Man Gray had said, and I'd feel a terrible longing for youth and age at the same time. I'd recollect what Ike said, and I'd see through his words into his visions, and feel disturbed.

Seemed like, too, as I drove home through the moonlight, that this day I had traveled a long ways futher into that strange country I'd come to the border of that Sunday in the church-house. And I seen opening before me a time when everthing I done would fall in a different light than it ever had before: like when you go to sleep under the shade of the porch roof on a moonlight night and have clearer dreams than any you could have in a dark room in bed, for the moon stays right with you in your sleep and shows you the way into what will be on the dream road ahead. It's like you could rise up in your sleep and step down off of the porch and walk a great distance through the glowing country, and as you walked, hours and days as well as yards and miles'd slip by you and you could live your life fast enough to see not just little parts of it alone, but long stretches of it all in one piece. From behind, as I rode home in the moonlight, rose up that Sunday morning at church, the swimming-hole, Mary or Sherry, all of them ready to make the future plain when the time come.

All of a sudden, as I drove past the cemetery lane, I recollected the tomahawk I'd found and hid. It dropped right down before my eyes heavy and dark, with the moonlight not able to make the grainy stone of it shine. Was it streaked with blood? I thought it was. But I couldn't go beyond that. I couldn't see how it entered into all of this, and I was afraid to see if I could find out. Yet I would find out. I'd have to. Because now I knowed good and well the tomahawk and all of the rest of the peculiar experiences of the past couple of weeks was signs of something fearful big yet to come.

9

After that night though, things cooled down some for a while. I didn't hear no more from Yas, nor from Ike nor Old Man Gray nor nobody else. I stayed pretty close to home, except for going to see Ellen. Me and her was getting along as fine as ever. The only thing anyways worrisome was I'd catch her watching me funny ever now and then, and I'd see with no doubts about it what was on her mind. She knowed something was wrong somewheres, and she wanted to say, the same as she'd said that Saturday on the way to town, 'What're you up to, Amon?', and get a straight answer. But knowing she wouldn't she just wondered and tried not to be too hurt about it. Just one of her funny looks was enough, though, to make me uneasy for a day or two, and in between I dreaded when one'd come next.

Well, the story concerning me and Yas kind of died down, as stories'll do, and the curiosity-seekers quit pestering old Haley so much, I was told. One thing that helped matters along was that people had something real practical to study and worry about now. The country was beginning to suffer for rain. We'd had less of that than we needed for a year or two already, and one more like them might put farmers in a hard shape sure enough, especially it being Depression times and all.

I worked hard in the field. Crops was up good by now but not growing like they ought to. I seen things turning dry and dusty. Still, I didn't see no need to worry about a drouth till one set in good and proper.

For several weeks there, I stayed away from preaching or any other place where I might run into a bunch of my neighbors together. I told myself if I was seen out and around, it might keep tales about that old house-place going longer. But the real reason was, I was just afraid of what the next developments in this whole situation might be, and I'd got to where I wanted to put them off as long as I could.

But things come to a head anyhow. It was one Sunday. Ellen had made it a special point to ask me, the day before, to take her to preaching that morning, a thing she didn't ordinarily do. My excuse for not being able to take her was I'd heard about some tractor attachments for sale way over east of us six or seven miles, and this was the only chance I'd have to look at them. So Sunday morning I drove over by Ellen's and got her in the notion of going with me over there instead of to preaching, and so we struck out.

The trip was mighty dusty. We hadn't got more'n two miles away from home when I seen the drouth was a whole lot worse in that neighborhood than it was in our own. It made me realize what we was in for ourselves if we didn't have some rain pretty soon. That old road hadn't been graveled in a good while, and the red clay that showed through everwhere was cracked and rock hard, with enough of it ground up by wheels to fly like powder when you drove over it. They was a jog in the road ever few hundred yards, with a bunch of hills to go up and down. A right smart of the country was in pasture that wasn't nothing now but dead ticklegrass and patches of moody grass looking singed and scraggly. Where they was fields, mostly planted in cotton and corn and a little dab of peanuts, you could see the worst effects of the drouth. The blades of the corn was beginning to crinkle and die along the edges, the cotton stalks was little old spindly things with leaves drooped down about half-wilted, and the peanut leaves was commencing to turn out the white underside, a thing they oughtn't to do till about thrashing time. I seen a good many dead trees, too, in the timber we passed through, because the drouth had been in effect so long.

We got to where we was going, and I looked over the attachments. I did need some of them, like the post-hole digger, but I didn't buy anything because it was such sorry-looking stuff for the money.

And so we went on back home, got there around dinner time, and being as Ellen had cooked the biggest part of it before we left, we wasn't long in setting down to the table. We didn't go out of the house anymore that evening, and Ellen didn't give me any funny looks. We just spent the time being full and lazy and close to one another.

Still, I left out early, about middle of the evening, because since we'd been together from morning on, I was just afraid she *would* give me one of her looks and ruin the day. Plus for the first time the drouth was beginning to worry me. I thought I'd go on home and do up the work—tend to the stock and chickens and all like that—and then just rest.

Out at the end of the lane from the Gray's house, next to the culbert, is a bunch of mailboxes on an old cultivator wheel and a post, fixed so the mail carrier can turn the wheel around and reach all the boxes without moving his car. A big old blackjack tree stands on the bank of the ditch right in back of the mailboxes. That spot, even more than any other one in that lane I love so well, always makes me feel good to think about it, because it's where you turn in to Ellen's house.

That evening Old Man Gray was setting there under the shade of the blackjack. As I crossed the culbert he stood up and motioned for me to stop, then he come straight over and climbed in the front seat without waiting to be asked.

"Amon, I want to talk to you again, and this time no two ways about it."

My mind caught a glimpse of him disappearing across the square that day he'd give me a going-over the first time. Now, though, he seemed to be a lot more worried than he was before. I didn't say a word. I just waited, kind of scared, the truth is.

"Amon, it's up to you to put a stop to all this, and I mean right now. This ghost business I'm referring to. Yas told me the other day that now Ike's been over there at that old house-place, and he seen one too."

"What's all this? When was Ike over there? I hadn't heard nothing about it."

He waved off my question. "It don't matter just when. But here's the thing. That place is unlucky, we all know that. But you didn't see no ghost there, and you know it! Yas told me how you come over there to his place and inquired around about that Tandrum bunch, and got him all worked up. The durn fool couldn't see you played a trick on him, but I could, just from his report of what you said. What in the devil did you want to start a joke like that for! You've got the whole country in a uproar. Too many people around like Yas and Ike, who'll imagine anything with a little help."

"What did Yas tell you about Ike?"

"Oh, how do I know? Some kind of a man-shaped thing he seen on the top of that old hill south of the house-place."

Just like I thought. Yas heard somewhere—no telling who from—about the round Ike had with the ghost when he was a boy, and Yas had it down as taking place recent, probably didn't even bother to ask Ike about it. But still I didn't want to say anything to straighten Old Man Gray out on it, because it might've meant spilling what Ike had told me, which I taken to be confidential. So I kep my mouth shut.

Old Man Gray was trying to keep ahold of his temper: "You're bound and determined we ain't going to talk about the main proposition, ain't you? But you're going to hear it, whe'er you want to or not. What I mean to tell you is this, you've got to make a clean breast of it about this. Tell people you was fooling, or else the thing'll go on till somebody does something foolhardy. Mark my words. Everthing that takes place over there makes somebody suffer. See if I ain't right. If you suffer, I don't give a dam. You got plenty of it coming, seeing as how you pass it out so easy to other folks. But I'm thinking about my little girl, and I swear to God if you cause her any misery I'll take a shotgun to you!"

I just plumb ignored his threats. Anyhow I was trying to figure out what was in back of all this. Here he was going on like the whole community was still tore up over mine and Yas's scrape, when he surely knowed the matter was settling down. No, he was bound to be bad worried about whe'er we really had seen a ghost or not, because otherwise he wouldn't've done so much inquiring around nor so much studying about it. Whatever he tried to tell me, all the same he sure was superstitious about that old house-place.

I thought I'd fix him, so I said, "What makes you so all-fired sure I didn't see a ghost myself?"

"Don't you start anything like that with me, Amon Lamb! You know Goddam well that was a pure-dee old lie!"

He sure was trying hard to make me agree with him. That old long face of his can get the most serious look on it you ever seen, and when he's mad along with it, the bones stand out white under the skin and his hair bristles out as stiff as it does on an old boar.

I was doing my best to think of something to tell him, but what? If I said I hadn't seen a ghost, that wouldn't've been true in the real sense of the word, and if I said I had, that wouldn't be so neither, exactly. The fact was, I didn't even know how to go about telling the truth anymore. It looked like I'd either have to lie by beating around the bush, the way I had with Ellen, or by making up a wild story, the way I had with Yas.

But what I would've done in that case, I don't know, for something happened to save me from having to go any futher. A car come along, started to pass on by, then stopped all of a sudden and backed up.

It was Ike. He got out and hurried over to where we was. You could see from a distance he was mighty upset about something. And he hadn't hardly come in talking distance when he hollered out, "Amon, I sure am glad I run into you. I need to see you right at once."

Old Man Gray sure got flustered. I thought for a minute he was either going to have a heart attack or just take off and fly.

Ike pulled up short. "Oh, excuse me, Mr. Gray. I was so bent on getting to Amon here I didn't even see you."

"That's all right," said Old Man Gray, which it didn't sound like, then he just set there like he was paralyzed. Ike come right up to the car and leaned on the door, and I was plain caught between them. All I could hope for was they wouldn't discover they both wanted to get on to me about the same thing and gang up on me—for I just knowed Ike had some new wrinkle on the ghost business he wanted to see me about.

It didn't take Old Man Gray long, though, to figure out the same thing. He taken a chance and said, "If it's any of my business, I judge you want to see him about what's been going on over at that old whatch-a-muh-call-it place."

"Why yes, that's right, Mr. Gray. How'd you know?"

Old Man Gray snorted. "Who don't want to see him about that? I just been getting in after him about the same thing myself."

"Well then," said Ike, "I don't suppose it'll hurt none for you to hear what I've got to say about it. Amon, I'm worried. About my boys, that is. What I need to know is, did you actually see something over there, or has Yas just let his imagination run away with him? I mean, to me it don't matter, but to my boys...."

I could've interrupted right there and said, 'You're a good one to ask me a question like that, after that story you handed me in town here a while back.' Seem like for the minute he'd deliberately put that out of his mind. But I let him go on.

"You know, my boys, when they first heard about that situation, went and gathered up a bunch more kids to go with them, and they aimed to go over there and spend the night. I got wind of what they was up to, so I forbid them to do it. But to my way of thinking they'll find some way to sneak off and go. I can't watch them ever minute. I don't care, of course, for them going over there in the daytime. I've got a pretty strong suspicion that's where they went to today, even the youngest one, and he ain't but ten years old. I was just on my way over there to see about them." (If he didn't care, what was he so worried about?) "But I seen you here, Amon, and I thought it'd be a good idey if you could talk to them, explain all this mystery. You know how kids are. If you laugh at them a little, and tell them it was all a joke, they'll forget all about it."

I thought to myself, 'Why Ike, you old so-and-so, you too! You're getting to be as big a liar as I am!' He thought I'd seen something, and he'd worried about it as much as Old Man Gray had. But he wasn't going to ask me to deny it direct to him. If he could talk me into lying to his kids, though, he could pretty soon believe it hisself.

All of which sure made me think less of Ike than I had been lately. But I reckon he thought less of me too than he always had.

All I said was, "Well, maybe we better go on over there and see about your boys."

Ike wasn't willing to press matters about what I'd seen, but Old Man Gray didn't have no such qualms.

"Hold on a minute," he said. "You ain't answered Brother Ike's question. Did you see something or not? Just admit it was a prank and be done with it."

And boy, that got old Ike! He seen his sideling around and trying to make me lie wasn't working. I could just see fear all over him that I'd break out right there with the story he'd told me, or maybe look him right in the eye and describe the appearance of a man in a big hat with blood like berry juice on his chin. For a minute I bet he wished a thousand times he'd never told me about that.

Well, I won't say I didn't think about doing just that, putting Ike in more embarrassment than he'd put me in, tit for tat. But I didn't do nothing of the kind. I set there, holding on to the steering wheel and looking straight ahead, trying my best, still, to think up a answer that'd satisfy them. They was both looking at me like now everthing depended on what I said, and of course that just made me more nervous'n ever about speaking up.

But then I seen keeping quiet too long would be the same thing as saying 'Yes, I did see something.' So I quick-like blurted out, "If we're going to see about them boys, we better get on over there." And at the same time I jammed my thumb onto the starter button.

I was hoping Old Man Gray'd say he had to get out and go on back home, but he didn't make no move to, just set there. So I drove off with him, Ike's car fell in behind me, and we tore out. Looked like Old Man Gray wanted to question me some more, but I reckon he thought better of it, because he clammed up.

When we come to the cattleguard opening into Haley Blair's place, I was glad it was a good piece from his house, even if it wasn't altogether out of sight. The pasture road inside the cattleguard led down to the branch and played out, but you could see where cars had been turning up the branch to get up as close as they could to the old house-place. I followed their marks on the grass as far as any of them went, and a little futher, till I come smack dab up again a ditch, about a hundred yards from where me and Yas was supposed to've seen the ghost rise up.

They wasn't nobody around, no cars nor anything. Me and Old Man Gray got out, Ike come up, and we all stood there looking around.

"Where do you reckon they went?" said Ike.

"What makes you so sure they come here?" I asked him right back.

"I'm satisfied they did."

About then I caught a glimpse of two or three boys up the slope in the edge of the woods, right there in that draw where Ike'd seen his ghost. But Ike hadn't seen the boys yet, and I was hoping they'd get out of there before he did, afraid seeing them there would scare him half to death. Anyhow, I remembered well enough about sneaking off places when I was a kid, and I wasn't in favor of giving them away. If I'd been them, I'd've hiked out for home through the woods and been there when the old man got back.

The boys give theirselves away, though. Probably figuring they'd already been seen and couldn't get out of it, they come out of the woods to face us.

"There they are, finally!" said Ike in a voice that was fierce but scared at the same time.

The three of them come poking down the rise, the biggest one in front and the littler ones trailing him, all of them dreading ever step that drawed them closer to us and the wearing-out they thought was waiting for them. I begun to feel right sorry for them.

But that march down the hillside of three guilty younguns broke up all of a sudden. I never seen anything happen so fast in my life. First, they was three boys dragging along, and then, like the earth had swallowed him, the smallest one dropped out of sight.

I didn't hear nothing. I just caught sight of him as he sunk straight into the ground, seen his arms fling out, seen a little puff of dust. And in one instant that spot, from where we stood, looked like it never had been disturbed at all. Only they was now just two boys dragging down the hill.

It didn't take me but a second to realize what had happened. He'd fell in that old well. And by the time I realized it, I was running as hard in that direction, already, as my legs'd carry me, without even informing Ike or

Old Man Gray what the matter was. The other two boys turned ever which-away, even started to run, I guess thinking I was running up there to give them a whipping myself. But when they turned around and seen what it was all about, they froze right where they was and didn't stir.

Now I could see the hole, four or five foot across and looking like it was ready to cave in some more at the edges. An old rotten end of log or two stuck out a little over the hole. I dropped down on my hands and knees and crawled up as close as I dared to get, but that wasn't nowhere near the edge. Another foot, and I felt sure them old walls would cave in and do away with any chance we had of saving the boy—if he wasn't drownded already.

I yelled out, "Georgie, are you still there?" Just the kind of a stupid thing that comes to your mind at a time like that. I don't know where else he could've been!

But I hollered it out four times before I seen how silly it was, and the fourth time I got a answer too, a voice weak and far off, "Yes, I'm *here,* I'm right *here.*"

Then he busted out to squalling and screaming. I commenced shouting, "Wait! Wait!" and kep it up till he finally settled down enough to answer. A little bit at a time I got it out of him that he wasn't in the water but up above it hanging on to another old piece of log that had wedged itself in between the rock walls in falling. He was laying on his belly on top of the log, he said, but of course they was no way in the world of telling how solid it was nor how soon it would fall, especially if he moved around any.

Ike had come up by now, and all this time I was having to hold him back from crawling right up to the edge, telling him over and over that if he done that, them old rock walls, which I was sure wasn't cemented in but just chinked together, might tumble in and bury Georgie. As I seen it, we had to find some way or another to go down straight and lift Georgie out.

Afterwhile I convinced Ike to go on back and pick up some ropes out of mine and his cars, and any old thing he could find to dig with. The two boys I sent skedaddling off to Haley Blair's, and to Gilbert Blair's too, to bring help and tools. Old Man Gray, so far, had just stayed out of the way, and I give him a warning look or two to remind him to keep on doing exactly that. Me, I stayed as close to the wellshaft as it was safe to, laying out in my mind the best place to set up a windlass, and at the same time ready to make some effort to save the boy if the walls started caving in on their own accord.

Seem like it taken forever and a day for help to begin coming in. The first one I seen was Haley Blair, tromping up the branch about where I'd seen him that day I found the tomahawk. He had a long rope twined around one shoulder, a axe in one hand and a shovel in the other. Haley's a big man, some taller and heavier than I am, and I ain't no runt. The tools and the rope made him look bigger yet. He stomped the ground as he walked. You'd've thought he was on his way to execute and bury somebody instead of saving them. When I seen his old heavy snout and the scowl between his eyebrows and his eyes staring frosty out from under the wide brim of his straw hat, I was about ready to conclude he was going to make a run at me with that axe, or walk right up and push me off in the well.

Pretty soon we all gathered in: Haley, his brother Gilbert—who's a whole lot milder and better fellow than Haley—Ike, Old Man Gray, Ike's two boys, and me. Old Haley was just glaring around in ever direction like a penned-up bull, but specially at me of course. But they wasn't no time to pay him any attention from now on, and he didn't offer no objection to me taking charge.

We all pitched in and cut some poles in the woods, dug holes on both sides of the well, pretty far out, and set up our poles sawhorse fashion. Then we taken a real long pole and slid it out over the well running from one of our crossed stakes to the other one. All we liked having a real windlass was a way to turn the crosspole. But it would've taken too long to fix up something like that, with a handle and all. The only way to work it was for all hands but one to stand a good ways off and let the one man down on a rope sliding over the crosspole. We skinned some of the bark off of it so the rope would slip easier.

Then Ike got plumb unreasonable again. He wanted to be the one to go down, and I might near had to fight him to keep him from it. I wouldn't hear of nothing but being the one to go myself. I knowed in reason that when Ike taken one look at his youngest boy down there, he'd fall in hisself and drownd them both.

I rigged up a kind of a noose seat and tied it around me. I clumb out along the pole and let myself swing down easy. Haley and Ike and Gilbert, with Old Man Gray holding on to one end of the rope but not contributing much, inched up bracing their feet like a tug-o-war team.

And there I was settling down into that black hole.

The first terrible fright I had was thinking Haley might trip them all and send me to the bottom for good. Then I got afraid that Old Man Gray'd do the same thing. I knowed they was crazy ideys, but I couldn't avoid them.

Then Godamighty! That strong suspicion come to me, for the first time, that I'd jumped off of a high place and couldn't know what I'd hit when I landed. In a instant the text of Ike's sermon come back to me. It was the pinnacle of the temple I'd leaped off of, and that few words kep running through my head. 'He shall give his angels charge over thee.' But I wasn't anyways sure He would. If some angel was down there, it was liable to be one sent by the Devil.

A few foot below the surface of the ground I yelled out for them to stop so I could get my eyes used to the dark and size up the situation. The walls, like I figured, wasn't cemented. I didn't dare to move, for fear I'd dislodge a rock and hit Georgie on the head, or maybe cause a whole section to fall. Nobody hadn't mentioned snakes, but we all knowed they might be some in there. If they was, all I could do was hope they'd be blacksnakes, as they most always are, and not cottonmouths or copperheads.

Now I'd been in wells before—that is, I'd cleaned out one or two in my time. I don't think, though, I'll ever feel like going down in one again. I couldn't keep it out of my head, the minute they started letting me down again, that they never would be able to stop, and in no time the sunshine would disappear from the hole above my head, and the rock walls'd get narrower and narrower, and the snakes'd start to coldstare me, and the smell of rotten wood and stagnant water'd rise up to choke me. Everthing would just grow darker and darker, till I couldn't see no water below nor the faintest light above. I'd be expecting to strike the water and sink into it. But I'd be waiting for the touch of that slimy water a long time before I come to it, for how many hours or days I wouldn't be able to count, because down here they wouldn't be no time like above the ground. They'd be nothing but blacker and blacker eternity.

Putting all this as far as I could in the back of my mind, I tried to pick out Georgie below. One thing I'd forgot was to bring a light, but it was too late now to go back after one. For what seemed like a long time I couldn't see nothing of him, nothing only the black shaft sort of lumpy on the sides where some of the bigger rocks bulged out from the walls, and then away down at the bottom of the shaft a few glitters of light skimming across the face of the water. Then I noticed off to one side where the glitters went out of sight behind something solid between me and them. As I squinched my eyes up to look closer, I seen the faintest kind of a light splotch. That turned out to be Georgie's shirt, and moving my eyes slow up and down from it, I made out the rest of him, twenty foot or such a matter below me.

I sung out for them to keep on lowering me down easy, and my voice shook some when I done it. My head swum for a little bit there, and seemed like Georgie was floating up to meet me in my fall. Now I could see him a whole lot plainer. He was hugging that old log for all he was worth, froze to the end of it next to the wall. The rest of that log slanted down out of sight, and the way it leaned it appeared like it was plunging right on down the tunnel carrying a terrified boy with it and pulling me right in after it.

Everthing was still as death. I couldn't hear no voices from above. I felt the rope jerk a time or two, and had to barely touch the walls to steady myself. Never in my life did I feel anything colder and slicker than them walls.

Sinking down and down I went, fighting the idey I never was going to stop, having all I could do to keep from bawling out for them to quit, long before I got to where Georgie was. Fear commenced to tell me loud and strong that they wasn't nobody up there on the other end of that rope, that even that little bit of connection between me and the normal world had been cut in two.

Finally, after what seemed like forever, I was even with Georgie and could call a halt. Before I thought, I yelled so loud I scared Georgie, who I don't think even knowed I was there before, he was so petrified.

He give a start, both arms come aloose from the log, and if I hadn't grabbed ahold of him just when I did, he'd've been a goner. But I clapped him right around the waist, and he made a wild clutch at me, wrapped his arms around my neck so tight he purt near choked me to death before I could tear them away and force them down to where he could clamp around my chest. I had a good hold on him, that was the main thing, though his added weight bearing down on that rope just about caused it to cut my butt in two.

I hadn't nomore'n guided his arms around my chest when his head got turned so he happened to look down, I'm satisfied for the first time. It plumb paralyzed him again, but he commenced to moaning and stammering, "Snake! Snake!" with a lot of other words mumbled and jumbled in.

That stiffened me up too. For a while I couldn't even holler for them to draw us up. All I could do was to stare down towards where he was staring.

I never was sure I seen a snake, but if I didn't, the snake my eyes made was worse than any real one. It was right at the face of the water, ten or fifteen feet down. The glitters and glimmers of the water danced off in rings away from the rock wall, and at the edge of that black core where they set out from, I seen a head poked out from between the rocks, as still as one of the rocks and as black, with nothing but the shape to tell you it wasn't a rock. And if I seen the eyes of it, they was shining with the same light as the ripples of the water. And what I seen brought up in me the strangeness and terrifiedness of this place, even stronger than I had felt them before. I could sense the massacre and the ghosts. I could sense that tomahawk, lodged in the rocks near the place where the snake was, with blood streaming from it into the water below.

If that rope hadn't been nearly cutting me in half, and that child getting heavier and heavier, I don't know how long I'd've set there looking, charmed and helpless as any bird.

But I couldn't stand the weight much longer. I called out at the top of my voice, "Pull us up!"

They started in, way too slow, but I hated to run the risk of asking them to go any faster. We rose up through the dark, dizzy and faint. We come to the top and the blinding sun hit us. It taken more effort than I ever thought I could muster to climb out and off of that pole. Still we made it. Georgie was altogether fainted with fear, and I was awful close to it. Climbing out on that pole, upside down, inching along gripping with my arms and legs both, with Georgie laying on my chest weighing me down like he was made out of rock, I could've swore that pole was a mile long. But it was too dangerous for anybody to come up close enough to give us any help.

I reckon I did pass out, for a second there, when they helped me off the end of the pole and up to the edge of the woods and laid me down in the shade of that old blackjack where I'd hid from Haley the day I found the tomahawk. I didn't know nothing about having fainted, if that's what it was, till I come out of it. Then I knowed I'd been drifting somewhere outside of myself. When I woke up, Haley Blair was towering over me, with his hard, burning eyes glaring down at me from under the wide brim of his straw hat.

First off, I wanted to explain to him, say I was sorry or something, though I don't know for what. And I just wasn't able to, couldn't say a word. Then I seen they was wrath sure enough in his eyes, and wrath commenced to swell up in me too. It was like he knowed everthing I'd felt and seen down there in the well, like it was something I'd taken away from him. I recognized that a fight between us was closer to happening than it ever had been, and they wasn't no question, now, about apologizing nor reconciling in any way whatever. He'd be out to get me from now on, whatever I undertaken to do. And the only answer was to give him right back as good as he handed out.

The time may come when I'll forget a whole lot of what was happening to me at that time. I'd already forgot a good many things that only come back to me now as I set here writing. But if I live to be a thousand, I won't never forget the look on Haley Blair's face that day in the edge of the woods, nor forget the words he said.

As we stared back and forth—it couldn't've been for more'n a few seconds, but it seemed like a day or more—his face turned fiercer and fiercer, like a thunderhead you see away off some evening about dusk. You cover up everthing with wagonsheets and shut up barns and sheds and check the rope on the cellar door so if you have to go to the cellar that night, and the wind gets up too bad, you can hold on to the door and keep the storm from blowing it away and the rain from pouring in. But no matter how many preparations you make, you know when that storm comes it'll lay waste to everthing.

And when that look of Haley Blair's had darkened up to its worst, his voice come out like low thunder:

"The Lord's been merciful to you once again, Amon Lamb."

10

As time went along, people in the community at large all begun to be concerned more and more about the drouth. You couldn't hardly get a word about nothing else out of nobody. The ghost and the accident at the well slipped on past and was might near forgot about. Ever time you turned around you seen crops ready to dry up and blow away, and pastures burned to a crisp, and the timber dying like a blight was creeping over the woods. The wind set in to blowing too, that hot dry wind that takes away ever breath of moisture they is left.

Now what come up next I don't have no clear idey what first made me think of it. The whole scheme was well along in my head before it ever rose up to where you could see it, you might say. I remember saying to myself one day, 'Wouldn't it be good if a man could make it rain whenever he wanted to?'

And then I remember being dumbfounded at finding a wild notion for trying to do just that floating around big and ready in my mind. And what it all come down to was that tomahawk I'd dug up and then hid away in a crack in the rocks.

Before long I got to where I'd lay awake of a night and study about that tomahawk, and then fall so dead asleep just before morning that Ma'd have to come in and roust me out like she used to have to do when I was a boy.

"What's got into you here lately?" she'd chirp out. "I declare, you're harder to wake up than a sulling possum." Then she'd light in to sweeping the room and stirring up so much dust I'd holler for her to quit and leave so I could get up and put on my clothes.

But before that, Pap's voice would come rolling in from the front room, "Let him alone. Let him sleep. They ain't no use in getting up and going to the field. The way the wind's blowing, in another day or two they won't be no field left to go to."

All I done during the day was piddle around the place fixing up little things that had been put off for a long time. About ever minute, though, I'd look off towards this field or that one and watch the dust blow. And at night again I'd lay and stare, and study about that tomahawk and the drouth, no more sleepy than a hootowl.

I got to where I could feel the dark like I never had before, like suddenly in the solid blackness I'd catch a glimpse of where one piece of it was joined on to another one. And I'd sense when one big bulk of darkness would shift a little in relation to the one next to it. But before I could see any actual cracks in it, the seams'd close up again, and still I was left with the notion that I'd slipped through without knowing how and reached some other piece of darkness not altogether like the one I'd come from. At the same time I'd twinge all over like I'd picked up some kind of electric shock from brushing again the sides of the crevice. The closest thing to this motion through the dark I'd ever lived through before was being let down in that old well. Only now the big difference was I wasn't hardly afraid at all.

I'd listen, too, till my ears rung, listen for some whispers besides the wind, and some I heard I couldn't tell whe'er the wind made them or not. I'd look, too, always straight at the ceiling, or, if I happened to have my head propped up on a pillow, at the wall before my eyes. Right square in front of me I never seen nothing out of the ordinary, but at the sides the big forms of blackness crowded in, like they didn't care to have me see them direct, like if I did look towards them they'd shrink back. And sometimes they'd give me a feeling I couldn't hardly control to get up and head out of the house to be in the pure blackness away from any other humans.

But then something told me that wasn't the way to do what I had in mind.

The wellshaft would come to my thoughts, and the shape on the branch, and the big monument, and the bees flying at the woods like gold bullets, and the tingle on my neck as I set on the log that Sunday in the thicket by the swimming-hole—ever strange thing that had happened to me of late come back heavy.

Most of all, though, the tomahawk.

It appeared before me in different sizes, sometimes so big I could feel the weight of it on my soul, oblong, tapering up from a jagged edge till it turned into a cylinder like, and then the notch for the handle, and above that the head like a knob. And now the seams between the giant bulks of darkness would open into crevices, and the tomahawk would cleave right through, and it was like I'd slide through along with it.

All of this kep on for several nights, a week or more, and then it reached the point where I couldn't keep my mind off of it even in the daytime. The light commenced to acting like the dark, with sudden shifts too of one big mass alongside another one. A joint would melt away, the mass would bulge a little and jell, and the same kind of feeling as in the night—that I had slipped through from one mass to another one—would go all over me. And that tomahawk become more and more of a weight on days and nights both, bearing down to divide parts of the day and night from other parts.

Maybe, I thought, I oughtn't to've dug up that tomahawk. Could be it was meant to stay where I discovered it.

But then that didn't appear quite right. It begun to seem like I'd hid it in the wrong place, and my next step, I seen, was to move it somewheres else, and maybe bury it again.

I won't say I had any conviction it would decide to rain if I moved the tomahawk, but still I didn't see no harm in trying.

I might as well admit, while I'm at it, that I could see one or two motives for acting the way I was. For one thing, my conscience never had quit bothering me, some, about what I'd done to the people of the community. I mean, I'd stirred up something by my antics, and as a result, a boy come purt near losing his life. I had saved him, yes, as it was my place to, but somehow or another I ought to try to do more to make up for my wrong, and for the drouth. For yes, I'd begun to feel like I was the cause of that too, maybe.

So I concluded I'd try to bring rain.

For another thing—and I reckon that was more important than I allowed myself to say most of the time—I knowed a battle between me and Haley Blair was sure to come. I'd taken something away from him when I dug up that tomahawk, and when I went down in the well, and he knowed it as sure as I did, even though I didn't reckon he knowed the tomahawk existed. The only answer he could think of at the time of the well incident was that bluster of his: "The Lord has been merciful to you once again, Amon Lamb."

But he wouldn't stop there. Sooner or later he'd make another move. So I'd better use what I'd taken away from him while I had the jump on him.

So, one morning about daylight, I hiked out for the hill where the tomahawk was. I scratched around in between the pieces of rock and pulled it out, almost as excited as I was the day I first dug it up. Till I had it out in my hand and was standing there looking at it, I didn't quite know what I had intended to do with it.

Bury it? Bury it where?

The idey had been in my mind that it would look different now, after all the strange motions it had been through in my imagination. But it was just the same. I'd forgot about the chip on the edge. It wasn't much of a chip, a little sliver broke off leaving a rough line nearly straight for about a inch, then the rest of the cutting edge jagged. The whole thing wasn't over eight inches long and maybe three inches thick at the round part, but a thing that heavy is hard to hide when you try to walk with it, and I wanted awful bad to keep it out of sight, if I could, till I got to wherever it was I was going with it.

I managed, though, by sticking it under the bib of my overalls and cradling it in my hands. From a distance anyhow, it would look like I just had my hands clasped together and was resting them there. Walking back home as fast as I could, I hoped all the way that Ma and Pap wouldn't be up yet. When I stopped at the car shed I didn't hear no noise from inside of the house, which give me the chance to start up the car and drive off before anybody could catch me.

I'd already decided, on my way home, to kind of backtrack and head first for the graveyard, because after all it was from there I'd started coursing the bees that led me to the tomahawk. When I got to the graveyard, I pulled up next to the fence and set there a while to decide what to do next.

That patch of wildflowers by the graveyard was of course all dead. A few summer weeds was still holding out among all the vegetation inside with the graves, but most everthing, because of the drouth, had done give up and died out. That old monument hadn't changed none, of course. The sides of it gleamed and the pillars of it set solid and sure, and the pyramid roof with the flat place chipped off on top rested there like it was waiting for the statue to come back.

Directly I got out and walked around, carrying the tomahawk in my hand and still wondering what to do next.

Was I supposed to bury it here?

Finally I set down on a footstone and turned the tomahawk over and over and around and around in my hands, but for the life of me I couldn't get no clear indication on what I ought to do next. A time or two, despair come close to getting the best of me, and I rued the day I'd ever found that cussed thing. Then I'd toy around with the idey of burying it close to the big monument, but still I couldn't see no reason why.

And because I wasn't watching my business, I just about got slipped up on. And by nobody but Haley Blair hisself. He's got a field over there in back of the graveyard, in a kind of a bottom like, pretty far separated from his other place, and that must've been where he was headed for. Lucky for me, I looked up just as he was about a hundred or so yards off, seen him before he seen me, and had time to slip the tomahawk back in the bib of my overalls and head for the car. Before I got there he'd done seen me, but I had just time enough, before he come up, to slide the tomahawk down in under the front seat.

I didn't reckon he seen it, because he never let on like he did.

Naturally, he was the last person I wanted to see, and I'm satisfied he felt likewise. But they wasn't no way to get out of speaking and passing a few remarks.

He said, "Morning."

"Morning."

"Dry as ever, ain't it?"

"Worse," I said, "I don't know what'll become of us if we don't get some rain pretty soon."

He stood there gazing around, didn't have his usual straight stare about him, the one that always looks ready to freeze your bones. I figured I'd better mention some excuse for being over here at the graveyard, though what I thought up wasn't a very good one:

"I'd kind of forgot what that old monument looked like, it's been so long since I was over here."

A blank lie, that was!

He didn't make no reply to that. I leaned again the car fender and said, "You checking your crops?"

"Yaow, I just wanted to see how near dead things is in that field down yonder."

Then he taken a sudden shift:

"Listen here, Amon, while it's on my mind. They's something I been thinking about, and I'll put it up to you ahead of anybody else."—He sounded friendly enough.—"What I been thinking about is whe'er it would be a good idey or not to hold a...oh, a prayer meeting. On account of the drouth I mean. The Lord...."

And he broke off right there. Maybe he seen right at once the effect his piousness had on me. I couldn't keep from showing it. And maybe it was then, too, he recalled, just as I done, his last words to me that day at the well: "The Lord has been merciful to you once again, Amon Lamb."

I answered as unconcerned as I could: "Praying for rain ain't in my line. You better see Ike about that."

Still lying! But then I wasn't going to confide nothing in Haley Blair.

He give me a straight hard look, now, then he took off his hat and rubbed around inside of the sweatband like he was doing something terrible important. All of a sudden he glares up and snaps out, "Maybe you ought to pay a little bit more attention to things like that. You might be better off."

Well now, that made me mad, so I sneered out, "You always know what the Lord says and does, don't you?"

He knowed now, if he didn't before, that I was making fun of him for that remark he made at the well. I seen him tense up and double up one fist. I just knowed it would come to a fight any minute now, and I wished I hadn't been so quick with my tongue.

He jammed his hat back on, them eyes of his in a fury and direct on me. "Amon Lamb, I'm warning you. One of these days you're going to overstep yourself. You come might near adoing it already. Keep that in mind. You've rambled around on my place just like it was yores, and never said a word to me about it. You been telling windies just to hear yourself talk. Till you got the whole community in a dither, and purt near caused a little boy to die. Oh, you went down and got him out of the well, yes, and made yourself look like a big hero. But if you'd kep your mouth shut, none of it never would've happened. I ain't the only one, let me tell you, that's on to your kind of tricks. You like to put things over on people, thinking you're better'n they are. But I'll tell you right out, and right now, that if any harm comes to me or any of mine because of you, you'll pay for it."

He'd done said enough, of course, for me to jump on him, calling me a liar and all. But I wasn't going to be tempted into striking the first lick, not unless he went a whole lot futher'n he had. Besides, I had a creepy feeling, knowing a good deal of what he said was right, even if I did hate like thunder to hear it come out of his mouth.

But I thought, If it's going to be a cuss fight, I'll mix it with him all right.

So I said, "Seem to me like a fellow that's had as much to do with accidents as you have ain't got no room to talk."

His eyes bugged out. "What do you mean by that?"

"I reckon you know."

He did know too. His face turned plumb black, and I could just see that whole episode coming up in his mind, as many years ago as it was: That Boland girl he was messing around with, her no-count brothers digging for gold on the old Blair place, his son Duncan shooting the girl accidentally when she come there one night to look for her brothers. Haley knowed good and well that me and some others had doubts as to just how accidental that shooting was.

Haley stood there purt near choking till he'd quietened down some.

And then be dammed if it wasn't that real pious voice of his that come out this time: "I don't make no claim I ain't a sinner. But I've repented of my sins, Amon Lamb, and the difference between you and me is, you ain't repented!"

"I reckon I can be the judge of that without any help from you, Haley Blair."

I called him by name because it grated on me the way he kep spouting out mine.

By this time he'd got hisself down to a long-suffering tone:

"Remember my warning, Amon, and mend your ways before it's too late."

And with that he turned around and walked off.

But then I got to feeling ashamed, not of myself exactly, but just that anybody would have a fight like that. Right at that minute I thought we was a couple of fools. I even hollered out after him, "If you want me to, I'll wait here and give you a ride back to the road, and we can talk this over sensible."

His answer was, "I'll be gone a good while. Just think over what I told you."

I leaned there again the car fender for a pretty long spell, my mind taking turns being mad and sorry, and as much as anything else, just confused. I didn't know what to do with my tomahawk any more than I had before Haley showed up.

Directly I wished I'd been a little prompter about getting up and leaving. Whatever made him do it, I don't know, but Pap had taken it in his head to follow me, because there he was jogging up the lane ahorseback. He gets on a horse so seldom anymore, for a minute I didn't recognize who it was.

I wondered what in the thunderation he was up to, and that's exactly what I asked him when he rode up.

His reply was, "I reckon I could ask you the same thing, the way you got out and drove off before day without letting out a peep to anybody. I thought maybe they was something the matter? Is they?"

"Not as I know of."

"What do you mean, then, scaring us all up?"

"Who scared you up? You expect me to make explanations ever time I drive somewheres?"

"Well, I don't know," he said in a kind of a weak voice. "I just thought maybe you might be headed over to Haley Blair's, and I followed to prevent any kind of a ruckus. I seen your tracks turn in here, and I just followed you."

For a minute I thought Pap'd been listening to mine and Haley's little run-in, but I didn't see how he could of. I guess he was just basing his suspicion on what he'd heard about me and Haley at the well. I don't know who he'd heard about that from, because I hadn't said a word to him about it.

"No," I said. "Haley Blair did just come by here, on his way to the field, but I got rid of him as quick as I could, for I've got better things to do than visit with him."

I meant for Pap to conclude I was on my way over to Ellen's, and looked like he did think that, for he shut right up, even if he did set there, for a little, gazing at me kind of funny, like he wanted to ask,'Then what're you doing over here at the graveyard?' But all that come out was, "Well, I'll be getting on back home. See you afterwhile."

And he rode off as puzzled, I guess, as when he come.

I let Pap get back to the main road before I budged, then I drove out and turned in the direction of Ellen's house and the church-house. After I'd gone about a mile and come over a hill where the road runs down and then up through a kind of wide glade like, I seen away off on the other side a man tromping along. It was good sunup now, and the man was too close into the light for me to tell who it was. Thought to myself, though, I never seen so much activity around here so early in the morning before.

Coming closer, I thought I recognized him, and sure enough, when I overtaken him, and him striding away from me with the breeze in his ears and not able to hear me till I was right up on him—it was Yas Bailey.

Of course, I stopped, to find out why, if I could, he was in such a hurry this early and so far from home. He said he was on his way over to see how Ike's boy was getting along, and he wanted to make it over there and back before the heat of the day set in.

I offered him a ride, and he of course taken me up on it, said his car was broke down at home—which wasn't anything new for Yas, with that old wreck he's got.

If it hadn't looked downright mean to do it, though, I'd've let him walk.

Not being decided as yet what I was to do with my tomahawk, I'd just as soon've been by myself. Still, I was curious to know the real reason why Yas would take his foot in his hand and walk about two miles each way to inquire about Ike's son's health, when the boy was already long over his shock, as far as I'd heard. To my notion, Yas wanted to find out whatever else he could about the hant. You could tell right away from his face he was so wrapped in that idey these days he never give hisself time to think about nothing else. He looked at you kind of wall-eyed and muddled, so much so I knowed I had to try and do something to straighten him out.

But while I was feeling around for a way to begin, making offhand remarks in the meantime about the drouth, Yas broached the subject hisself: "You been back over there lately?"

"No, Cephas, I ain't. Not since the boy had his accident, that is. And I don't aim to, neither."

"I wish I could talk you into the notion of going back over there with me just one more time."

"What for? Ain't you seen enough?"

"No, I ain't. Say, stop a minute here, will you? We'll be at Ike's place before you know it, and I want to talk to you for a minute private first, if you don't mind."

We was right at the church-house, so I pulled up under one of the big postoaks on the grounds. He said, "Yas, Amon, what I want to find out I wouldn't tell anybody about but you, and I'd just as soon you didn't let it go no futher. The thing is, I want to know if they's any connection between what me and you seen and what come up on my doorstep one time several years ago. You remember me telling you about that right after it taken place, don't you?"

I answered yes because I'd heard it not only from him but from a dozen other people besides.

"But listen here," I said, "how in the world do you expect to find out such a thing as that? Are you going to ask that hant?"

He kind of shuddered. "I ain't got the least idey how I'll find out, but they must be some way. What I was hoping was, you might be able to help me. And then of course, they's Ike's boy. He might of....Oh, well, I don't know."

I guess I knowed in reason before I started it wouldn't do no good, but I done then what I ought to've done a good while before. I taken a deep breath and flew in to telling Yas that the whole thing was a trick, a prank I'd played on him, that they wasn't a word of truth in it. I begged his pardon for doing it, and swore up and down I'd made up ever bit of it out of my head. I lied—again—so far as to say I hadn't seen nothing the night me and him was at that place, but just pretended I did to carry him high. That'd make him mad, I knowed, but at least it might put some sense into his head. I must've talked for fifteen minutes, repeating, in as many ways as I could think of, that they wasn't a bit of truth in anything I'd said or done.

And Yas set there quiet through the whole spiel. When I finally shut up he still kep quiet, looking off up the road we'd come over. Directly he turned around chuckling, with his face scrooched up in a kind of a sneer. Then he throwed up his hands with his elbows stuck out like he wanted to fly and come down to slap both of his knees with a loud smack. He snorted a couple of times and twisted in his seat. I got afraid I'd drove him completely out of his mind.

What he said, finally, was, "Drive on over to Ike's and let me out. I ain't got no time to fool around with such a feller as you!"

I started up and drove on, keeping my eye on him close. I was uneasy. I figured he might jump on me any minute. But in a little while he had stiffened up, with his arms akimbo, his head away up in the air, a set expression on his face and a wild look out of his eyes like you better not touch him or even speak to him. And he didn't say a word till we pulled up in front of Ike's.

Then, just before he climbed out of the car, he turned to me and said, high-pitched, "You're lying to me, Amon Lamb! You seen the thing, all right, and now you're insulting me by denying it. And why? Because you and a whole bunch more fools around this part of the country think I ain't to be trusted with knowing things like that. Think it's better to keep me in the dark by telling me lies like you would to some kid that's seen too much for his age. Think I'll let you get away with it too. Yas, but you've got another think acoming, the whole passel of you! If you was really my neighbor, you'd help me find out what I need to know. But I wouldn't ask you to now, not under no circumstances, and wouldn't let you if you begged me to. And that's my final word on the subject!"

With that he swings out of the car and slams the door and walks off towards Ike's front gate.

I wanted to scat out of there myself before Ike come out and stopped me and maybe seen me and Yas'd been having a fuss. So I didn't turn around at the house, but tore out straight on east down the road.

Now I wasn't thinking about anything but the trouble I'd had with Yas, but when I drove by that old empty church-house where the lane opens up to the swimming-hole, my heart commenced to beating faster.

Down there was where I ought to be going with my tomahawk.

But of course I couldn't go right then. Part of the way down I'd be in full view of anybody looking out from Ike's house. Him or Yas or one of the boys'd be sure to see me pass. The tomahawk would have to stay under the seat where it was till I had another chance, when I could catch Ike and them gone from home.

But now I knowed for certain what to do when the chance did come.

Be danged if I didn't come might near running into Haley once more before I got back home. I'd made a big circle around and was back at the fork of the road by the church-house when I seen him. He was ahorseback. He'd already made the turn and was riding off with his back towards me in the direction of Ike's house. I thought to myself, Bet he's on his way over there to hit Ike up about that prayer meeting.

And so it seemed to me like I couldn't waste no time in putting that tomahawk where it had to go.

As it turned out, though, they held their prayer meeting before I could take care of the tomahawk. I heard all about the meeting from Old Man Gray, who was there, and who come out and stopped me when I was leaving Ellen's house one time. He looked awful worried about me, and not mad neither. Seemed like me and him was getting to be better friends, at least, out of all this.

He said Haley had got up at the prayer meeting and made a long speech, beginning with how necessary it was to humble theirselves before the Lord, letting Him know they didn't deserve no favors from Him. Said he couldn't stress too much how they'd have to ask for rain in that spirit if they expected to get any. But what seemed funny to Old Man Gray was the way Haley went on to spend more time than anything else talking about them that follow the Devil and get what they want thataway. He give them a long rigamarole about pride and how some in the community was suffering from it, and how their disobedience was harming the community—responsible, as he put it, for the drouth. He must've been pretty emphatic about it, without mentioning no names though, till it begun to look, Old Man Gray said, like the meeting was going to turn into a session for condemning everbody in the community that Haley Blair looked on as sinners, forgetting all about the purpose the gathering was originally called for. I understand Ike finally set him down by telling him they was supposed to be praying for rain in a humble spirit, like Haley had said at the start, and not to be setting theirselves up as judges over other people. Ike even asked him who he was talking about anyway.

I wished I could've seen Old Haley's face when Ike give him a dressing down. But I do have to give him credit for one thing. He wouldn't say who it was he had in mind. As far as I could judge from Old Man Gray's report, Haley left the impression, though, that he knowed a whole lot more'n he was willing to tell, and warned them all to watch out.

I seen I'd have to be on my guard more'n ever. No telling what Haley was liable to take a notion to do.

As the days passed, I itched more and more for the opportunity to slip down to the swimming-hole unbeknownst, thinking I might be too late al ready. But looked like I never would have the right kind of luck. Some of Ike's was always at home during the daytime, and it'd be a hard matter to ever make it down there at night without somebody from Ike's catching you. The house was built so close to the lane any light'd give you away. If I'd knowed it in time, the night to go down there was when the whole bunch was at the prayer meeting. But you see I didn't think.

Anyhow, I finally settled on Saturday as the best day I'd be likely to find everbody gone at once, and accordingly, I drove by there of a Saturday evening, right after dinner, for three weeks straight. Getting that tomahawk down to that hole of water come to seem like the most important thing on earth. I found myself getting irritable. Ellen and me got to where we quarreled and spatted about ever little thing that come up, her not knowing what I was up to and me so mad at both of us because I couldn't find a way to tell her, that I taken it out in jowering with her.

It was the fourth Saturday before things come around right. I'd just drove over the hill and come in sight of Ike's, as luck would have it, when out of the house piled Ike's wife and ever last one of his kids. Into the car they climbed and off they went in the opposite direction from me. I was so happy to see that, it taken me a minute to begin wondering, Yaow, but what about Ike hisself? Was he already in the car, behind the steering wheel, or did the oldest boy do the driving, and was Ike still at home? Unless he was off in the field someplace, of course.

I passed by the house, turned around by the old empty church-house, and drove by again. No stir, no more than if the place was plumb moved out of.

My patience was might near gone, anyway, I was so anxious to do what I had to do. The third time I passed by the house and come on down to the lane, I twisted the wheel and dabbed right into it.

But right at once I thought better of that, and even fuming the way I was, I made myself take a minute to find out for sure whe'er Ike was at home or not. I turned right around and drove up there, went into the yard, knocked on the door. I had it all made up to say I'd come to borrow his posthole digger attachment for a tractor, if Ike come to the door.

But he didn't. The house stayed dead still. So I could go on about my business.

I drove down that lane just like I'd done that Sunday when all of this started, parked my car in the same place, picked out as near as I could the same trail through the open woods. I was carrying that tomahawk under my arm pressed up again my ribs, all the time afraid I'd drop it or it would someway fly out of my grip on its own accord. Ever step of the way I felt a kind of pressure on all sides of me, one that would squeeze in close and draw back, over and over, and when it was tight again me, ever muscle and pore and vein would twinge and glow, and then cool for a second when the pressure drawed off, running a cycle the way your breath does going in and out. And during the inflow the flesh and blood of me changed for a second, from the touch of some holy thing, into all the flesh and blood that had ever lived.

Ever step carried me through time along with distance, like what had happened to me that moonlight night driving home from Ellen's, and along with the beating of that holy rhythm was a fearfulness that around the next tree I'd meet the source of it face to face: if it wasn't already slipping up behind me, ready either to pounce and devour me, or else with its power to turn me into a thing no longer human. What it would look like, if I was ever allowed to see it, I didn't know. It might be the ugliest thing, or the most beautiful thing, in the universe. Or it might be both.

As slow as my steps was, I was panting like anything. Everthing about this place come back to me: the naked boys chasing up and down, the peculiar light of green and brown, the watermelon rind I'd set next to the big elem tree, Mary or Sherry in their own light in the schoolhouse, the baptizings we used to hold on the creek in the tender grass. But now I seen that all these things made up a foreground for what I'd never remembered before: men in animal skins seemed to be running along the banks of the creek hunting food with flintrock knives, and fighting with tomahawks like the one I had under my arm. The blood they had shed of men and beasts seemed so real I imagined the tomahawk warm and sticky under my arm.

Back futher in my head I seen animals I'd read about or dreamt about, filling the woods and even the sky, kind after kind gathering like they'd answered the call to go into the ark: great horses, and cows and camels, and bears, and wolves, and tigers, mammoths and elephants, reptiles flying and crawling, great birds of ever description. Life had been so thick in these woods that it was all I could do to force my way through.

I picked my way down a gash in the bank and crossed the sand of the dry creekbed, and tore out a path through dead ironweeds and kerkleburrs and bloodweeds, not hesitating nor looking to one side till I found the open place in the thicket and the log I'd set on that Sunday. Under the big old tree I knelt down and scooped out a hole two foot deep or more in the sand, till I reached where the ground was still moist. Next I gouged out the bottom into a lengthy place that would hold the tomahawk laying flat, put it in, and covered it up.

When I'd got rid of as many signs as I could that I'd been there, I hurried back to the car, trembling with fear and joy, but most of all with the feeling I'd accomplished some great thing.

At the end of the lane by the county road, I pulled up behind the old church-house and got out to piss. I guess I'd been busting to for a hour or more, but I'd been so wrapped up in what I was doing I hadn't thought about it till now.

When I finished, I happened to look around the corner of the building, before I started back to the car. Did I see somebody looking out through Ike's kitchen window? Or was it the reflection of the sky in the glass that looked like a man leaning forward, then drawing back? Was Ike really gone from home, or did he deliberately fail to answer my knock because he suspicioned me and was laying low to catch me?

I drove on off at a regular speed, didn't even look when I passed Ike's house....

That night was strange but peaceful. The darkness rubbed its sides together like before, only now I knowed that for the time being I was in control of it. When I'd think of the tomahawk dividing the dark, a tired and calm feeling would come over me, and I'd remind myself again that I'd accomplished some powerful thing.

Sleep hit me pretty early, but out of the window, before I dropped off, I could see the sky growing blacker and blacker, and once I spied a glimmer of lightning. I slept and I dreamt. I sunk into sleep and dreams, settling down through a long distance. And what I dreamt about went on outdoors too. The lightning played and the thunder tumbled all around the sky. The wind blowed through the elements, a moist and a curing wind.

And the rain was freed to fall.

11

Yes, it did rain that night after I buried the tomahawk. It come a regular downpour. And it didn't stop when day come neither. It kep on till along around sundown, when the rain quit and the clouds split up and the light spilled through the big gashes. The sun went down burning like a flame at first, then a coal throwing the purest red light across the whole country. The air looked heavy and fertile, and you could already see the crops that was left alive coming out of their misery.

But then two days later it rained again. And the day after that some more. And on and on like that it went. We'd have one or two pretty days, but we couldn't get on past the third one, seem like, without at least a shower. The weeds and grass sprung up, and they growed faster'n the crops did. Fields needed plowing bad, but the ground stayed so boggy you couldn't get in them with a tractor.

The first week, naturally, everbody was happy. Let it rain while it's in the notion, they all said. It'll change its mind soon enough. But by the end of the second week everbody was wishing it'd fair off and stay thataway for a month.

I'd've give anything, along about then, to hear what Haley Blair had to say about the situation. But since I didn't want to go around him, I had to work Old Man Gray into talking to him and then reporting to me. Which he done, because we'd got in the habit of meeting and talking out by the road about ever time I went over to see Ellen—out there by the road because I guess he didn't want the old lady to know how thick we was getting to be.

The old man said Haley was all hepped up thinking the prayer meeting had turned the trick, and slapping hisself on the back for calling it. Give Old Man Gray to understand that "All things work together for good to them that love the Lord." Even hinted it was his speech condemning sinners that was more responsible than anything else—though I don't know how he made that jive with what he'd said about humility—and said when you come right down to it, Ike ought to tend to his business of separating the sheep from the goats a little better than he'd been doing it.

I sure would like to've seen old Haley's face if I could've walked up and told him my idey of what caused the rains.

But I was in for a comedown, as I seen when it kep on araining and araining. Before long me and everbody else forgot they'd ever been any such of a thing as a drouth, like it had been damp and steamy this way forever, with clouds threatening ever hour of the day, or if they didn't, late in the evening a line of thunderheads bumping up in the north that you knowed would blow in before morning. A time or two we had gully-washers, with creeks getting out of banks and stock drownding, and terraces busting in the fields and leaving the crops in low places standing in a slough of water.

Happen so I went to preaching one Sunday, taking Ellen with me. I didn't figure to be facing stares from my neighbors now, because the business about the hant had died plumb down. But I was wrong. They did look at me funny, some of them did, and as soon as I laid eyes on Old Haley Blair planted over there in his usual spot and seen him squirm just a little, I knowed the source of the funny looks. It had to be he'd been spreading rumors around about me.

Well, the whole community was there for a bigger turn-out than usual. You take when people are uneasy about something, the way we'd been uneasy first about the drouth and now about the floods, they'll head for a church ever time. Ike give a strong sermon that day on mankind and the weather. He made mention, quite a bit, of the prayer meeting, but he didn't come right out and state it was the cause of the rain. Fact is, he played it down. Said present circumstances just went to show you how little man knowed about the ways of God. First He'd sent us drouth and now He'd sent us flood, and it was up to us to make out the best we could with both of them. He wanted it understood to begin with, though, that he didn't mean God was doing us dirty by giving us too much of what the whole community had asked for. Said it might even've been going too far to organize that kind of a thing, especially if we condemned others by doing it. Yes, we might've overstepped our bounds by praying in a whole bunch for what would bring us more money and make things easy for us. Things wasn't meant to be easy for us. And the Lord knowed what we had need of—to save our souls with, that is—before we asked for anything. And he ended up by saying he didn't know but what it wasn't a good idey to let things be, as they was bound to be, in the hands of God. *He* knowed how the world ought to go and why, and clamoring to Him for a bigger share than what we was due might not set too well with Him sometimes.

Yes, it was a strong sermon, all right, or that is, Ike meant it to be. But I don't think he seen what the natural conclusion might be: not to pray nor do nothing, but just let things take their course—which didn't sound at all like Ike, nor any other preacher. Still, I for one knowed what he meant to do. He meant to get at me and Haley both while he had us in the same building, and he didn't know quite how to go about it. I was satisfied he'd felt all along that Haley's instigation had put too much 'Take care of your chosen people, oh Lord. Don't you see how much better we are than everbody else?' into the proceedings. And as for me, he seen that in some kind of a way I'd taken matters into my hands that I didn't have no business to fool with.

Right then and there I decided it *was* Ike spying on me through the window of his house the day I buried the tomahawk.

Haley's part of Ike's eating-out sure got through to him all right. He's a man that can't prevent hisself from looking mad when he is, and he looked mighty frowned up, let me tell you, when he come out of the church-house door.

Before me and Ellen made it back to her house good, it had already set in to thundering and lightning and coming up a cloud. By the time dinner was over with, it was pouring down like it never did aim to quit. Me and Ellen set on the duofold watching out of the window at the rain falling. That day, so far, we hadn't bickered none, and after the sermon—a sermon always relaxes me, when I listen to it, even if I don't agree with a word of it—I'd commenced to hope I could tell her my problems and do away with all these growing doubts and suspicions.

Ever little bit, a streak of lightning would claw out somewheres, and a regular explosion of light and noise'd paralyze the sky and the ground for the batting of an eye. And always high up and all around, the thunder boomed out like ever storm from here to Jericho had run together headon.

I had my arm around Ellen and she was rubbing the nape of my neck with her fingertips. Without no warning she spoke out more open than she ever had: "Amon, sweet, I don't know what's the matter with you, or what's come over us of late. We always seem to me to be halfway at outs, even if we don't have words very often. Can I do anything to help you?"

There was my chance, come about so easy it plumb startled me. All I had to do now was open up and tell her everthing. I thought about it a minute.

I decided she'd be able to understand, after all, strange as the whole business was. Because I was certain they wasn't nothing Ellen couldn't understand if she was a mind to.

But I didn't do what I decided to. No, I didn't! By God, it's enough to make you tear your hair out. Just look at how I tried to tell her at the graveyard, and how if I had of, she'd've been in it with me from the start. And then everthing, I know, would've taken a different course. Just look at how I'd been waiting and itching for the right opportunity to confide in her all along, knowing we was drifting apart because I hadn't. Then why couldn't I tell her when the time come?

Well, I can't say in so many words. You see, I'd taken to doing everthing by just the way I felt at the moment, no rhyme nor reason to it. And after all that big decision I made in my minute of thinking about it, I just didn't feel like opening my mouth. The lightning flared and the thunder cracked and the rain poured, and I was afraid. What I had stirred up was too close by, right then, for my tongue to move. I was dead certain that if I opened my mouth about what I'd done, the lightning would strike me down.

So all I finally answered was, "No, I don't reckon I need any help. Why?"

"Why was it Brother Ike looked so much at you and Haley Blair when he talked?"

"He did?"

"You know good and well he did."

"Oh, me and Haley had a kind of a little tiff a few weeks back."

"What about?"

Of course, it wasn't nothing but coincidence, but right then the lightning struck a tree out by the main road, the same blackjack Old Man Gray had waited for me under, the Sunday the boy fell in the well. All the same, I quivered like it had hit me. Ellen jumped, herself. My voice was mighty quavery when I said, "Nothing that amounted to much. Forget about it. I'll tell you sometime."

And of course she didn't forget about it. She was pretty cool to me the rest of the day. We just moved around the house kind of uneasy in the storm, and even though we didn't have no open fuss, it was mostly tensed-up looks that went back and forth between us.

Still I stayed, because the weather wouldn't let me leave. That night after supper the rain let up enough for me to slip and slide home through the mud.

Coming in sight of the house, I was surprised to see a lamp still burning. It was Pap waiting up for me, a thing he hadn't done in long years. And we set up for a hour at least talking about the terrible rains and what would become of the crops. Then he got off into other wet years, and dry ones, times when I was a baby or before I was born or when him and Ma first married. I listened to him, for he didn't seem to want many answers. Now that I recall, he kind of told the story of my life before I come into the world, if you can put it thataway, and before I was big enought to remember much, all of it in relation to years of drouth and flood.

But if that was about all he said, it wasn'ty all he meant—if he even knowed what he wanted to mean. He was concerned, and they wasn't no direct way of saying so. I was seeing in him what I'd commenced to see in other people at preaching that day, and soon was to see a whole lot stronger, in Hap Carr and Gil Blair and others I didn't meet up with very often. And before long even in Old Man Gray, just when we'd got a little used to being on a friendly standing. Yes, Pap was concerned and uneasy, but the rest of them soon begun to look at me like I might be some kind of a freak, and maybe dangerous along with it.

No doubt about it, it couldn't've been nothing but Haley Blair spreading bad stories about me around the community.

The way the rest of them looked at me, suspicion everwhere, and one rainy day after another one, sent me off into a deep gloomy spell. And that kep up till one day I lost control of myself, a day that purt near done me in before the consequences of it let up. I say lost control: what I done was leap into something I ought to've taken more time to consider. But again, you see, I was at such a pass I couldn't arrive at nothing by any kind of a sensible means. Even when I was set again something, I'd act and then wonder how I could've been so foolish, always when it was too late to call back what I'd done.

As I laid in bed at night now, again I couldn't get off to sleep and couldn't stay long when I did, just like when the drouth was bad. The dark again moved in pieces in upon itself. The tomahawk sunk through and cut one mass off from another. Only now the strongest sense I had of the dark's motion was through my ears—a scraping or a screaking or a sliding. Sometimes it was might near unbearable. Cool as it was with the rains, I'd lay and sweat, for the notion kep coming to me, like a fire set in my nerves, that I might be going crazy, as if all the great things I'd experienced up to this time was a mockery that had finally caught up with me and I was doomed to run mad like a dog with hydrophoby. When I couldn't stand that feeling nomore, I'd get up out of bed and tiptoe out on the porch, to steady myself, hoping I wouldn't wake up Ma or Pap while I was at it. At the best, they'd think I was sleepwalking, and that opinion wouldn't've helped matters much.

You can just stand so much, and then you have to do something. An idey hit me one day while I was out fixing the cowlot fence, working hard under the blazing humid sun, trying to get my mind off of things if I could. Before I altogether knowed it, I was in the car and speeding off down the road. In no time I was past the church-house and Ike's place and the old rotted-down church-house and in the lane running down towards the swimming-hole.

I didn't tarry nowhere nor for nothing. I just parked, run down, waded the creek and fought my way into that thicket and got down on my knees and scratched that tomahawk out of the ground like a wild man. By the time I had it in my hand I was shaking like a leaf all over.

I hiked out of there as fast as my legs'd carry me, beating the vegetation, sloshing through the creek again, gripping that tomahawk in my fist and up under my armpit. I was so give out when I come to the car, I had to set down and blow a minute before I could drive off. I hadn't made no effort at all to hide what I was up to. I even just laid the tomahawk on the seat beside me. When I drove by Ike's house, he was standing on his front porch trying to wave me down. But I acted like I didn't see him, kep aracing the motor and spinning on through the mud of the road.

By the time I made it to the roadforks near the graveyard, I'd quit shaking on the outside, but they was a tremor flashing through my breast and down through my bowels that stayed with me the whole rest of that day.

Instead of going towards home, I turned down the road leading to that old house-place, and when I pulled up by the cattleguard opening into the pasture, I seen they wasn't no use in trying to drive through down there in a car, for they was washed-out places and bogholes everwhere. So turning around and beating it back, I went to the lane on my side of the linefence that me and Yas had taken the night of our scrape, and drove into the woods. At least I had enough sense about me not to leave the car on the main road in plain view of everbody.

I taken mine and Yas's route afoot, easy enough going in the woods, but once I come out in the open pasture, it had rained so much since we was there, it was a matter of wading through a rank growth of weeds, and on the far side of the simmon thicket I commenced to hit muddy places and sinkholes and stretches of slough water. I had to pick my way around the best I could. The closer I come to the channel of the branch the worse things got. I fooled along stepping from one little tuft of grass to the next, weaving a path through a regular loblolly. The bed of the branch, plumb full of course, was anyhow sluggish where I happened to strike it. A big old drift had about halfway dammed it up.

With the help of a pole, I blundered across on the drift.

By the time I come up to the old house-place, I was good and ready for a spell of rest, and I wanted like anything to struggle on up to the big blackjack for that purpose, but first I at least wanted to locate the spot where I'd dug up the tomahawk, because my idey now was to put it right back where I'd found it. But you know what? The rock I remembered turning over wasn't there, and having to search around for it drove out any thought of a rest right at the time.

There was my rock, all right, but away off to one side. Somebody had lifted it out of the ground and toted it off a few yards just outside of where the old house had stood. I thought it must've happened when we tore up the place making ready to rescue Georgie out of the well, though we didn't make no use of it as far as I could recollect. And all the rain had softened and smoothed the ground so much, in that sandy soil, that you couldn't nomore tell than anything where the rock had been.

I knelt right down on the ground the way I had the day I discovered the tomahawk, at what I thought was the right location. But I just couldn't be sure, and a terrible feeling struck me that if I buried the thing in the wrong place, matters'd be worse off than ever. I shut my eyes while I was kneeled down there, thinking and thinking and hoping I could see in my mind the whole layout, so then I could open my eyes and glance to the very spot.

But it was no use. The ground I seen with my eyes shut was altogether different from what I seen with them open.

The worst, though, was yet to come. What made him show up right then I don't know. He could've just chanced by, or he could have been laying for me. Anyway, Haley Blair come along while I was still in a quandry. I mean to say, he drove by on the road, stopped by the cattleguard, and was standing there watching me when I first noticed him. It was a long ways off, so it was a easy enough matter for me to keep the tomahawk out of his sight. But just the same, I sure was caught in an awkward shape, kneeling down like that on the wet ground.

And so, burying the tomahawk now was out of the question. Haley couldn't miss seeing me scratching around in the dirt. I could manage leaving with it, by heading for the woods and taking a roundabout way back to my car. With my headstart and dodging around in the timber, he could never hope to catch up with me, no matter how hard he tried.

But the thing was, I couldn't take the tomahawk away now. It had to be left, if I only knowed exactly where that was, in its own place.

The only shot left was the old well. Haley hadn't got around to filling it in yet. He'd just built a stout barbwire fence around it, taking in a space about six foot out, all around the shaft.

I walked up to the fence, with my back to Haley, pitched the tomahawk into the well, and heard it hit the water with a spat and a splash. If Haley seen me and asked me, I'd say it was a rock I throwed, just for monkey-work, to see how much the water level had rose since the floods.

Then I hiked out for the woods. Because Haley, I noticed over my shoulder, was walking off down in my direction, and not under no circumstances did I want to face him right then. And it's thankful I was I'd hid my car where I did. He never did backtrack enough to discover it. I had to tromp over a mile or two of woods to make it back to my car without him seeing me, but I did get clean away.

The tremor deep in my guts was still with me when I went to bed along in the night. In one way I was calmer, yes, but I sure did wish I could've done this thing up right, thinking maybe if Haley hadn't come along when he did, I'd've found the right location and reburied the tomahawk in it. Because now I was commencing to feel I'd done absolutely the wrong thing by throwing it in the old well.

And then, when I was about halfway asleep, the tremor turned into the sensation of falling. Falling, falling. I dozed off and woke up falling.

I grabbed on to the bedstead. It wouldn't stop me. A rainstorm had set in. It and the bedstead and the room and the dark and all things fell right along with me.

Lightning begun to streak and flash. Pap stepped into the doorway of my room, in his white nightgown, like a ghost the lightning had brought. Some time had passed, I realized, and the storm was heavier.

Pap said, "Amon, maybe you better get up and come on in here with us."

The storm was growing worse by the second. I jumped to my feet, snatched up my britches, and hopped across the floor working my legs into them.

A big crash of wind, rain, thunder, and lightning hit.

Pap was shouting, "We ought to get to the cellar! How can we get to the cellar?" And his white nightgown lit up and faded and lit up in the dazzle of lightning.

I seen how fearful a time we was in for, and I knowed I'd brought it on us. I never seen such a rain fall. The wind drove it in masses. The thunder bounced and whammed like it was throwed from cloud to ground and bounced back up, striking terrible blows through the whole elements. And the jagged cracks of lightning from the hammering of the thunder flew all up and down and across the sky ever second or two. Before long the whole sky would be beat to pieces and fall to the earth in slivers, letting all the waters above the firmament descend in a gush.

Now all three of us had collected in the front room, Ma with a dark coat wrapped around her, stock-still and straight in the middle of the floor. Me and Pap went up and stood on either side of her.

The body of the storm was on us. Rain in torrents. Wind like a sickle. Wham after wham of thunder. In the continual blaze of lightning you could see the trees whipped and the ground cut in gashes by the flood. Familiar buildings looked strange and threatening: the carshed, the henhouse, the smokehouse, the barn futher off. The next time you looked they might be in splinters and flying at you through the air. And the tearing and the wrenching of the wind on the house was terrible.

The one thing I could think of to do, we done: I run around and commenced to jerking featherbeds and quilts and pillows off of the beds, and Ma and Pap, seeing what I was up to, followed suit. We throwed them all in a pile in the center of the front room and crawled in among them, keeping some of the stuff below us and drawing the rest of it in around our shoulders with just our heads sticking out, and ready to duck them in if the walls or the roof started to go.

I just knowed the house couldn't stand up another minute under all that. Somewhere in that cloud they must be a twister, marked, I was right sure, for me.

The wind screamed across the house, with a shifting and groaning of rafters and joists, playing a terrible squalling tune down the stovepipe. The rain slammed into the walls and the roof in waves, and the noise of thunder far and near was like the tide of more water rushing in. Even if you could've kep your eyes shut, you'd've been convinced the lightning was out to blind you, flash to flicker, flicker to flash, and the thunder out to deafen you with its lashing and crashing.

Still, afraid as I was, I wasn't trembling nomore. To face death by a storm wasn't as fearful as the steady facing of the other powers I'd come to know about.

In a flash of lightning I seen about half of the chickenhouse scoot away from its foundations, then lift up and skitter towards us. But in the next flash of lightning it crumpled and dropped just before it hit the house.

Afterwhile it begun to settle down a little, and we thought it was safe to crawl out of our hole. The roof was leaking in several places, so we brought out ever pot and pan and bucket we could lay our hands on and caught what we could. Outside, in ever direction, was a sea of water appearing in glance after glance of lightning. The yard was standing full, a swelling stream had tore out down the driveway. I couldn't see far out into the fields, but I knowed they'd be lakes and ditches, and few crops at all left standing.

In a half an hour or so the wind died down to about normal, the lightning weakened, and the thunder moved on away. The rain smoothed out to a steady light fall. Me and Ma and Pap set in chairs pulled up in a circle in the front room, after we'd put back the bedding and cleaned up the mess from the leaks. Pap smoked his pipe, and all three of us tried to ease down so we could go back to bed.

One time there the rain quit altogether for about ten seconds, then it started back real slow once more.

During that breathing spell, a voice inside of me said, The big rains is over with.

We did go back to bed directly. I felt calm, but I didn't figure on sleeping much the rest of the night. And I didn't. I laid there bug-eyed for I don't know how many hours.

About the time you could begin to see the gray creeping into the black, I heard splashing and plopping, and the last thing I expected to see come up the driveway—a man ahorseback.

When he rode up to the yard gate and hollered, I was already halfway to the door, buckling my overalls and stuffing in my shirt as I went.

It was Haley Blair.

"Amon, come on over and give us some help. Cephas is lost. We can't find him nowheres."

I didn't stop to ask no questions. Pap had come to the door right in behind me and heard what was said. I left him to explain to Ma, and I run out, first towards the carshed, but soon as I realized you couldn't drive a car noplace now, I lit out for the barn. The stock was all huddled up next to the cowshed, so it wasn't no trouble to catch the horse. I saddled him and overtaken Haley a little piece down the road, where he was waiting for me. I asked him a question or two as we went slopping and sliding along through the mud and water—at least the rain had stopped—but he wouldn't hardly say a thing. I concluded I oughtn't to've gone with him at all if that was the way he was going to act, even started to feeling like he didn't want me to help, but had come after me for some other reason. All I could get out of him, in so many words, was what he had yelled out from the front gate: Yas was lost, they couldn't find him nowheres.

We kep on ariding as fast as our ponies could go, and that wasn't none too fast, till we come to the cattleguard where people had been going into Haley's place to look for the hant a few weeks back. As soon as we come in sight of the cattleguard I seen others waiting: Gil Blair and a couple of his oldest boys, and Yas's oldest boy too. They was all wet and dirty, and all standing still like they was planted in the mud, looking uneasy towards one another and off down towards the branch, which was out of banks and spread all over the bottom. Gil Blair come out to meet us, sloshing along on the berm of the road: "We been up and down it from one end to the other, close as we could get to it, that is. He ain't there, I tell you."

"He's there," says Haley, not looking at his brother but at me, and smiling awful grim. "Where you think he'd be?"

"It's a false alarm, someway or another," was Gil's answer.

"It ain't no such of a thing," said Haley, clamping his jaws shut and giving me a dead cold stare.

So now after we'd about broke our necks getting here, didn't seem like Haley was in a hurry nomore. Without batting a eye, he commenced on me: "Amon, I got you over here to help us look for Cephas, like I told you. You know what happened last night? Cephas's boy says his dad come off over here along in the night to look for whatever it was you tolled him over here to see some time ago. Then when it come up a cloud, he must've been caught out in it, for he ain't come home this morning. I just thought you'd like to know the particulars before we set in to looking for him."

Then he just stood there staring at me level and accusing.

"Well, for the love of God!" Gil busted out. "If we're going to look some more, let's get at it. No use in standing around here and jawing about it."

"Thought you said it was a false alarm," Haley kind of sneered.

Gil throwed him a sharp look, turned to me and said, "Why don't you and the boys take this side. Me and Haley'll cross down yonder at the culbert and come up on the other side. I reckon we can wade all right along the road. But look out about getting too far out in that water. They's sinkholes everwhere. And cottonmouths too. I done seen a couple of them."

I was doing the best I could to keep from jumping on Haley. This wasn't no time for losing tempers. But that sonofabitch practically laid the blame on me, at the jumpgo, before he even knowed what had happened!

We worked our way up the branch from the culbert northwest, split up in bunches like Gil Blair had told us to. And it was hard going, let me tell you. Water had backed up for a good thirty or forty yards on each side of the channel, thick brown and full of logs and limbs, nasty at the edges with foam and silt and trash. In towards the bed it was running fast, asucking and agurgling. They was pecan sprouts and blackberry tangles and willow thickets we had to get around the best way we could, or fight our way through. If you didn't watch out, you'd break a leg in a sinkhole, or worse than that, step on a snake. Because the cottonmouth moccasins was out sure enough. We carried clubs with us. I killed two snakes and Haley one before the whole thing was over with.

Our way of going about it was to struggle along a few steps, then come to a halt and one group of us look out over the water towards the other one, pointing out and comparing what we could see, especially around the big pecan and elem trees, or wherever happened to be any drifts. A half an hour or more went by before we come up opposite the old well and the old house-place. On up above a little ways, they used to be a spring right on the branch. Haley had dammed it up for a tank a good many years before, and the dam wore down in the course of time to where they wasn't nothing left but a kind of a low bank a few foot high and pretty long. In dry weather they'd be a tank behind it about as big as your hat. The dam was showing above the water now, but you could see from the gashes and the drifted grass on top that the worst part of the flood had covered it. Right now what was left of it was standing out like a island between the water dividing and gushing around it on either side. The only funny thing about it was, close to the top of that mound they was a stob asticking up, real clean-looking, like you'd taken your pocketknife and peeled the bark off of a green stick.

"What do you reckon that is?" I hollered across to Gil and Haley.

"What?" said Haley.

"That stob. What's it doing there?"

Haley stopped to study a minute. "If I ain't mistaken, they used to be a bush there....Yes, they was, a thorn bush."

I seen right then and there what had happened, but I wouldn't admit it to myself till later on because I didn't want to believe it. All I said, out loud, was "They ain't no use in going futher upstream."

And so we turned back, nobody asking me why they wasn't no use, because I'm satisfied most of them knowed too. Anyhow Haley did, and the rest of them wouldn't go again what me and him thought.

We retraced our course real slow, back to the culbert again, only when we got to that I motioned for us to cross the road and keep on agoing downstream.

They was a big old elem right below the culbert, and on down from that a dogwood thicket. A drift had piled up thick next to the dogwoods. Right where the water was pushing hard and slow at the drift, we found Yas. His face was buried in the drift and his arms spread-eagled again it, like he himself was trying to push his way through. A crawfish, drove up to the only safe place he could find, on top of the drift, was poking around at Yas's ear, and backed up with his claws lifted when he seen us coming, curious, I reckon, as to how that thing got there and what we wanted with it.

• • •

Nobody knowed much, of course, about how Yas got drownded. It wasn't till after we'd pulled his corpse out, and all the pains we had to go to to get ahold of the rest of his folks, and send for the undertaker, and all like that, till I had time to think about it. And then I wished I didn't have the time.

I hadn't seen Yas since that day I give him a ride to Ike's and he told me where to head in. Ike told me how Yas had questioned his boy as far as Ike'd let him on what the boy had seen. Ike then tried to convince him to forget all about it, but he didn't have no luck neither. Yas's wife said no, said he'd been agoing over there ever night or two. Told her he kep a look-out some, from up there by the simmon thicket. Nobody could say for sure if he'd gone to the branch and the house-place itself before last night. My guess is he hadn't.

Oh, I didn't have no desire to build it up in my mind, the way it come about, and I don't want to write about it now. But I did build it up, and I will write about it.

No, my guess as to why Yas didn't go to the branch till that night is a straight shoot from his reasons for hanging around that spot at all. Yas believed in hants and he was scared to death of them. The only one he knowed he'd seen was that one that walked up to his steps one night when he was laying on a pallet, the cause of him busting his fist on the door facing. When he convinced hisself they was another ghost in the country, the way I see it from what he said, he couldn't rest till he'd proved to everbody it was there, and to hisself he wasn't afraid of it.

Because he *was* so afraid of it, if you see what I mean.

To my way of thinking, Yas finally got up the nerve to face the territory around the old house-place the night he died. He went off down there and set for a while on the dam by the thornbush. Maybe he didn't pay no attention to the weather, or maybe when he seen the cloud acoming up, he just taken for granted that was a natural part of the scene for the hant to appear in. Or maybe he even thought he'd seen too much, and the storm was on its way to get him, and he was too petrified to run—or I don't know what.

But it had to be he wasn't in his right mind somehow, or he'd've seen the bad spot he was in and at least've moved fifty yards away to where he'd've been safe. And even when the water first begun to rise, if he'd had any judgment about him, he could've swum his way out, big and strong a man as he was. But no, he just set there, and when the water come over the dam he grabbed on to the thornbush, wore the bark off of it and the skin off of his hands—we seen that—till the bush broke and he was washed away.

While I was helping to lift out Yas's corpse from the drift, I just couldn't look at Haley Blair.

But he wouldn't let matters be. Not that he said anything open, now. If he had of, I don't know what I'd've done. Maybe he seen it was too dangerous to talk. I expect he did. He kep on ahanging around me afterwards, though, giving me hard looks in such a manner as I knowed what he was thinking:

There's a man you killed, Amon Lamb. How do you like it, having to handle a man you killed?

12

I went to Yas's funeral, of course, because I couldn't afford not to. But if they'd been any way to get out of it, I would of. In plenty of eyes I seen the blame laid on me. Oh, I knowed well enough it was Yas's own foolishness that brought on his death. But no denying I put him on the road that led him so deep in his foolishness, and folks was bound to count that pretty heavy.

The one thing I could do to help Yas's family I done. They was in a hard enough shape with Yas alive. I had to dig into some savings to do it, but I give them about four prices for the crop Yas was making that year, which was at least twice as much as it would've been worth in a normal year. That was the only way I knowed of to repay a little bit of the loss without offering the family money outright, which they wouldn't've taken. A little later on they moved off of the place and out west of town with her folks, who ain't too bad off.

One more thing I done too, which nobody don't know about but me and my lawyer, Old Man W. D. Clagg. I scraped up some more money and bought each one of Yas's kids a hundred-dollar savings bond apiece, fixing it up to where they wouldn't get them, or even know they had them, till they was twenty-one years of age.

I pitched in to working what was left of my crops, and of Yas's, though his was might near a losing game. One good thing about it anyhow. The rains quit coming.

But then I have to begin at the funeral to get to what taken place next.

They put Yas away in the little graveyard next to the church-house, because that's where most of his folks had always been buried. And they was a bigger crowd present than I reckon ever showed up for any event held in Yas's honor while he was alive. The standbys of the community was all there, of course. And lots of others that come out of curiosity. Because the thing had been blazed abroad over a couple of counties. Cars stood thick on the grounds of the church-house and overflowed up and down the road in all directions from the forks for quite a ways. Everbody couldn't get inside of the church-house, but with the double doors throwed open, some of the bunch left outside could push in on the broad steps and kind of follow what was going on.

If it had been just me by myself, I'd've come late apurpose and stood outside with strangers. But of course I had to take Ma and Pap—for one time, Pap didn't complain about highbobbling around—had to drop them off, then go pick up Ellen, because Ma never would ride in the same car with her. By the time me and her got back, the church-house was filled up excepting for a few spots in the far corners, and we was among the last ones to get seats at all.

They had two preachers, Ike and a fellow from Milcourt. Brother Cartwright his name is. He retired a good while back from holding down a regular church, but he still preaches a good many funerals. I been to at least a dozen where he presided, myself. And he's good at it, quiet and straight out. You can tell the minute you see him near a coffin he's conducted hundreds of people underground. I reckon that's one way a preacher along in years has of getting used to the idey of dying that the rest of us don't have. I never heard Brother Cartwright waste no time on big spiels for people that didn't deserve them. I ain't exactly sure what Yas had coming in the way of a funeral sermon. But you could tell, more by what Brother Cartwright left out than by what he said, that he thought Yas died as a result of his own foolishness. Knowing he agreed with me made me feel some better, because he's in ever way a reasonable and a sensible man.

Ike's part, of course, was a good deal harder, because he was more directly involved in the circumstances. I seen how he'd picked out ever word with care—he had most of his talk wrote down and laying in front of him, a thing I never knowed him to do before—and how uneasy his eyes kep roaming around the crowd. It wasn't till later, though, that I knowed just how much reason he had to be worried.

He repeated a whole lot of what he'd said in that sermon several weeks back, his big point being that nothing couldn't be helped, everthing was the will of God, and all like that. Again, he aimed some of what he said at me, but more so, this time, at Haley. The word "accident" kep cropping up mighty often, I thought, and I soon knowed he was throwing it in to Haley over accusing me.

Now we was a good distance from the pulpit, but Ike had seen us go in there and set down, I know for a fact. During his talk he'd cut his eyes in my direction now and again, but never looking direct at me. Of course he gazed most of the time at Yas's family on the front row of benches, but ever once in a while he'd cast a strong look over towards his left. It had to be at Haley, but I couldn't see him till I finally creened my neck enough to catch a glimpse of not only Haley and his wife, Flora, and their two young kids, but also a stranger setting beside Haley. The man was big and rough-faced, holding a white Stetson in his lap like he was afraid somebody might try to steal it. His eyes hardly ever blinked, and his lips was set for what ought to've been a smile, but looked more like he'd happened to get serious all of a sudden and just forgot to change his expression, so his face froze thataway.

At the graveside itself Old Haley was in there close, right next to the family. He bowed his head lower'n anybody for prayer and swept his hat around from one hand to another. For a fellow that paid so little attention to Yas Bailey while he was living, Haley Blair sure let on like he was grieved. It wouldn't have surprised me if he'd busted out crying.

And that big man with the froze face stayed right next to him, looking on at everthing and not being affected by nothing.

It wasn't till late that evening when I found out who that man was, and Ike was the one that told me, come all the way over to my house to do it. It was a deputy sheriff, he said.

"What in the devil was he doing there?" I blurted out.

Me and Ike had gone off out to the barn to get out of hearing of Ma and Pap, and was setting on the edge of a manger in a cowstall. Ike looked up and said, "That's why I come to see you, to put you straight on a few things."

I wasn't as surprised as I let on like, but I wanted Ike to tell me all he knowed, and that's what he done:

He was running a big risk, he knowed, of starting bad trouble, but if he didn't step in now, they might be worse. He might as well be frank about

Haley, who'd been doing a lot of talking about me long before Yas's accident, telling how I'd spread lies that his farm was hanted, how I'd monkeyed around and might near caused Ike's boy to get killed. (Ike put in right at once he didn't hold me responsible for that. Not minding was what had caused the boy's trouble, and for God's sake, I saved him, didn't I!) And so Haley had talked and talked, to Ike hisself twice. The last time Ike had told him to lay off of me unless he had better reasons to condemn me than the ones he'd give. But of course Haley just throwed up his head and left after that.

And now, the day after Yas's death, Haley had taken it on hisself to try to get me criminally prosecuted. He'd laid the whole matter before the sheriff and the county attorney, and it was his idey for the deputy to come to the funeral.

"Why?" I said. "He never made no move to arrest me, never even paid me no attention."

"Oh, I think he come just so them laws can say they been on the job all along, in case they do decide to prosecute. But then, I don't think they will, no matter how much Haley presses them. And even if it was to get as far as the grand jury, I don't believe they'd bill you. And to consider futher, if they did, you'd come clear. Haley knows that too. But it'd be a kind of a stigma again you, and that's what he's working for.

"But now my idey's this," he went on, "I want to stop this bad blood before it goes any futher, if I can. If you'll agree to it, I'd like for you to go over to Haley's with me and talk to him. Maybe we can settle it peaceable. What do you say?"

I didn't hesitate. I said, "It's all right by me." Because while I knowed it wouldn't do no good, Ike was still on my side, and I wanted to keep him there if I could.

That Goddammed Haley Blair! He was sneaking around all over Milcourt trying to have me arrested, trying to get the law to take up his grudge. That's the way of it with a low-downer like him. He can't be satisfied to hate somebody and let it go at that. He's got to have the laws and the preachers and everbody else in it with him to make it seem right. I got so mad thinking about it, while me and Ike was driving over to Haley's, that if I hadn't felt more'n half guilty concerning Yas's death, I'd've put a stop to Haley Blair's capers right then, if I had to beat him half to death.

The only way I could keep control of myself, during that little call we paid on Haley, was to let Ike do the biggest part of the talking. He put it up to Haley like he said he would, tried to make him understand that I hadn't broke no laws. Said foolish things had been done and foolish remarks made on both sides, but now was the time to realize that if matters went on like they'd been agoing, bad trouble was certain to be the outcome.

Haley heard him out, but when it come his turn, you could see Ike's talking had just made him harder set than ever. He come right out in the open, suggesting I was trying to hide behind the preacher, blaming me all the way for Yas's death, said he'd done everthing he could, and would still do everthing he could, to see that I answered to the law for my crime.

I couldn't even look at the bastard. If I had I'd've gone crazy and tried to kill him. Ike hisself was clean dumbfounded by how bold Haley talked, didn't seem to have no answer for him.

So finally I did speak up. I looked at Haley too, just long enough to say he'd better consider well before he carried out his threats and be prepared for consequences he probably wasn't looking for. But he just set there and sneered.

I couldn't stand it no longer. I got up and headed off down the road afoot, my head reeling and my ears ringing and my eyes half blind with rage. Ike hollered at me and Haley give a kind of a jackass laugh. But I wouldn't've turned around for nothing in this world.

Ike wasn't long in following me, drove up beside me in his car. I got in, and I didn't draw a free breath till we was entirely off of Haley Blair's land.

Ike looked pretty glum when he let me off at the house and drove on. I didn't blame him.

Haley kep his word. I don't know how much cane he raised in Milcourt, but anyway in a few days here come that man with the froze-up face—I found out then he was one of the Andrewses from up on the river—driving up to my place in a sheriff's car. I was in the field, down by the road a good piece from the house, I'm glad to say. He'd been on his way to the house itself, but he seen me and stopped.

He come up swinging his big white Stetson in his hand, and I thought I was in for it good and proper. He begun to ask me some pretty direct questions concerning me and Yas, and I told him everthing he wanted to know. He was nice enough about it, making out like it was more or less of a routine check-up they always had for any accidental death. The only time I come might near losing my temper was when he pumped around to find out if me and Yas had ever been enemies in any way, but I got past that too without cussing and raring, and all the time he was there, nothing was ever said about arresting me. He just left like he was more or less satisfied.

But still Old Haley wouldn't give up. I heard he hung out around the county courthouse for several days, seeing anybody who'd talk to him: the sheriff, the county attorney, the county judge, the foreman of the grand jury—which happened to be in session right then. But they finally seen through his particular scheme. I understand the county judge, in the end, give him a dressing-down, forbidding him ever to bring up that business again to the county officers.

Well, that might've shut him off from using the law, but it didn't put a stop to his tall talking. For a while I still heard reports from Ike and Old Man Gray and a few others. But then in the course of a week or two, it got to where I couldn't pull nothing out of them neither. No, everbody commenced to acting suspicious around me, so I knowed mighty well Haley was beginning to convince even my supporters about some wild story, I didn't know what.

In all my studying about the problem, and you can bet I done aplenty of it, I seen any kind of a fist fight was out, unless he jumped me first, which of course he wouldn't do. So the best thing I come up with was this: When I figured he'd gone too far and slandered me, I'd put a piece in the paper laying down the facts of the case as I seen them, and coming right out in the open to say Haley'd been spreading tales, adding in how the law had refused to charge me, and ending up by demanding for him to either shut up or I'd bring legal action again him. I had the piece about all wrote out in advance, and the time wasn't long in coming when I figured I ought to publish it.

First off, though, I went to Milcourt and talked to Old Man W. D. Clagg. We went over everthing in his office, and worded and reworded my notice till it suited him, and set the day after the next as the proper time for it to appear in the paper.

It sure tickled me to think how Old Haley would have to come out from behind his gossip now. No more sneaking around. It would either be shut up or risk putting his old pious self in court.

But then that notice never did come out in the paper. It wouldn't've been of no use anyway, and that was clear enough the very evening I come home from talking to W. D. Clagg.

I taken the roundabout way and went by Ellen's house. Because while I was setting in the lawyer's office I said to myself, 'The time's come to make a clean breast of this to Ellen.' And right at the time it seemed like all I had to do was go out there and explain everthing to her in a natural kind of way, I mean including the business with the tomahawk and everthing—just explain and she'd understand.

I found Ellen in her flower garden, in jeans and a wrinkled shirt, her hands covered with dirt and a streak or two of it on her face. Her hair was tumbled ever whichaway. I walked up and reached out for her, not saying anything but smiling like I was plumb tickled to death about something.

But she wouldn't have nothing to do with me. Dammed if she didn't jump up on the steps and slip inside of the screen door and hook it and stand there looking at me funny, mad for one thing, and even scared.

For the first time I thought, 'My God, the strange stories have got to her too!'

She said, "You're not touching me! You're not even coming in this house till you swear you'll explain to me. And don't you dare say, 'Explain what?'"

"But sweetheart, that's exactly what I come over here for."

"It's about time."

She unhooked the door and I went in, but she kep her distance, made me set down on a chair across the room from her. I begun my tale, but I was already losing heart before I got good and started.

Ever since that Sunday of the storm, the last time I'd come close to confiding in her, we'd acted cooler'n ever with one another. The bickering and little quarrels hadn't got no worse, but they sure hadn't got no better. And while I set there talking, now, I seen what a fool I'd been to think I could explain it all away. Instead, it looked to me like the time had come for a big falling-out sure enough.

But I went ahead and told her everthing, like I'd intended to, beginning that Sunday when I first went to the thicket and working right on through. I tried to be as honest as I could, not making no bones about how strange all my experiences had been lately. I included the coursing of the bees, finding the tomahawk, the prank on Cephas, the well accident, the drouth, the floods, the part Haley was playing, and all the rest of it.

And when I finished, I could see in her face before she opened her mouth that me and Ellen had just parted company, and behind that I seen, besides, that I was going to part company with the whole community. Putting that notice in the newspaper wouldn't do no good. Nothing wouldn't do no good.

So I taken what she had to say in silence:

"Amon, I thought all along that your peculiar actions could be blamed on wanting to have it out with Haley Blair. I know you don't like him, and he hates you, and I don't blame you for being mixed up in that. But what do you mean about ghosts and that tomahawk causing it to rain? Do you really believe all that? Amon, that's crazy! What I've been hearing about you's true. For God's sake, Amon, you're insane!"

She even tensed up, like she wanted to be ready to bolt if she had to. I still didn't say nothing. I just set there staring at the floor. She got up slow and went to the door. My eyes was half full of tears. Before she spoke again, she went out on the steps and stood holding open the screen door: "You have to leave, Amon. That's all they is to it."

I walked out. As I was in the car and starting up to drive away, she come running over, and standing a few foot away, she said, "Watch out for Haley Blair. He's going to try something else, I don't know just what. And listen, Amon, I know you're not crazy. You couldn't be, no matter how funny you act. Forgive me for saying so, Amon. But I've got to think about this for a little while. Do you understand? It's led to so much strain between us, I've got to think it over. No, don't get out of the car. Go on. Go away. Let me think. And you, you've got to beat Haley Blair, and you've got to do it without turning violent."

And that's the last time I've seen Ellen. They wasn't no time to get in touch with her before I left the country. And anyway, from the last thing she said, she may have me down as a regular coward for running. Still, she told me not to turn violent. And *she's* the one that told *me* to leave her alone, which left the situation, I thought and I still think, so that it was her place to come to me. Now that I've run over it all, I'm surer than ever she's let me down. W. D. Clagg must've told her where I am, like I asked him to, and she ain't wrote me. So there you have it....

When I drove up home from Ellen's, Pap met me at the carshed:

"Listen here, boy, you got to do something about that Goddam Haley Blair! You know what he's up to now? He went and called a meeting of the whole community to try and get people to take some action again you. Ike just come over here and told me. It's going to be held at the church-house this very night. It's serious, boy....But here, let's get away from this carshed. Ma'll see us talking and wonder what's up."

So we wandered off out to the barn like nothing unusual was going on. We set down out there and talked for a while. At least Pap didn't think I'd gone out of my mind. Yes, but if I'd told him all I'd told Ellen, wouldn't he've come to the same conclusion she had? And she *did* think I was some on the crazy side, even if she did deny it as I was pulling out.

What Pap had in mind was they might even lynch me, even if he didn't say so in so many words. He thought the best thing for me to do was to skip the country for a while and lay low till the whole thing kind of blowed over.

But that went too much again the grain, right then, that running away. I said, "No, by God! I'll just go over there and stand up to them, that's what I'll do"—because I couldn't believe they was all that much danger.

But Pap hollered out, "No, son! That's the most dangerous thing you could do."

But I wouldn't have it any other way, I told him. And he said all right then, he'd go with me. I didn't want that, but he wouldn't give up on going along till I promised him I'd look over the lay of the land good before I taken the risk of going into the church-house.

Like I say, I just couldn't believe they was all that many of my neighbors that had it in for me.

So directly, then, me and Pap went on to the house, where Ma had supper about ready. And as soon as we eat I struck out.

It was right after sundown now. I drove the car along real slow by the graveyard lane and the turnoff towards where the Blairs live, and then over the ridges on east. The warm daytime air poured through the car with the last of the sunlight, and when I eased down into Coon Creek bottom, the night air and the dusk hit me cool and dim. I was going along so slow I noticed the change might near as much as I used to when I was a kid, when we'd be going to the revival meeting of an evening in the wagon, with me setting in the back end of the wagon swinging my feet over the open tailgate and watching the daylight drop back behind us over the hills while night come up to meet up out of the creek bottom. I used to wait for just that minute when the edge of the night cool'd slide over me from below and push out the heat of the day. I used to think about God walking in the Garden in the cool of the day, the time when he called out for Adam and Eve and they hid from Him. Back then I didn't look on it as unbelievable at all for God to hunt out a cool dim bottom after a long sultry day as close to the sun as He lived. And now, right now, for that night at least, I thought I could believe it again. I don't know just why. I guess I seen my lot might be lonesomeness and danger, but one thing about it. Seem like that idey give me sharp and clear my own way of looking at things like I'd never enjoyed it before. Even suspecting the worse might be ahead, I couldn't feel anything but peaceful about it all, or maybe not peaceful but strong and fit to bust with life.

Now I didn't know what time the meeting was supposed to commence, but not especially wanting to run into anybody on the way over there, I hunted me up a lane into a back pasture. It was over on the Carson place, a good ways from any house. I pulled into that as far as a strip of woods and stopped out of sight. And there I set till a good while after night, till I judged it was between seven-thirty and eight o'clock. Then I went on back to the main road and drove on to another lane about a half a mile from the church-house, left my car hid there and hiked out afoot.

I went along the road till I seen lights in the church-house, then I stopped. I had just turned the last corner coming in from the south, and from there on it was a straight shoot to the church-house, without hardly any grader ditches to hide in if I needed to. So I decided I'd better cut across someway and sneak up close to check, like I'd promised Pap I would.

Some renters named Kyle lived in a shack of a house about fifty yards off to my right, and they was a garden between me and the house. From the looks of things they wasn't nobody at home, or nobody up maybe, because they wasn't a light nowheres. Old Man Kyle had a hound or two, though, so I had to work mighty quiet as close to the house as I had to come.

So I creeped along in the dark till I come to the garden fence and straddled over it. The ground ahead looked bare to the fencerow of the little graveyard that lays just south of the church-house. But dammed if they wasn't some old dead watermelon vines in my way, too near the color of the ground for me to notice in the dark, till I was right in among them. They rattled like anything around my feet, and out come one of them hounds abarking and araising sand.

He stopped a ways before he got to me. I stayed still, waiting him out. He barked and growled and fussed around for some little bit, but I never could catch a glimpse of him, because he was under some trees at the edge of the yard. And I don't reckon he ever seen me neither. Finally, when I couldn't hardly stand still no longer, he give up, and a minute or two after I quit hearing him, I inched on. It wasn't no easy matter to keep from making a noise. I managed the best I could by lifting up my feet and easing them down, testing to make certain I wasn't on none of them vines before I set all my weight down. Seemed like it taken me forever to cross that garden.

From the fencerow of the graveyard, I could make out a little of what was taking place, through the south windows of the church-house, both of them raised, but about all I could see was shadows and dim forms. The fencerow was tangled up with briars and wild pea vines and bloodweeds, all that heavy growth the rains has brought up and now dry enough to be noisy. I tore my shirt, stuck myself with briars, scratched my hand on the barbwire. And then, once I got inside the graveyard, I was faced with stumbling over tombstones. I fell down four or five times, till I finally had to slow down to just creeping along like a blind man on the edge of a cliff, feeling for everthing with my hands and feet. Because the tombstones was so near the color of the ground, like the melon vines had been, that I run into the same trouble with them.

Ever minute or so I'd stop to get my bearings again, and the church-house would look just as far away as ever, far enough to keep me headed towards it all night and never get there, till daylight come and they'd catch me in the middle of the graveyard.

Another thing that made me even uneasier was that if they'd been a hole in the ground, a cave-in caused by the rains, I could fall in it and down among the coffins and bones before I could do a thing to save myself.

I don't know why it taken so long to come to me, but when it hit it was all of a sudden. I remembered Yas was buried here. The thought struck me so hard, and scared me so much, all I could do was fall down on my knees, too weak to stand up anymore. I put my hands over my face and moaned. Waves of sickness and dread whirled all around me. If his hand had reached out and touched me or his voice called out, I couldn't've been no nearer dead with terror than I already was.

Two or three times I tried to get up, and ever time I did I sunk back trembling. Finally I commenced to crawling, till I bumped headon into a tombstone and pulled myself up by it. I looked around, and when I recognized the tree that Yas's grave was under, a good ways off to my right, I breathed a whole lot easier. I'm satisfied I said something to that grave, but I don't know what it was. It may not've been any more than a moan or two, but it quietened me down enough to go on.

Time went by and kep agoing by. After what seemed like all night, I come up to where the light from the church-house lantern cast a little reflection on the top wire of the fence that run a few foot from the building wall. Staying out of that glow, but using it as a guide, I snuck up to the fence and crawled along it to find a way through, not wanting to risk opening the gate and having it screak on me.

The lowest section of the fence was hogwire around knee-high, with two strands of barbwire above it. I could've straddled the hogwire, but I was afraid it might screak too. Directly I found a washout under it and slid on my belly through the gap. Then I had to worm my way back down a few yards till I was square under one of the open windows of the church-house.

I couldn't raise up to look now. It would've been a dead giveaway. But in all my eukering around I'd noticed they was thirty or more men inside. I'd picked out Hap Carr and Gil Blair and Old Man Gray and Ike, and a bunch more. As far as I could tell, they wasn't a one among them a stranger to me. And, of course, Haley was right in the big middle of them, standing not in the pulpit but close up beside it. I'd seen others raising up and setting down, arm motions, heads turning. And now if I was too near to risk looking, I could sure hear well enough:

"...a sneak and a snake...," I caught that coming from Haley, and just then Ike cut him off: "Brother Haley, I think we have to keep one thing straight. As I understand it, this meeting is for the purpose of deciding whe'er Brother Amon's crazy or not. Now, if he is, then being a 'sneak and a snake,' as you call it, ain't got nothing to do with the case, because a crazy man's not responsible for what he does. If he's mean, that's one thing. If he's crazy, that's another. Brethern, we've got to keep that difference in mind. Now in my opinion...."

"Just a minute, Brother Ike," Haley broke in. "I'd like to say that I see you're entirely right. I just lost my temper there for a second, because you see, I've had so much trouble with him. And I don't mean to cut you off, neither. But if you'll just allow me to kind of summarize what I've said, why then I'll set down and let somebody else have the floor."

A sort of a muttered agreement went around the room. He sure did have them under his thumb. And on he went: "Now friends and brethern, my main point is this: Amon Lamb's actions of late show as clear as anything that he's insane, and may be dangerous, and still we can't get him sent off, I don't expect, because our county officers are too sorry to take a hand in this matter at all. But just let me summarize why he's crazy. First there's that lie he told poor Brother Cephas about hants, which is something a kid might do, but not a grown man in his right mind. Or even granting a sane person would, just as a kind of a joke, wouldn't they try to put a stop to it as soon as they seen the danger they was getting the person they told into? Well, Brother Amon had ever chance to do that, and he didn't lift a finger to. When the word spread around the country and everbody started running into my place out of curiosity, he was even warned to do something—Brother Ike, you said sometime back you'd hit him up about it. Did anybody else?"

Old Man Gray kep quiet, I'm glad to say.

"Well, I did," said Haley. "I talked to him one time when he knowed beyond a doubt he ought to do something, because it was after your boy, Brother Ike, fell in that old well. Yes, I know Brother Amon went down and pulled him out. I know that. But I was there, and I'll swear to you that when I seen him climbing out of there with that boy, he looked plumb wild out of the eyes. I believe to my soul that if the rest of us hadn't been astanding there, he'd've throwed the boy right back in."

And I'll be dammed if everbody didn't swallow that! Even Ike didn't say nothing.

The meeting, of course, had been in progress for some time when I got there, but I'd surmised at first, from what I heard, that Haley wasn't making as much headway as he wanted to, judging from the way Ike shut him up on that 'sneak and snake' business. But I soon seen that wasn't really the way of it. Some of them still a little bit favorable to me might object if they heard Haley condemning me as a pure-dee bastard, but everbody, seem like, was more'n half convinced I wasn't in my right mind, so much so they'd take in a flat-out lie.

"And so," Haley run on, "I don't need to tell you it was negligence on his part, at the very least, that led to Brother Cephas's death. I think it was more. I think it was deliberate. But wait! Hear me out!" He got real loud to squelch some mutters that commenced to spreading around the group.... "Now, as some of you've heard, I thought at first it was because they was enemies for some reason I didn't know about, that Brother Amon planned it all, and that he ought to be tried for murder. And I don't hesitate to say I done all I could to have him charged. But the more I studied about it, the more I decided they wasn't no reason—no sane reason, mind you—for him to want to get rid of Brother Cephas. And when I come to that conclusion, brethern, I quit trying to get the man charged. I concluded he was suffering from some kind of insane motive that me and any of you wouldn't understand, and that it wouldn't be right to try him for it...."

How do you like that! They run him off from the courthouse, that's why he dropped the idey of getting me hung for murder!

"...But brethern, listen to me, and listen carefully. They's one thing I ain't brought out yet, and if you don't go along with anything else I've said tonight, this ought to cinch things for you. I swear to it now, and I'll swear to it on a witness stand. I don't pretend to understand the workings of a crazy mind, now, but I will give you the facts, and you can judge them for yourselves.

"The first time I seen anything strange about Brother Amon was one day when I was walking along the branch right over there by that very old house-place under discussion, looking for a cow, I believe I was. Well, I seen somebody scrooched up behind a tree up there in the edge of the woods above the house-place. All of you know that spot well enough, and how uneasy it can make you, because nobody can go around there without remembering the massacre that taken place there. And so anyway, at first I didn't recognize who it was, but I didn't let on. I just fooled around up and down the branch for a while, finally went up and set down at the foot of a tree a little ways along the woods from where this person was. He hid hisself, or thought he did, by hugging the trunk of that blackjack on the side away from me.

"Now I didn't know quite what to do. I was even a little bit leery of accosting somebody that might be crazy, from the way he acted, or anyhow was up to no good. What I finally done was to get up and leave out like I was headed for home. But then I turned off into the timber right away and circled back up to the head of that draw running up through the trees to the top of the hill. And this time I recognized him. It was Brother Amon, and he was heading out for home across my pasture, carrying some kind of a heavy object in one hand.

"Now then, you can imagine how mystified I was, brethern. Even after I'd investigated around some, all I knowed was that Brother Amon had been digging in the neighborhood of the old house-place. What he carried away, whe'er it was something he'd dug up or been carrying with him all along, I didn't know. That heavy rock of a looking thing was, and still is, one of the biggest mysteries of this whole business.

"But that ain't the end of it. One day I come up on Brother Amon at that old graveyard over there on my place. Close to the end of the big drouth, it was. And the same day I warned him to set Brother Cephas straight. Now when I first seen Brother Amon, he was setting down on a tombstone, and why was he doing that, in God's name? He had his car a little piece off. He rushed back to it when he seen me coming, and shoved something under the seat. Now again, all I could see was that the object was like a rock, gray and rough, only this time I seen it was oblong and round-like.

"I left him after having a few words with him, and went on to the field where I was started to, but I stayed where I could see him drive off. I ought to include, though, that I suppose his dad, Brother Henry, was worried about him too, for he rode up on a horse and talked a while before Brother Amon sent him home...."

For a second I wished Pap could've been there. Oh, what a look on his face if he could've heard 'Brother Haley' call him 'Brother Henry'!

"...When he did finally drive off, he went towards the east, and that evening I saddled up my pony and rode off to inquire. You see, that stone-like object had me wondering something fierce. Brother Ike, I don't guess you knowed, till now, why I asked you about Brother Amon. It was that day we decided on the prayer meeting to ask the Lord for rain, remember? And you told me he'd give Brother Cephas a ride up to your gate and then left out. Well, anyway, I kep an eye on him after that, mostly from that field I mentioned. Two or maybe three different Saturdays I seen him drive over in that same direction, and I got to timing him to see about how far he went before he turned around and come on back. The last time he went, I went over his ground that very evening ahorseback. I'd taken note of what kind of tires he had on his car, you understand, and while of course I couldn't follow them on the main road, I could check ever turn-off on east of you, Brother Ike. And I didn't have to look far, neither. He'd drove through the grounds of that old vacant Mt. Carmel church-house and down that lane on the other side of it. I tracked him to where he parked his car, not far off from that old Monroe swimming-hole that all of us knowed quite well as boys. I couldn't follow him no futher, though, not right then.

"Well, to shorten this some, suffice to say I kep checking back there, ever day or two. Now then, I want you to note that the very day before Brother Cephas was killed that night, I seen a mighty strange thing, and I come might near missing it too. I just happened to drive by that cattleguard of mine that leads down to the branch, in time to see Brother Amon up at that old house-place again. Down on his knees, I want you to know. And what for? I ask you. When he seen me, he got up to his feet, went to the old well, and throwed something in it. Now I couldn't see what it was, and he lit out for the woods before I could ask him. But I'll tell you this much: that very evening I made tracks over to that swimming-hole, thinking he might've been there. And that's right. He had been. This time I tracked him across the creek itself and into a thicket, and there I found a hole scooped out, like he'd dug up something that was buried there.

"Now brethern, that's about as much as I know. What he dug up, I don't know. What he throwed in the well, I don't know. But none of that don't matter, when you come right down to it. The thing is, his actions just ain't the actions of a sane man. And they're more'n just peculiar. Why is so much tragedy connected with what he does? I mean, first Brother Ike's boy. But most of all, Brother Cephas. What Amon Lamb has done the law won't touch him for, but I say if we don't do something, we'll all end up in danger from this man. We've got to protect our wives and children, because the law won't. And before we get off into feeling sorry for a man that's out of his mind, we've got to remember that our first duty is to our loved ones and the good of the whole community. I say we've got to get rid of him, friends and neighbors. We've all got to stand together and drive him from our midst. And we can't waste no time about doing it."

Godamighty! I was clean paralyzed for most of the way through Haley's spouting-off, and cussing myself for being outwitted at ever turn. He'd been watching me all the time, and laying for his chance, and it had come. And how!

Of course, I could see, even at that, that he had some reason, from his point of view, for putting me down as crazy. But he was pushing it so hard that I didn't hate him any the less.

I could hear shuffling all over the place now, and others talking, but Haley's voice still cut in ever now and then above the rest of them.

So I was done for. Any idey of going in there would've been plumb silly. If I'd busted in and tried to explain, all they'd've done was grab me and like as not tied me up. And they might've taken me to the county line or they might've taken me to the nearest tree, in spite of all that talk about not holding me responsible. The only one that could've helped at all was Ike.

But as soon as the voices toned down a little, and Haley asked him—you see how sly he was, he never did give up the floor at all, no matter what he'd promised—I say, as soon as he asked Ike if he'd seen me going to that swimming-hole place, it come out he had. Ike said yes, he'd seen me go down there once or twice, even admitted he'd stayed at home one day when all the rest of the family had gone to town, just to watch me, and seen me go down there. Tried to holler me down, too, the last day I went there, and couldn't get me to stop.

So it was Ike, and not any reflection from the sky, I seen that day when I stopped to take a piss by the old ruined church-house.

And so, things went from bad to worse. It turned into Haley questioning Ike about why he hadn't reported my strange actions, and Ike not being able to do nothing but back down. Till Haley might near had him implicated in concealing the suspicious doings of a dangerous man!

I don't know why that Haley Blair didn't make a lawyer out of hisself!

Well, they wasn't no use in staying around any longer and running the risk of getting caught if they broke up the meeting sudden, as they was likely to do. So I crawled off, and this time I didn't go back through the graveyard and the garden. I followed the fence closest to me over to the road, walked slow up that till I figured the noise of my feet on the gravel wouldn't carry back to them, and then I lit out at a dead run. That dam hound commenced to barking again, but I just charged on, hoping they was too busy at the church-house to pay me any mind.

I made that old car hum, let me tell you, to get home ahead of them, just in case they decided to come over and capture me that very night. Pap was still up, and in no time flat I put him wise to what was up. Ma come bouncing out too, and we all got me a few clothes together, and a little food, and what money they was in the house, which, because of Ma's habit of hiding money around in the kitchen cabinet, was enough to keep me going for a while till I could let them know where I was and they could send me some more.

So pretty soon I was ready to go. My intention was to head for the river, that being the state line, and use the best way I could find to mix up Haley and his bunch if they come after me. For I didn't know but what he wanted to get his hands on me, whatever he said about just running me out of the country.

Nothing would do but Pap had to go with me. What I wanted was for me to leave the car at a certain place, and for him and W. D. Clagg to go over there and pick it up in a day or so. Because he can't really see well enough to drive of a night. But he pled so hard, I had to let him go along, only getting him to promise to wait till daylight to drive home.

We taken off, made it through Milcourt without being interfered with. It was just a few miles on north to the river, but instead of going there on the highway, we taken a roundabout way and ended up in Sagamore Bend where the dirt road dips down to a low-water bridge. I'd fished there, and I knowed the spot pretty well. I got out, showed Pap a place to hide till morning, and shook his hand goodbye.

We didn't say much.

Then I went down and crossed the bridge. It had been under water a whole lot during the summer. The river had just barely gone down enough even yet to leave the top of the bridge clear of the water.

Like I said away back yonder, as soon as I'd crossed that river I felt like all my troubles had slipped back a thousand miles behind me. I never had felt so free in my life.

And so all that night I slep in the woods under a cool sky with the stars quivering and sending out sparks, and it was like the whole sky was rolling to carry me and the stars on a good long journey with some kind of wonder at the end of it.

PART II

1

Lord, how long is it now since I wrote anything in these tablets?

Nearly six months it is, when I stop and count it up. But then it seems like a whole lot longer'n that. And with all that's taken place in that time, I don't hardly know where to start to catch up. Don't know, as a matter of fact, if I ought to start writing again at all. But I will. I'll try it for a little while anyhow.

Some big changes, you see, commenced right after I finished up writing what had happened back in Milcourt up to the time I left out of there. These new changes put writing clean out of my mind, and for a long time there I couldn't see no reason to ever go back to it at all. I'd done finished up what I started out to do. Like I said away back yonder somewhere on one of these pages, all I started out to do was kind of lay out the whole mess in my mind, with the help of a sheet of paper, in hopes of seeing it all a little better. Well, I done that: that is, I wrote it all down. I still didn't know if I seen it any better. But no matter. I was supposed to do now what I'd said I would when the writing got done: I was supposed to make up my mind either to go back home or take an altogether different course. The way everthing worked out....

But here now, I've got to come at this slow, and in the right order. I had better say, though, just why I've picked up writing again after so many months.

The main reason, I guess, is this: during the time when I was writing on what taken place at home last spring and summer, I got into the habit of kind of thinking of myself as two people—the one that had done all that bunch of things, and then the one doing the writing about them. I did forget about such a thing, all right, when I found myself all tangled up in this bunch of new happenings. But now seeing as how they've all settled down, and other important things have happened too, and now when it seems like I'm in a sort of a lull, I keep feeling like I deserted part of myself, and I've just got to take ahold and finish telling what I done. Even though I still suppose nobody'll ever see these tablets but me.

So I have to go back to the time when I finished up writing the first part.

It was the dead of the night when I finished, nearly a month after the night when I first started, or that is to say, about two months after I'd left home to begin with. It was around three weeks after I'd swore I wouldn't have nothing more to do with Dilly, and so far I'd kep my promise.

Turned out, though, that she really had been out at her Grandma's for a week, after which she showed up back at Bee's rooming house again. I checked up and found out. Her Grandma had taken sick all at once that Sunday, the day after we was out there that Saturday night, and Dilly had gone out there to see after her. And when the old lady was up and around again, Dilly still couldn't persuade her to move into town.

But I also imagine Wert spent a right smart of his time out there. And me, I just went on my way acting as unconcerned as you please. When Dilly moved back into Bee's, she did seem to be a little uneasy around me. I was just civil to her, and that was about all. I'd meet her coming in or going out once in a while, I'd run onto her downtown ever now and then, and a few times when I dropped by the cabstand, she'd be there. For you see, I wouldn't've made it look like I was trying to stay out of her way for anything in the world. If I happened to catch her at the cabstand, I'd pass the time of day with her and Mrs. A. a little bit, and then I'd be on my way. Not in all that time did I ever see Dilly just the two of us by ourselves. And I didn't make it by the cabstand all that often, neither. Because most of the time, you see, my mind was just completely taken up with writing in my tablets. All I done, outside of that, was to go up to Bick's and eat, or stroll around town some when I couldn't stand my room nomore, or check at the post office once in a while. And the deeper I got into that routine, the less I cared whe'er Dilly and Wert was hanging out together or not. Because it was like I was living all over again what had occurred at home, like being there and at the same time looking on from another place far off. And when the misery and the blues would creep in on me, now and again, I'd begin to look harder at what had come to pass at home, and how I could make it clear in my tablets, and then I'd forget all about the misery and the blues.

But then I finished up writing—like I say, away along in the night—and after I'd set there and stared at the wall for about a hour, I had to admit I didn't know what in the world I'd do come tomorrow. For I didn't feel satisfied the way I'd expected at all. In fact, it was like I'd been plumb lost for a long time and had just now come to realize it. In a minute's time there, I jumped from one extreme to the other. Glumness couldn't take ahold of me at all as long as I was writing, but the minute I put up the finished tablets, it bound me up completely.

I did get tired enough, finally, to crawl into bed. But I just turned and tossed, and if I did manage to drop off for a while, I had bad dreams I couldn't remember when I woke up, dreams I had to fight my way out of, one after another, only to come up again the next one, dreams that come at me like so many hands reaching for you as you fall from a steep place, and you don't know whe'er they intend to catch you or knock you around. A time or two, when matters come to their worst pass, I'd about half wake up and about half stay asleep. I'd know I was in the dark of some room. I'd catch a tiny bit of a glow on the windowlights, like it was painted there. I'd hear the wind on the increase, and I'd say, 'It's bringing dust thicker and thicker.' Maybe you can dream and remember at the same time and maybe you can't, but anyway that's the best I know how to describe it. Different times back home got twisted up with times now and come in on me from all sides to tear me betwixt and between them, yesterday and today in a spin and me caught up in the middle of them, falling but still not going anywheres. I never felt the sickness of that falling any worse'n I did right then, and all the time I knowed I was in the dark of a room touched by a little bit of dirty light at the window, and the wind was stirring up more and more dust to blind and choke me.

About daylight that morning I give up trying to sleep, snuck out of the house and walked weary up to Bick's Cafe. They wasn't a soul in the place except for Bick hisself. He was on the stool by the door, hunched over the counter and turning regular as clockwork the pages of an old magazine, and staring at them with his pooched-out eyes.

"We Never Sleep," it says on a sign tacked up behind the counter, and it seems like, sure enough, Bick hisself don't. I know in reason he can't be present ever one of the twenty-four hours a day the place is open. Still, I never go in there but what I find him, and I never seen him do more than doze a little bit behind the counter. That morning when I looked at Bick with his big old gray head and his bulged-out eyes, and heard his gratey voice say hello, I just knowed he stayed around all the time to keep the grub as bad as it was. If he went out for a minute, somebody might improve it, and then he wouldn't be contributing his part to the suffering of the world.

Me and Bick usually have at least a few words to say to one another, but that morning it was just hello and nothing more. I ordered, eat, left. Coming home past a few street lamps over sidewalks as empty as the ones in a ghost town, I had some doubts about what I was to conclude from my dreams. It was that feeling about leaping from the temple again, and right then I felt like I was headed for sheer destruction.

I drug up to my room and set by the window till sunup, knowing very well I was in too much of a wrought-up shape to think, and yet spurring myself to think anyway, and just not able to stop spurring. It's a good thing a person can wear theirselves out pretty fast doing that, because when they're completely tuckered they can lay down, like I did, and fall off to sleep.

When I woke up this time, things looked a little better. But not much. And for several days, there, I just slouched around, not going nowhere to speak of. I even just about quit going to the post office, a habit I'd kep up about halfway while I was writing. But in all that time—a month, mind you—I still hadn't heard a peep out of Ellen. I had heard from Ma one time, and right away I telephoned W. D. Clagg again, to let Ma and Pap know through him that I was still all right. But I'd sure seen, since I'd quit writing about home, how cut off I was from it. I thought, 'It's just gone, that's all. That's a part of my life I'll never live over. That's a place I'll never see nomore. I spoiled myself into thinking that writing about it could take the place of being there. Only now I know better. So the thing to do is turn to something else.'

Then again I'd think, 'No, by God! I'll go back there anyway. I'll face up to Haley Blair. Let him do his dammedest. I'll get the best of him someway or another.'

Only it didn't take me long to get out of the notion, because I never was long in remembering that Ellen didn't care a thing about me nomore, and I'd remind myself I didn't give a hoot in hell about going back there if she wasn't a part of the bargain.

Practical matters, of course, did have to be considered sooner or later. Pap had hired the crop gathered that fall, mine and the one I bought from Yas, what they was in the way of crops in such a sorry year, and hiring hands taken a pretty big bite out of that. Ma wrote me how much money they was in the bank—my part, their part, and all like that. But it would mighty soon be time to think about a crop for another year, and what was to be done about that? Pap sure couldn't make a crop by hisself. We'd either have to rent out the land or sell the place, and we'd have to decide before the first of the year. Ma and Pap could, I guess, have realized enough out of the rent money to scrape by on. But I'd about decided I was in favor of just putting the place up for sale. Land wasn't bringing no big price, but still Ma and Pap would get enough out of it, I was satisfied, to live on for the rest of their lives.

As for myself, I wasn't worried. The money I'd brought, and what Ma and Pap had sent me out of my savings, and now with the crop money too in the Milcourt bank—no more than I'd be spending I could make out on that for better'n a year, if I had to.

But then, I couldn't decide on nothing, seem like. The main trouble was, I didn't have a blamed thing to do with myself, now, except lay around. I might've picked up some kind of a little old job if I'd just looked, but I didn't want to.

I like to pulled out for Chicago one morning, was halfway bundled up and ready before I changed my mind. I didn't know what in the devil I'd do in a place like Chicago, a country fellow like me. Oh, work wasn't that hard to get. Depression or no Depression, they'd put me on in some factory or something, I felt like. My brother Reed could get me fixed up, and I could stay with him and his family till I got things smoothed out. But just the very idey got me down. I never had been in a city the size of Chicago, and I knowed good and well I wouldn't like it.

A few times during my moping around I thought to myself, 'I know a farm I could work, I'll bet.' And of course what I had in mind was the place Dilly's Grandma lived on. It was a good-size farm, and the renter they had had about half let things go to the dogs. But then I knowed, too, that they'd be a whole lot more to work there than a farm.

It was Dilly, just the same, that finally pulled me out of the dumps. She'd gone to work, you see, at Bee Coleman's beauty parlor. I guess the little money she had had give out, and she had to do something. She wasn't no beautician, but I found out Bee was training her, so she could get her a license and be able to support herself.

And so, one day about middle of the morning, when I'd might near sunk to the bottom and was plumb disgusted with myself for not coming out of it, I was setting in a booth at the Frying Pan Cafe, and in walked Dilly, white uniform and all, a silk or rayon-like uniform that flared out just enough from her curves to let you know how luscious they was, and that dark blonde hair pushed up in thick glossy waves and her eyes soft in the morning light.

I jumped right up and cabbaged on to her. Taken her by the hand as she walked past and led her over to the booth.

I just said, "Come over here. I want to talk to you."

She laughed, like she was real tickled, and said, "Why, Amon, I didn't see you there!"

I made her set down, without saying anything, for the fact is, it taken me a little bit to pick up my wits, because I'd flew in without thinking. Then I put on this grin that I'm satisfied was kind of foolish and said, "Seems like we both been pretty busy. What've you been up to?"

"Well, as you might imagine, nothing important. Working, mostly. And what is it you've been so busy at, anyhow?"

'Uh-oh,' I thought. 'If I don't watch out this'll turn out to be another one of them I-ask-you-a-question, you-ask-me-another'n times.' So I just commented, "I see you're making a beauty operator."

"How do you know I ain't one already?"

"Well, nobody could look more like one," I said, "nor any prettier in the uniform that goes with it, neither."

"Amon, you are the funniest man. You don't say a word to a person for weeks and weeks, and then all of a sudden you're passing out the nicest compliments."

I liked her better serious. When she flirted around like this, she acted like a high-school kid, and it didn't become her.

I'd ordered some coffee for us, and when the waitress brought it over, Dilly said, "Oh Amon, honest I have to go back to work. I told Bee I was just going to step over here after a package of gum."

But still she didn't make no move to leave.

I stirred my coffee, not taking my eyes off of her, and said, "How's your Grandma? I heard she got all right, but is she completely well?"

She blushed, I swear, but still no more than she would've from just being glad I'd asked: "As well as she can be at her age, I suppose. She asked me about you the other day."

And then, "Listen, Amon, not to change the subject, but you know you've sure got Bee's and Boggs's curiosity up, and mine too, for that matter. We all wonder what you're doing with that bunch of tablets. Bee thinks you're hid out here writing a book or something, and just making out like you left home for some other reason."

I laughed right out loud, a little too loud, I guess: "Writing a book! Do I look like the kind of a fellow that'd be writing a book?"

"Oh Amon, you look like you'd be capable of doing anything!"

Now a thing like that embarrasses me. I thought to myself, 'Will you quit trying to be cute!' But I was sucked in just the same, by her soft eyes and her warm voice. All I said, though, was, "I wish you and Bee and all the rest of them'd quit making me out to be such a mystery man. It's a simple matter, I tell you. I come up here, like I told you, because I had a fight with one of my neighbors, and we're both kind of cooling off. It's so tangled up I don't want to explain it, but believe me, they ain't much to it. I may go back home pretty soon, and I may sell out what I've got down there and move on somewheres else. I just ain't made up my mind, quite."

"That makes it sound like you run away."

"I did run away! What do you expect, with one fellow again everbody else in the country?"

"You said a minute ago it was just one neighbor. You even told me his name one time, I believe."

"Haley Blair."

"Yes, Haley Blair. So how did these others get involved in it?"

"Now look," I said, "I'll just tell you this much. Me and Haley Blair got into a ruckus, and he kep blowing it up till he made it into a big thing to the community at large, and if I hadn't left when I did, they's a good chance I'd've been rode out of town on a rail. As for what that ruckus was all about, that's something between me and Haley Blair that we'll have to settle between ourselves one of these days.

"Now then, about the tablets you and Bee and Boggs're so itchy over. They don't amount to much neither. I'm just writing up something that...happened a while back...in my family...just to give me something to do. So it ain't nothing for you nor them to bother about at all."

"It's a kind of a family history, you mean?"

"It's a kind of a history, yes."

So there I went again. I made what I had to say sound a whole lot stronger than I really meant to, too much 'mind your own dam business' about it, and I done it to throw her off. But here I was again telling about one-fourth of the truth, one more time doing what I'd caught myself doing so much of late, not coming right out with a bare-faced lie, but wording things in such a way they sure stayed a good ways from the truth. I mean, what I was writing didn't exactly take place in no family, and it wasn't exactly a while back. It happened I thought of Grandpa's tablets, is what made me say it the way I did.

Oh well, anyway, I couldn't afford to tell her too much of the truth right then.

What I said didn't hurt her feelings at all. She taken up the line I was thinking along right away: "All right, Amon. My goodness! I didn't mean to meddle in your business, so you don't have to get huffy about it. But say, look who's coming in the door."

For one time, accidental or not, I had forethought enough about me not to turn around.

"Who?" I asked.

"Nobody but Wert."

She still sounded calm enough, but something in her voice changed. That high-school flirty tone was gone all of a sudden, and in the place of it I could've swore I heard her voice quiver with fear, away down deep.

I ain't sure if he knowed we was there when he come in, or just when. But he headed straight for our booth, I know, because it wasn't a second after she spoke when I looked up and there he was, stepping to her side of the booth and leaning his elbow on the high backrest behind her, not paying no more attention to me than if I hadn't've been there. Grinning kind of foolish and mad at the same time, he said to her, "I come over to the beauty parlor to go get a cup of coffee with you, and you wasn't there."

Which was pretty obvious, wasn't it?

Dilly looked from him to me, like she was leading his eyes over: "You boys know each other, don't you?"

He growled out, "Yaow, we're acquainted. How're you?"

"Tolerable well. You?"

"Fine."

If he'd waited for me to ask him to set down, he'd've stood there a week. Dilly sounded uneasy when she said, "Why don't you set down, Wert?" and slid over next to the wall.

"Ain't got time."

"Cab business must be pretty rushing," I put in.

"Enough so to keep me out of other people's affairs."

I sighed out real loud. "Ain't it a shame, though, how everbody seems to have so many troubles of their own?"

He didn't know what to make out of that, you could tell: whe'er I was backing down or whe'er I'd found some roundabout way to insult him. I reckon he must've decided I meant it insulting, because it looked to me like he was about to spit out something sure enough nasty, when Dilly stopped him: "I really do have to go back to the beauty shop. Wert, why don't you walk over with me?"

I wasn't going to let him take her away from me that easy. I said, "You can't go off yet. You ain't finished your coffee."

"She can go when she feels like it," says Wert.

"Not if you're just out to make her leave, buddy!"

Dilly jumped up right quick. "Please now! You boys quit it. Nobody's making me go, and nobody's making me stay. I've got work to do, that's all. And I just come over here after a package of gum. So both of you stop it. It's been nice seeing you, Amon. Come on, please, Wert. Walk back over to the beauty shop with me."

"Okay, let's go."

She said, flirty sounding again, but I swear frightened, "Goodbye, Amon."

"Bye bye."

They left out. I set there drinking coffee till I'd cooled off some. Then I went out to walk the streets some more.

By the time I'd gone not many blocks, I decided one thing: Wert Fleming wasn't going to have things as much his way as before. Because I'd come to the conclusion, from the way Dilly acted in the cafe, that she didn't like him as well as she sometimes let on she did. And I thought to myself, 'What's this acting scared all about? We'll have to find out what this is, if nothing else.' And I wondered if it didn't have something to do with that former husband of hers. Wert had been a big friend of his at one time, she told me. I begun to imagine all kinds of ways, some of them downright silly, where he could've been holding something over her head. When you ain't got nothing else to do, you can make up the dammedest stories.

Anyhow, the first thing I done was to march myself right over to Bee's Beauty Parlor. Wert had done gone, as I figured he would be. Thimblebrains like him're liable to think it's womanish just to step inside of a beauty shop. But I went in, embarrassed as I was to have to talk to Dilly up there in front of a bunch of other women. Lucky for me, I didn't have to. She was busy giving a permanent in one of the booths, so Bee said, and she'd be tied up a half an hour or more. Bee looked pretty startled to find me barging in and asking to speak to Dilly, when I hadn't been in the habit of paying her no attention at all. That was part of my idey, though. Because if word got around town, as it sure would, that Wert had taken Dilly plumb away from me in the restaurant, I wanted it noised around too that I wasn't out of the running yet. And I didn't see no better way to get the news on its way than to let it slip in Bee's Beauty Parlor.

What I done then was go down to the bus station and call Dilly from a telephone booth, knowing she was still busy, but just making my point to Bee again that I sure wanted to get in touch with her. And I set right there by the phone booth till she called me back. Without cutting any didoes about it, I asked her to go to the picture show with me that night.

Well, she said she couldn't, said she was busy.

"A date with Wert, I reckon," I said, dry-like.

"Oh Amon, now quit it!" But she didn't say it wasn't Wert.

"All right, how about tomorrow night, then?"

And that was okay. We fixed it so I was supposed to come by her room about eight o'clock the next night and pick her up.

Later on, I thought once or twice about asking Mrs. A. for her car, but then I decided they wasn't no point in it. It'd be better anyway, for us to be seen as much as possible around town, to let people see we was keeping company.

And so the next night we went to the show. They was just one movie house in that burg, plus the drive-in. They showed the general run-of-the-mill stuff: western stories, detective stories, musical pieces where it always comes out just right for the man or woman to sing a song ever few minutes. None of them didn't ever interest me much, and the one that night—it was a western story, is about all I remember. I found us some seats away off in one corner, and we set there and necked during the whole thing.

Dilly was dressed in that floweredy dress again, the one I'd first seen her in. In the show it was just dark enough to imagine the glimmer of her dress, with its pale background and the flowers just visible, as a part of her, and not like something she wore. I seemed to draw away futher and futher from the everday world, to where is was just dark and there was Dilly, and through the night all around, her lips reached out, moist, warm, clinging to mine. Night was wide, and her tender lips was in ever corner of it. And arms, arms that when you barely touched them underneath above the elbow, they was softer than you thought human flesh could ever be. And yet arms that when they squeezed around you, you could know how strong they was.

The noise of the show was another world, one that you didn't care about anymore.

A long time passed before we come out of that show. I was so happy and bounding inside of me, I wanted to go over by the cabstand—I said to say hello to Mrs. Armbruster. But Dilly wouldn't do it. She said no so strong and appealing that I never mentioned it nomore. And she didn't want to stop anywheres for a cup of coffee or something neither. She wanted to go right straight home, and that's where we headed for.

It was a still night, for once, and cloudy. Walking slow and holding one another's hand, we went down the whole length of the main street, and it being so late, we nearly had the town to ourselves. The thump and scrape of our feet on the gritty sidewalk you could hear reflected off of the building fronts. Boggs Coleman drove past in his taxicab, but he didn't see us. Being might near as big a talker as his wife is, he was yapping his head off, you could tell, to whoever he was hauling in the back seat, some old man I didn't recognize. Bick looked out of his show-window at us, with his old pooched-out eyes, and waved back when we waved at him.

The streetlamps thinned out considerable after we went by the hotel and crossed the railroad tracks, but with it being low cloudy, they was enough glow cast back from the town lights we could see where we was going pretty well. I put my arm around Dilly then. The feel of her soft, solid body, the working of her hipjoint along my thigh as we walked, the brush of her hair now and then on my arm—I was walking inside of the first hours of happiness I'd seen in months. My mind run on away ahead of me, seeing us together time after time in the future, imagining us when the arms and the lips and the night was shut up in a room and wrapped up in a bed, when the working of her hips and that luscious ass would be to press all her naked flesh against my own. I seen us beginning what would be for both of us a new life. I seen us married.

And that minute, good God, Ellen! I'd tried not to think about her, and I just about hadn't. Only now, I couldn't keep from remembering how long we'd been in love and been together. And I hadn't married her. Yes, but that was as much her idey as it was mine, more so, in fact, I argued to myself. And right at once, as they always will, all the arguments I'd made up to protect myself from feeling guilty—most of them hanging on not having heard from her—they come to my rescue.

Me and Dilly was at the darkest spot between the railroad tracks and the bridge over the creek. I stopped and grabbed her, squeezed her as tight and kissed her as hard as I could, and she give back everthing she got, for a little bit, till she realized before I did that it would be a pretty out if a car was to happen along just then. So she pulled back, wrapped both arms around one of mine, give me a real quick wet kiss on the ear, and said, "We better go on home."

But they was something I suddenly wanted to mention, and I couldn't keep from busting out with it: "You afraid Wert'll come along and see us?"

She got mighty tense.

"What's the matter?" I said.

"I wish you wouldn't bring up his name."

"Why?"

"Just because."

"Well," I said, "sooner or later you're going to have to stop seeing me or him one."

She had her head about half down. They might've been tears in her eyes, it sure sounded like it in her voice.

She said, "I may go out with him once in a while because I almost have to, but I wish you'd understand they's nothing between us."

"You sure? Then why do you have to run around with him anyway?"

For a minute she didn't say nothing, like she was wondering whe'er to tell me or not, or just fixing to tell me and trying to think up what to say. We'd come to the bridge by now, and had started across on a little walk bordering the car lanes, her being on the inside. I glanced at her one second and seen her again a mixed-up bunch of trees and a wooden freighthouse and a weedy lot. I glanced at her a second time, and she seemed to be balanced unsteady away up high, with on the other side of her the skeleton of steel banisters, tops of trees rising from the creekbed below us, a stone facing of the channel away down below, and everthing tipped half over with me and her ready to fall along with it. A sudden dizziness hit me. The scenes I'd made up of me falling from the temple rushed in. I gripped at her tighter before I thought. She looked at me funny, and I guess forgot any notion she might've had of telling me about her and Wert.

I got ahold of myself and was just about to ask her again why she had to associate with Wert. I was all ready to keep on till I found out something at least. But about that time, before I could say anything at all, a car swung around past the railroad station behind us and bumped across the tracks and come on to overtake us, going medium fast. We'd just reached the far end of the bridge, and when whoever was in the car seen us, it slowed down real slow and idled along past us. They was two men in the front seat, but it wasn't nobody's car that I'd ever seen. I looked at them hard, and I couldn't make out nothing. They wasn't enough glow for that.

Dilly never paid them no attention at all. They didn't say nothing, neither, although they was close enough to. They just looked, and I looked back, and then they speeded up and went on.

I might've knowed one of them'd be Wert, though like I say, I didn't recognize him. But Dilly knowed good and well it was.

"You see there," she said, "he follows me around."

"See what?" I come back. "You mean because he stops to gawk at you like a idiot when you're walking along with somebody else, you're supposed to be scared to death and run back to him? I never heard of the like!"

"That ain't all of it," she said, real low. "I just can't explain how it is right now, Amon. You'll just have to please believe me when I say even if I do go out on a date with him once in a while, it's nothing to keep me and you apart. If you'll just please trust me, I'll make it all right, honest I will. Please, Amon darling."

She stopped right on her last words and turned around facing me. I taken her tight in my arms again, and we stood there on that sidewalk hugging and kissing for several minutes. It wasn't till we'd about finished when I realized we was standing nearly under that streetlamp that shows me all I can see of the town late at night from my window. Somebody else might've been watching too, but now I didn't let it bother me none.

When we finally walked on, I wasn't hardly stepping on the ground at all. She'd just pulled me into believing everthing she told me, and I felt so full of love and joy, right then, she could've said the sky was below us, and I'd've believed her.

At the door to her room we stood and clenched as long as we dared to, not wanting to wake up Bee sleeping just down the hall a little ways. We didn't say a word, but we didn't need to. I'd lost all account of time, anyhow. When we did break it up, it was pulling apart real slow, with several kisses while we was at it, and some hand squeezes as she opened the door to her room and I begun to back up along the hallway to the stairs.

In my own room and in bed, I found out I wasn't falling anymore but floating. I laid there uncovered and naked, the dark around me warm and close, turning my body now and again from side to stomach and then from stomach to side. Any new part of the sheet I touched was cool to my hot flesh. My head and all of my blood seemed to be balanced and trembling in the purest kind of rhythm. The curves of her body that my flesh remembered from a little while back came to me nude and warm, and in my slow turning in bed it was like I was thrusting into the deepest kind of union with her.

It wouldn't've taken much, let me tell you, to send me down there and into her room, and let all the dammed consequences fall where they might!

Ellen appeared awful far away, right then, and Dilly like the only woman I'd ever want. My heart would falter when I'd think how unhappy Dilly had been, with a husband gone insane, and for some reason I didn't understand yet, forced to be nice to a despisable bum like Wert Fleming. But soon all such troubles would be cut out of her life and mine, and we'd be together for good. I drifted off into imaginings of me and her on that farm of her Grandma's, of the house all fixed up, of the prettiest children you ever seen, of how I'd love her and she'd love me.

And of course, a big part of it was, I felt like I was rescuing her from sorry rakes and crazy people that had made her life a misery.

The wind begun to stir a little before I finally dropped off to sleep. As I imagined how it ruffled the leaves and waved the limbs of trees under the streetlamp down there, where we'd stood and kissed, the motion of the wind in the leaves and the limbs carried me along with soft rocking through the most passionate kind of dreams.

2

They ain't nothing in this world like falling in love strong and simple, no matter whe'er you're justified in feeling that way or not. It looks to you like everthing you want can be put in a few clear terms, and ever problem can be explained in the same terms. But to feel like that, of course, you have to take might near no account of anything else in the world except what's right in front of your nose.

And that's how I got to be about Dilly. I guess I'd been cooped up in that room with my writing tablets so long, driving myself half crazy mulling over my past troubles while I scribbled at them, that when I did break aloose I went on a tear sure enough. You couldn't've done anything on earth to convince me, beginning that night when we went to the show for the first time together, that Dilly wasn't some innocent victim of a whole lot of evil circumstances she never would be able to get out of without my help.

I won't even pretend I can explain all the reasons behind it. Mostly I'll just try to put it down like it was. But they was one thing, I know, that entered into it. One strong enemy, Haley Blair, has pushed me out of a place that was mine, and while I was still trying to make up my mind to go back and fight him, or what, along come another enemy, Wert Fleming, where it looked like it was easy to choose sides and to know how to fight and to see what the rewards would be.

And so, after complications so thick you couldn't count them in that business back home, everthing here looked straight and plain as could be, and let me tell you, I was ready to jump into that fight for all I was worth.

For a while they wasn't any what you'd call fighting to do. It appeared like we might have Wert buffaloed. I seen to it that me and Dilly was out doing something purt near ever night. Only, now and then, Dilly would say to me some night that she just had to go out and see her Grandma, and that Wert was going to drive her out and back. She seen that made me suspicious, and she give me to understand this was the best way, all around, to do it. Said she had to hold him at arm's length, but she could do that from now on, and for me not to worry about it.

When I let on like Wert Fleming didn't strike me as somebody that'd be satisfied just driving a girl around to see her Grandma, Dilly laughed like it was a joke and said I didn't understand Wert's sort of people. It looked to me, then, like she was fixing to defend him, so I commenced to get a little bit riled and was about to demand to know the whole story as to just why she couldn't brush off Wert altogether. She seen coming what I had in mind, and she headed it off by turning real lovey-dovey. With that she sure enough did shut my mouth for the time being—we was setting, at the time, in the swing on Bee's front porch, on a cool, clear night, with the stars looking bright for fall overhead.

But that was one of the very few times when I had a sneaking suspicion I might be a sucker.

Whenever I did see Wert, around the cabstand or anywhere, he'd scowl and as a usual thing not say much. But at that he didn't look much more surly than he always had. I reckon he must've thought I'd take a gentle hint like him driving past in that car, and eventually let his supposed-to-be girl friend alone. Him being, or so he thought, such a fierce hombry. One time he did pass a remark, in the presence of Mrs. A. and some others, that he'd heard of fellows getting shot for not letting other people's women alone. But I made out like I didn't hear him at all.

Most of my time, as you might imagine, I spent in studying about Dilly. I'd lollygag around up and down the streets while she was working, being right there to meet her when she got off for dinner, and we'd head out for Bick's, or sometimes the other cafe, and eat. And then that evening, when she was back at work, I'd walk some more, or I'd stop and talk to old nesters around town. I'd sometimes go to the show by myself, but generally I wouldn't, because chances were I'd done seen it with Dilly, or else I was about to right soon. For another thing, I'd go to this kind of a public library they had stuck off in one corner of the courthouse basement, with not much in it in the way of books. I'd set around there and read some, but to tell you the truth, I can't remember any more than just snatches of anything I read, my mind was so taken up with Dilly. Looking back on it now, I seem to remember a whole lot more about how I stared at this thing and that thing out in the town itself, reconsidering it like. And when I did, I felt relieved that I'd recovered from the dumps I used to be in. I'd see how the world was looking brighter and was shining more all the time.

That town, that dusty, windy town—to look at it then, I wouldn't've knowed it for the same place it used to be. Seemed to me like the weather got better, but I don't expect it did, not very much. It was just that whichever way I looked, now, whichever corner I happened to turn, whichever street I glanced along, it all brought Dilly to mind, and joy to everthing before my eyes. If the lawns all up and down looked parched and bald, it just meant, now, that wanting them different might've meant wanting the whole town different. If the buildings was dingy, and the pavement, where they was any, was rough, it just meant, now, that wishing them to be clean and smooth would've been wishing for this town to be taken away and another one put down there in its place. And another town would've meant another life, and another life couldn't've included the same Dilly. Even old Bick, with his pooched-out eyes and his heavy way of setting and looking out up and down the street, or turning the pages of his magazine, I didn't want him to change none either. Overnight, you might say, the town had turned into my town, with the touch and sight and smell of it new like it had been born again. Old Bick still set there and stared out of his window, or at his magazine, but I never passed there, now, by myself or with Dilly, but what I chuckled and felt sorry for Bick, because he had his sad, bulged-out eyes fixed on something that didn't really exist. He was living in the town that used to be, and I was living in the town that was.

With Dilly before my eyes and always on my mind, Ellen faded and faded, and along with her my life back home. And even the tablets I'd wrote begun to seem as old as Grandpa's tablets. Like I'd lived through the years of a whole lifetime in a little while and gone on to another lifetime as quick as you can catch a ride from one town to another one.

Mine and Dilly's situation was kiddish in lots of ways, of course. I mean we necked and spooned a lot in the show, and walked holding hands down the street, and grinned all over ourselves whenever we looked at one another. But that's as far as it went. Oh, I'm satisfied that even then, if I'd just've made a point out of it, I could of taken Dilly to bed with me. She never did make no motion to stop me, no more than the usual kind of pushing away of your hands that just means "come on" instead of "get away." One night we did come mighty close to ending up in a naked clench.

I'd gone in her room with her when we come home from the picture show, a thing I didn't ordinarily do. The moon was shining in through the window and across her bed. They wasn't a place in there big enough for two to set side by side except on the bed, and we didn't want no better place. Nor we didn't turn on no lights, neither. We set down on the side of the bed in the dim moonlight and kissed and hugged till we was both might near out of our minds. Pretty soon I had her dress halfway up her legs, and halfway undone above—that floweredy dress again—and was kissing her between the breasts. Inside of a minute we'd've been in the bed and at it good and proper. The moonlight on her legs made me plain delirious. But then once when I happened to glance at them, I remembered the night me and Ellen had come home from town, and how the moon had shone in through the window on her—and that was the end of that. I lost interest so fast that it looked to Dilly like something was wrong sure enough. But when she wanted to know, I couldn't tell her. All I could do was stay and smooch a little longer, not very heavy, and finally go to my own room.

Now after matters had stood about as I've described them for a few weeks, with me not much troubled by Wert, one night I run headon into him at the cabstand. And this time him and Dilly were just fixing to leave for her Grandma's. I'd been downtown in the library calling myself reading, but mostly just looking at pictures in magazines, when I jumped up and struck out for the cabstand all of a sudden, bothered as hell about Dilly going off with Wert, realizing, moony as I was, that however it was she was supposed to get rid of Wert, she sure hadn't been doing much about it.

When I walked in they was both standing up ready to go out of the door. I caught a look on Dilly's face, which was turned towards Wert, before she knowed I did, and it didn't appear to me now like she was at all unfriendly to him. And Wert, I guess feeling braver'n usual all at once, said, "Well, if it ain't Mr. Sheep!"

I don't go for people making fun of my name, even if it is Lamb, so I fired back, "If I was so pea-brained I couldn't think of a better joke'n that, I'd keep my mouth shut."

"Aw, you boys hush up," says Mrs. A., cool as you please. "What's the use in picking on one another?"

Sounded like she thought we was just two more similar to her boy, and she could try to correct us the same way—maybe with better luck.

Dilly spoke up too: "We'd better be going, Wert, or we'll be late."

I didn't like the sound of her voice at all, which made me keep on.

"How's everthing out at Grandma's?" I said, thinking they could take it any old way they liked it.

Wert give a real loud hoot of a laugh, so onery-sounding I like to lost control of myself. Me and him both was getting worked up pretty bad, and it just didn't make me no difference. I was ready to have it out right there in the cabstand, even if we both got throwed in jail. I got so mad it jolted me out of the foolish notion that I was supposed to be saving Dilly from Wert's clutches.

And lo and behold, there she was as cool as you please, and she didn't seem to be in no great hurry about pulling us apart if me and Wert was to happen to tangle. Mrs. A. begun to look kind of worried now. And Boggs Coleman, who'd just drove in, was standing in the doorway like for once in his life he couldn't think of nothing to say.

Then Dilly she said, "Amon, Wert really does have to drive me out to Grandma's."

But I swear her eyes was shining as she looked from one to the other of us in such a way that I got a scary feeling she wanted to stand right there and be fought over. The look wasn't all neither. A second later she added, prim as you please, "This is not the time and place to settle this."

I say "scary," and that makes it sound like I was afraid of Wert. But that wasn't it, by no means. I begun to see plain, now, what I'd been hiding from myself for a couple of weeks. And all in the same breath, I seen myself as a fool and a dunce and a idiot of the worst description. I didn't know what to do, so I didn't do nothing, and I didn't say nothing more. It must've looked to Wert, I know, like I really was afraid of him, because all of a sudden I didn't show no more life. Him and her walked out and got in his cab and drove off. They was clean gone before I paid any attention to what I was doing. Then I went over and set down in a chair and kep on studying about my situation. Mrs. A. would give me a look ever now and again, and so would Boggs. But neither of them didn't say nothing.

The phone rung. Mrs. A. jumped like she'd never heard such a sound before in her life. And I reckon I did too.

"Taxi?...Yes, we do....Where'd you say?...All right. He'll be right down. Boggs, 212 East Oak."

I listened real careful to what she said, just like it was the most important thing in the world to what I was thinking about. When she got through, and Boggs had gone, and me and her was by ourselves, I said, "You'd never think some people're as big a fools as they are, would you?"

"Who do you mean?"

"I reckon you know I mean myself."

"What've you done that's so foolish?"

"Do you mean to set there, ma'm, and tell me Dilly's not two-timing me?"

"I think you're all wrong about that."

"Well, what does she keep going around with *him* for?"

"With Wert? Well, they's more to this situation than you might imagine. Why don't you ask her? I can't tell you."

"Ask her! I have! And all I get's the run-around. But then what's the use in asking you, anyway. You wouldn't tell me if you knowed."

"What do you mean?" she said, bristling up. "Just why wouldn't I tell you? Anyhow, I'll tell you this much. Dilly's a straight girl, and nothing'll make me believe she ain't. She's had a hard time of it, with a husband that went crazy and then having to be good to a no-count like Wert. And then, to top it all off, when she meets up with somebody worth associating with, like you, to have him suspicious over ever little thing she does."

That time I like to busted out laughing. And still I was pretty mixed up. Just to hear Mrs. A. talk, you could've swore she was telling me a out-and-out lie, apurpose, and expecting me to be galoot enough to swallow it. But I knowed that couldn't be the case. I mean, sure, I'd been acting mighty dumb about Dilly, I knowed that. But I hoped not that dumb.

So I just come out as frank as I could: "Looky here, Mrs. Armbruster, seems like to me you're saying two or three things at once. You call Wert a no-count, and then in the next breath you say running around with him is a little thing. Now just what is it you're supposed to be getting at, if you wouldn't mind telling me?"

I expected that'd make her hum and haw. But no, she pitched right in: "Amon Lamb, let me tell you something about women. You take Dilly. Ever since she growed up she's had to put up with men like Wert, because let me tell you, her Daddy's pretty sorry hisself, lays out drunk a whole lot and chases ever old slut that'll have anything to do with him. I knowed them when Dilly was just a little girl and they lived out there on her Grandma's place. Dilly's mama died right after they moved to California, and there was Dilly, not much more'n a child, left with a boozed-up daddy to take care of. You can just bet she married that Orville because he was supposed to be one of these religious guys, and because he followed them from here to California just to wait for her to grow up. And that's a fact, he did. Then, as you know, it didn't turn out good at all.

"Well then, after he might near killed her and she had him sent off, she comes back here. And there's Wert ready to step in. But now you come along, and she don't exactly know what to do. A person like you she ain't never run into before—I mean, a man like you. But now Wert, he's a whole lot like her Daddy, and even some, I reckon, like her first husband. Mean and sorry men she understands, but decent men she don't. For all she knows, you may be just stringing her along. You might up and go back home and leave her high and dry...."

I cut in: "Did you get all this from her?"

"No, of course I didn't. I'm surmising, but I've seen enough in my time, Amon Lamb, to know what I'm talking about.

"No, now listen," she went on, "she still thinks she's got to be nice to Wert because he may be the only kind she can ever have, don't you see? But let me give you a little advice. If I was you, I wouldn't let a girl like her get away. I'd step right in and tell her what's what. Let her know you'll marry her, and fix it so Wert'll get the idey too, and the whole situation will be right in your hands.

"Now then, there it is. I've told you, and you can get mad at me if you want to. But I had to tell you sooner or later, and this was as good a time as any."

I was about to open my mouth, but before I could make it, she added on, "Oh, and they's something else I meant to tell you. Her old man ain't in the asylum nomore."

For a second I didn't catch on at all, then when I seen she meant Orville, I said, "What do you mean, her old man ain't in the asylum nomore? You mean he got away, escaped?"

"No, I mean they let him out, the asylum did. Said he was cured."

All I could think was, 'Well, that adds a little twist or two to this matter, don't it?' And that's what I said.

"Not if you don't let it, it won't. He can't give her no trouble. They was divorced, you see. That is to say, the marriage was broke up—dissolved, is what I'm trying to say—when he went off to the asylum."

"Yaow, but he might have different ideys about that. He may want her back no matter whe'er she wants him or not, or he may still want to get even with her someway or another."

I didn't say all I thought about it, but the situation looked dangerous to me. I didn't have any idey if Orville really would want Dilly back, but he didn't sound like somebody that would forget what'd taken place, jealous as he'd been, and considering Dilly was responsible for him being sent off. Besides, if he was as crazy as she made him sound like, he couldn't've been cured in no few months' time.

"No, sure enough," she went on, "they say he's cured. The only thing they made him promise was to stay away from Dilly and leave her alone, and he swore he would. That church out there in California that he's such a big member of, they're taking the responsibility for him till he proves out all right. Dilly got a letter from the asylum, and one from the church, and even one from Orville hisself. She showed them to me, and it all looks like it's been worked out so they won't be no trouble from Orville."

Dilly hadn't said a word about none of that to me, and I wondered why.

But anyway, Mrs. A. talked like she was pretty anxious about it, no matter what words she said. What she wanted couldn't've been no plainer, of course. She wanted me to take charge of Dilly, marry her, get her away from Wert. And save any possible trouble from Orville, she hoped, at the same time. You could just see the wheels working in her head. And I must say, I felt like all at once that Mrs. A. wasn't no friend of mine. Seemed like to her I was just somebody that could do the best thing, she thought, for Dilly. It sure annoyed me, but then again, I had to admit they was plenty of reason for her thinking the way she did. Mrs. A.'d had a husband about Wert's caliber, and now to look at her boy, you could tell he wasn't liable to be no better. And seeing what she thought was a way to save a girl like she'd been from a bad life, she didn't hesitate a minute in taking it.

A little earlier, I might've believed everthing Mrs. A. told me as strong as she believed it herself. But not now.

I jumped up out of my chair.

"Where you going all of a sudden?" Mrs. A asked in a scared voice, like I was swimming off before she had me all the way on the hook.

"Could I borrow your car?"

"You're welcome to it, of course. But do you mind if I ask you what for?"

I popped out with the first windy that come to mind: "I can think better when I'm driving around, that's all. And I've got some thinking to do."

Flimsy as that sounded, she didn't seem to know if she ought to believe it, or what. But she'd got so anxious not to cross me, hoping to drag me in where I couldn't get out, she just handed me the keys, with, "They's plenty of gas in it. Just try to come back here before twelve o'clock comes, and time for me to go home."

After pulling out and circling around the block a time or two so she'd see me and think I really was riding around to think, I headed out of town on the highway towards Dilly's Grandma's. For I'd done made up my mind to check up on Dilly and Wert, a thing I ought to've done a good while before, and would of if I hadn't been so knuckle-headed about wanting to believe everthing she told me, and—even more so—about all the moon-eyed things I'd made up to describe mine and her situation.

It was a mighty dark night, and they wasn't no traffic to speak of on the highway. Seeing I hadn't been out in that direction since me and Dilly was there that one time, I recollected all we'd done as I rode along. I passed the road we drove up and the cafe where we eat. It hurt me to remember.

I crossed the creek, and in no time I was idling along past Dilly's Grandma's house.

Just like I suspicioned, Wert's car wasn't nowhere to be seen.

A half a mile or more on up the road I turned around and headed back. On my way up, when I'd passed that bunch of beer joints on the creek bank, I'd looked all around for Wert's car there too. But no sign of it. When I made it to there on my way back, though, I taken a notion to stop anyhow. I picked out the biggest and the glariest-looking place, parked away back in the edge of the trees, so nobody couldn't recognize Mrs. A.'s car from the road, and into the place I went.

Inside, it was the next thing to empty. They was a cross-eyed woman with hair like dead cornsilks doing the serving. Two farmers, one of them booze-fat and red-faced, and the other one bone-thin, was perched up side by side at the bar. A slouchy-looking girl in a floursack dress—I expect the cross-eyed woman's daughter—had tolled a truckdriver off to a corner table and had her chair up so close to him her breasts bulged out over the table and him both. He had about a half-idiot face that he must've thought was handsome, the way he had it decorated with a spindling mustache and real long sideburns. Looked like he really thought he'd made a killing, being with the girl—and he'd end up, I didn't doubt, with that wench rolling him for his money.

Not having had nothing to drink, I durn near throwed up to see all that sorry bunch gathered in there in this dimmish light. Everthing—the tables and beat-up chairs and bluish-colored bar and warped floor—it was all dirty and sticky and smelled of ever rank odor humanity can have, most of all the stink of piss reeking out of two filthy white doors marked for restrooms.

But what really got me was a boy about ten years old, I judge the son of the cross-eyed woman. He was playing at a funny game, and while he done it, you could see by the leer on his face he'd already been a witness, time and again, to the lowest kind of going-ons, and wouldn't be long in following suit. Somewhere or another he'd got his hands on some tinfoil badges with "DEPUTY" printed on them. He'd been going around the room and pinning them on the customers. The two farmers wore them on the bib of their overalls. When I first come in, the boy was making a big to-do out of sticking one of his badges on the truckdriver's shirt, sounding off in his scratchy little old voice, "I deputize you in the name of the law!" And the truckdriver, he went along with the game, guffawing like he didn't have good sense.

Then the boy walked over and offered me a badge, like this was some kind of initiation you had to go through to join this outfit. And when I just shook my head no, he give me the hatefulest look I ever seen on a little kid his age.

The cross-eyed hag brought me a bottle of beer, grinning, and when I didn't grin back forgot all about me, went off to work on the two farmers at the bar. I didn't have nothing better to do than set there and watch her.

The truth is, I never felt more stymied in all my days. I'd jumped so quick from one attitude to another one, about Dilly, that I didn't know yet where I was. All I could muster up in the way of comfort was a dim idey that maybe, after all, everthing'd work out for the best.

But that didn't last no time. Because Hell! I just knowed, as sure as I was setting there, that Dilly and Wert was off someplace in the bushes.

It had crossed my mind they might show up at the beer joint, but I didn't have no real reason to expect it. So I nearly fell over when, about a half a hour after I arrived, and had drunk one bottle of beer, why in they walked.

Wert was about half-lit and weaving around. Dilly was cool and steady as you please, but her clothes looked mussed up to me.

Time to duck out of sight was what I wished for, but I didn't have it. Her eye lit on me just about as soon as they come in the door. She marched right over to my booth, with Wert staggering along beside of her. In what little bit of time it taken for them to make it from the door to the booth, all my notions of her being innocent died, and it was about all I could do to hold on to myself. What's more, that bold business of heading right for my booth give me the idey stronger'n ever that she meant to agg us on to fight over her.

But I wasn't aiming to be the first one to lose my head. I raised up to my feet as polite as you please and said, "Set down, the both of you. I was kind of saving this place for you."

She didn't let on like she took it to be sarcastic atall. And Wert, I don't think he even knowed yet where they was. She set down beside of me, and left him the side across from us.

She said, "I wanted to go on home, but Wert made me stop here."

"You driving?"

"Oh sure, I always do whenever he's like this."

"Must be pretty strong stuff your Grandma serves."

"We didn't stay at Grandma's but a minute or two. Wert had to run on up to Pawnee to see about something, and while we was there he got ahold of a bottle."

Wert come out of his daze. "A bottle?" he says. "That's a good idey. Let's have us a bottle of beer. Hey, ain't this Dan's Place? Why, sure it is. Where's Mabe? Mabe!"

The cross-eyed hag slid off her barstool, where she'd been concentrating on the bony farmer, and come traipsing over, grinning and glittery-eyed.

"Why, hello, Wert!" she squawks out. "How in the world are you, sweetheart?"

She throws her old skinny arm around his shoulder and bends over him and he stares back at her goofy and babyish like some depisable kid waiting for a witch to tell him a dirty bedtime story.

Mother Goose and one of her littleuns, I thought to myself.

When her and Wert got through greeting one another, she brought us some more beer. It was while she was gone after it when Wert first noticed I was there. I was crowded in next to the wall, with Dilly on the outside, and him setting across from us. He commenced to looking at me like he was addled. Dilly didn't say nothing, and I didn't either.

"Who's that setting next to you?" he said in a low-like voice. "And don't tell me they ain't somebody there."

"It's Amon, silly."

"Amon?" He thought it over for a little, then cawed out, "Oh, you mean Mr. Sheep! Is that you, Mr. Sheep?"

"It's Amon Lamb," she says quiet-like, "and you be decent to him."

Mother Goose set down our beer, I paid for it, and she went off. But not till she'd give me a couple of dirty looks. She'd had it in for me right off, I reckon, ever since I come in and wouldn't pay her no mind, and wouldn't play sheriff with that sneery kid of hers. And now I was looking hawk-eyed at her buddy Wert.

I wasn't even going to talk to him. What I'd made up my mind to do was stay put, not drink more'n two bottles of beer, not say no more'n I had to—and then settle things with her tomorrow, for good and all.

Only that ain't the way it worked out. I just couldn't hold my tongue after all. I said, "Wert must come purt near drinking up all he hauls back."

And that cooked them both, let me tell you! It was the one thing that would stick in that liquored-up head of Wert's. He'd been to Pawnee, you might know it, to pick up a load of whiskey and bring it back to the dry territory across the creek. If him and Dilly done it this way as a regular thing, I don't see how they kep from getting caught. Just imagine if a law stopped a taxicab being drove by a woman, with the cabbie drunk beside of her, and them hauling bootleg whiskey!

Oh well, the law around that place was pretty lax, and I'm satisfied they was some kind of a pay-off involved.

Anyhow, Wert kind of sobered up. Dilly's eyes growed a little bit wider.

Finally he said, "Mr. Sheep, you been listening to bad tales. Whoever told you we'd haul stuff like that around?"

I made out like I didn't hear him. I turned to Dilly. "Seems to me like you and him go a pretty roundabout way to get to your Grandma's and back."

"Oh, Amon, don't talk like that now. This ain't the time nor the place."

"You done said that once tonight."

All along, I was getting more riled, and telling myself more to settle down. Still I said, "I hear your husband's out of the asylum too. That's going to put you with three men stringing after you. How're you going to manage all of that?"

She didn't say nothing, but she sure didn't look cowed neither. She'd had her eyes on Wert. Now she turned them on me, then leaned over and said low in my ear, "They's only one of them I care anything about, Amon, and that's you. Stay with me and help me get him home, and tomorrow we'll set everthing straight, honest we will."

"We sure as hell will!" I said.

I guess Wert was still trying to decide what to do about me knowing he had bootleg whiskey in his car, and guzzling beer while he thought. But when he come out of it long enough to notice Dilly talking in my ear, he reached over and grabbed her shoulder and jerked her back upright: "Here! What do you think you're up to, mumbling in Mr. Sheep's ear."

"Say, is your name Sheep, sure enough?" comes this voice from over my head. I looked up and dammed if it wasn't Mother Goose standing right over me!

I just ignored her. Dilly cut her eyes up at her right sharp, and Mother Goose started to go back to her farmer, but Wert pulled her back. "Just a minute, Mabe. What did you say about Mr. Sheep? Come here. What was it?"

Mother Goose stood there and looked at me sidelong. I had her about halfway scared too now, as well as hating me, because she couldn't figure me out.

Mabe pulled aloose and went on off, and Wert he got up and followed her, still asking her what she'd said. She led him off down to one end of the bar and set him on a stool and commenced to talking to him, part of it anyway about me, because she looked in my direction once or twice when she thought I wasn't noticing them.

I said to Dilly, "I've put up with about all of this Sheep business I intend to. If you really want to get him home, the only way I know to do it is to let him drink enough to put him out. Will he keep on agoing long enough to pass out?"

"If I'm around to watch after him, he will."

"Seems like you're the best kind of influence on him, don't it? And him on you, I might add."

She had the nerve to set there and look like she was being put upon in the worst way in the world. I couldn't stand it nomore. I lit into cussing: "Goddamit, woman! What do you think you're up to? You hand me this big line about how you love me, and all the time you're tagging after Wert Fleming, letting on like you have to in some real mysterious way, and me stupid enough to believe you. Well, that's enough of that. So come on. Out with it! What is it makes you have to be so good and kind to our boy Wert? You tell me, or I'm walking out of here, and that's the last you'll see of me."

A person oughtn't to make threats they don't intend to carry out. She could see I wouldn't walk out. At least though, she did give up some of the mystery stuff. She said, "Me and Wert've knowed one another ever since we was little kids. Him and Orville was good friends, too, and Mama and Daddy always liked Wert. I just hate to see him go the way he has, and what I'd like to do, if I can, is help him improve some."

And right there she stopped. Me, I just set there bumfuzzled, thinking surely she had more'n that to say—and even that didn't jive with what she'd once told me, that she hadn't knowed much about Wert before she come back from California, that he was just a big friend of Orville's.

So, when she kep on abeing quiet, directly I said, "And you mean that's all they is to it? That's all they is to this big mystery you been stringing me along with?"

"I'm afraid that's all."

By God, I didn't know what to say! All that time I'd spent working out and studying about a great big romantic scheme, how she was innocent and how she was a victim of some kind of ahold Wert had over her, and what it turned out to be, in the end, was *this*. Oh, I don't mean that big sister business, neither. That was a lie so bald-faced she just hoped to get away with it. No, putting together what Mrs. A. had told me, and the cagey, meek way Dilly was acting now, and everthing else I'd seen with my own eyes but never would admit, I seen all at once what she was like and what a God-durn fool I was. She was a natural born two-timer, and good enough at it to fool not only men, but even women, Mrs. A. for instance.

While I was trying to wake up to all this, she leaned over towards me and said, in a low sweet voice, "But all I really want, Amon, is you."

That jarred me so, since I was thinking of her just the opposite to the way she talked, that I could've come right out and hit her. What I done, though, was set real still, stare at my beer, and straighten out things in my mind as best I could.

Because, in a way, she meant it, you see—right then she did—and her saying it helped me complete the picture. I never in my life seen plainer how some women can look to be one thing on the surface, and mean to be—for that minute—while underneath it all they're something else. She could talk like she was being mama to Wert as pure as you please, and chances are—I'd've bet on it right then—she was screwing him regular. He was a good example of men as she'd always understood them to be, just like Mrs. A. said. His kind of a man was a habit with her, one that ever once in a while she might've liked to get rid of, yes, but of course she never would. Her daddy was a drunkard, and after his wife died, when Dilly was still little, he probably laid up in his own house with this old slut or that one. Her husband had been crazy jealous and terrible in lording it over her. And now then here was Wert, who maybe seemed like both of them put together, again as Mrs. A. had said. On one side of her nature, I guess, she hated and despised him, and she really did want me. But on the other side she wanted Wert to mistreat her and she was a little bit ashamed of me because I didn't act like a 'man': that is, I showed her some respect and I didn't wobble around sloppy drunk nor hit her, and up to now I hadn't even been very jealous.

'Why shit!' I told myself. 'I could've pushed her into bed anytime I felt like it. Why didn't I at least do that?' But I put that aside right at once. Because I knowed so much of it had to do with Ellen, and things was already bad off enough without bringing her to mind.

Anyhow, Dilly, no matter what she done, no matter whe'er she made love to either one of us, or to both of us at the same time, she'd talk and act mild and innocent. And she wasn't doing it to be outright deceitful. What I mean is, she was more deceived by it herself than anybody else could've been. She'd worked it all out so long ago, to make herself fit into a world of such men as Wert—worked it out without hardly knowing what she was doing—that now it just seemed like the natural and normal thing to do....

Mother Goose had already brought us some more beer, and I went to swilling it pretty heavy, forgetting the two-bottle business. Dilly commenced to chattering about Boggs and Bee, and Mrs. A., but I don't remember a word she said. I reckon she could see I wasn't listening, but she went on talking anyhow.

Wert and Mother Goose had broke up their confab by that time. She'd gone back to the bony farmer, had her stool drawed up real close and was rubbing up again him. Wert he was being made a deputy by that sneery kid, who was deviling the life out of him.

As I drunk more beer, it all come clearer and clearer to me. I could've broke out laughing. The life I'd led for the past few weeks commenced to seem more like a dream than any I'd lived through up to then. The whole world and all of my life turned into one dream after another, a long and miserable string of them. I could just about have got up, walked over to Wert, and said, "You're right. I am a sheep," and then slunk out of the place and crawled off in a corner somewhere to die.

Just like I hadn't already guzzled too much, I ordered some more beer. Had some trouble attracting Mother Goose's attention this time, because she was working hard on that farmer. The floursack girl had wheedled the truckdriver out of the money to play some tune on the jukebox: fiddles and old electric guitars loud enough to bust the eardrums of a normal person, and a high voice screeching about love. I don't reckon that same tune played all night long but seemed to me like it did. They was a few words at the end of the chorus I couldn't understand at first. Sounded like it said "When I *felt* so hard for you," but what it finally come out to be was "When I *fell* so hard for you."

Now I wasn't the only one that heard it wrong neither, because after I'd got up to go to the toilet, holding my nose all the time I was in there except for drawing a breath now and then when I had to, I come out to find the record had stopped playing, and Mother Goose was holding up her beer and waving it in front of the thin farmer, screeching out in a half-tune, "When I *felt* so hard for you!" And in between repeating that, laughing her fool head off.

Some people's idey of a joke. Godamighty!

I couldn't stand to hear them, let alone look at them. Fast as I could, I went by and over to the booth and set down. I'd drunk about five or six beers in a row, and that, added to having to go in that cesspool of a restroom, and seeing that weird pair at the bar—I'm satisfied I'd've gotten sick pretty soon, if I hadn't noticed Wert on his way back to our booth, and that sobered me up some.

I didn't feel like a sheep nomore, though. Just the sight of Wert—that rough face, that hulk of a body—was enough, now, to set me off. He was taking the girl, and I was letting him. She might be a whore, in a way, yes, but she could've been something else if it wasn't for him and his kind. It come to me again: what Haley Blair had done to me at home, Wert Fleming was doing to me here, both of them driving me out and taking what rightly belonged to me. My head, my whole body, got to be steady, and burning mad. I watched and set quiet as Wert weaved around towards the booth. I still had just enough gumption about me to realize he was drunker'n I was, and I ought not to jump on him.

But I sure give him ever opportunity to jump on me. I let him get set down, across from us like he had been, before I said, "I thought you and Mother Goose had struck up a big friendship."

He blinked like a goof. "Mother Goose? What do you mean, Mother Goose? Are you casting slurs at my friend Mabe?"

I just looked at him.

He kep on. "If I had a name like yours, Mr. Sheep, I wouldn't give funny ones to other people."

I reckon I just wanted to think he was sobering up some, but his voice did sound like it.

Wanting Mabe to be in on all this, he turned around to call her over. Dammed if her and that bony farmer wasn't dancing, or trying to, and without a sign of music, because the jukebox was quiet for a little. Her eyes was all bulged out and glittering. His face had a skeleton grin plastered on it. Ever now and then, as they stumbled around the floor, she sung out, "When I *felt* so hard for you."

Finally Wert half stood up and yelled out, "Mabe! Come here!"

Her and the farmer stopped, she kind of guided him back to his stool, and come on over to us. "What you need, Wert?"

"This Mr. Sheep here is referring to you as Mother Goose. Don't you think we ought to take him down a peg or two for that?"

She looked at me more hateful than ever, but then she didn't want no brawl, because I guess she'd been closed up for that before, and so she commenced trying to smooth things over. "Aw, he's just fooling, Wert. Let him alone. Besides, if his name's Sheep, he ain't got no room to talk, has he? Is your name Sheep, sure enough?"

"You asked me that once before," I said.

"No," Wert put in, "it ain't. He ain't even big enough to be a sheep. He's a Lamb."

You take somebody as stupid as Wert, if they ever think of something even as clever as that, they can't afford to let it go. So I knowed he'd be at that Sheep-Lamb business till he was shut up once and for all.

But I still wasn't going to hit the first lick.

About that time, too, I looked at Dilly long enough to see she was enjoying the quarrel, and to see how right I'd been in suspicioning she not only wanted sorry men to mistreat her, but she wanted them to mistreat each other for her sake. I don't think, as of right then, I had any idey at all left of winning her away from Wert, nor any reason left to want to. But I was sure going to fix it where I'd get in one lick at least.

I don't know what made me do it, but it proved out to be just the thing. That tune was going on the jukebox again.

I said, "Dam that sonofabitching record! I can't put up with it nomore."

I raised up out of my seat, made Dilly move to let me out, walked over to the jukebox, pushed the reject button, and stood there holding it till not only the jukebox went quiet, but so did everthing and everbody else in the room.

I turned aloose of the button, swung around holding on to a boothback to keep myself from staggering, looked the room over. Wert was standing up with his eyes bugged out at me, but Mother Goose had ahold of his arm. The two farmers looked pretty uneasy. The truckdriver had the floursack girl in his lap. The sneery kid set with his hands full of tin badges and curled up his lips at me. Another boothful or two of people had come in, but I can't remember what they looked like.

I don't remember, neither, what my original notion was. When you're drunk you get some queer ones. But somehow or another, I wanted to speak out, and the tablets I'd spent so much time writing on got tangled up with that notion, and it seemed all of a sudden to me like a great sin and still a great attraction for me to tell all of these people a story: like it was the worst thing I could do to Wert, and to Haley, and at the same time, with the Devil whispering in my ear, like it was tempting God in the most forbidden way. It was like I stood on the pinnacle of the temple, and before I leaped, I wanted to address the multitude.

So I yelled out, "Listen here, everbody, I'm going to tell you a story."

I reckon that was the last thing anybody expected. Mother Goose was the first one to try and meet the situation. She busted out in that screechy kind of a laugh, then, "Listen. Listen, Mr. Sheep is going to tell us a story."

People commenced to commenting, but in a low voice. I all at once realized I didn't know what story to tell. I sort of wanted to be able to say, in a minute or two, all I'd put in my tablets. At the same time, I wanted to tell some tale that would show up Wert Fleming and Haley Blair for what they really was.

But then I didn't have time to do neither one. Wert jerked away from Mother Goose and made a lunge towards me: "No Goddam sheep ain't going to tell nothing!" he hollered out. "He's just going to get his fucking head bashed in!"

He come at me with both fists out. It wasn't no trouble at all for me to dodge one, knock the other one out of the way, and smash him right in the jaw so hard I thought I must've broke his neck. He went all the way back again the bar, stood there in a daze for a second, then come at me again.

He was just as easy to hit the second time as he was the first. Only now he plopped right to the floor. I couldn't tell whe'er I'd knocked him out or not—though I found out later I had—I couldn't tell because just as he struck the floor, something struck me, right on top of the head, and down and out I went....

When I come to, I was setting on the floor leaned up again the wall. My face and the front of my clothes was all wet and sticky. My first thought was, Blood!

But no, it wasn't nothing but beer they throwed on me to bring me to. Mother Goose and a lot of the others was standing around not saying much. Dilly and Wert was both gone. Everbody, Mother Goose in particular, looked relieved to see me conscious again. Dam her old soul, she was the one that hit me, still had the blackjack in her hand she done it with. And to top it all off, she rushed over to me now and lit into me good and proper about starting a fight in her place, and how she kep that blackjack around especially for troublemakers like me, and how she had a right to use it to keep order—making all that noise, of course, because she was afraid I'd bring in the law or something.

While she was mouthing, my head cleared up some, though God! how it ached.

Directly I interrupted her, "Where's Dilly and Wert?"

"They went on home. And I'd advise you to stay away from them and leave them alone."

I got up slow and lurched around till I come to a table to set at. Mother Goose brought me a beer, piping out to everbody, "On the house," just to show what a generous, forgiving soul she was.

And dam me if I didn't set there and drink it! I reckon just because I had so much to think about and no head to think about it with.

By the time I finished the bottle nobody in the room wasn't paying me no attention at all. But I was at myself enough to leave the money for the beer on the table before I got up and went, not wanting no gifts from Mother Goose.

She didn't pay me no mind whatever. Her and that bony farmer had gone back to dancing, with music to keep time to now—that same infernal song, and her screeching out that same verse ever now and then: "When I *felt* so hard for you!" Like it was some magic saying she'd used to call up a skeleton out of the grave and had to keep on repeating for as long as she danced with him.

3

My head like to killed me all the way home. I parked Mrs. A.'s car a little ways up the street from the cabstand, and as luck'd have it I was able to walk in, hand her the keys and leave out while she was talking on the phone and couldn't ask me no questions.

Then I hobbled on home and went to bed.

The next morning I didn't have the headache nomore, just a awful sore spot on my skull. But then that soreness wasn't nothing compared to how I was feeling deep down inside of me. I'd built up so many dreams so fast—like I always do, for God's sake!—that seeing them all ruined at once hit me hard. It was like you had a fine crop all planted and worked and might near ready to lay by, when along come a hailstorm and beat it all to pieces.

Since they wasn't no reason to be in any hurry about getting up, I laid there in the bed for a good while, waking up about halfway and then dozing off again. Once I thought it was close to sunup, the light was so bright, but then a little later on seemed like it got dark again, and I couldn't think what was wrong, as crossed up as I was. It wasn't till I heard the wind flying in gusts around the house and a few sprinkles of rain hit the roof that I knowed it was clouds making the room dark, and a pretty brisk norther was blowing in besides. By the time I crawled out, it was away after sunup, the clouds had passed over, and the north wind, I seen as I looked out, was sweeping along first one place and then another through the trees, carrying dead leaves with it, the wind puffing through the bright sunshine, blowing leaves in place of the dust, because enough rain had fell to lay the dust.

It was a day just made for feeling good, but they's been few times in my life when I felt worse.

From force of habit I put on my clothes and got all ready to strike out for Bick's. Remembering Dilly, though, I waited for a little bit, sprawled out face down on the bed, to make sure she'd gone to work and I wouldn't bump into her on my way down. But I didn't look out of the window to watch till she passed.

Come to find out about it, Dilly hadn't been home that night at all. I got that much from Bee later on in the day, who come up to me on the street and wanted to know if I'd seen Dilly. I just said no, short-like, and went on my way.

Wert and Dilly made it in along in the evening, I heard later, and went the rounds of the beauty shop and the cabstand and so on, informing everbody they'd got married that morning. I didn't know nothing about it, myself, till the day after, when I seen the two of them moving Dilly's stuff out of the room she'd had at Bee's.

From then on, Dilly stayed out of my way, and I stayed out of hers. I seen her just one time, to talk to, after that. She come back to Bee's three or four days after she married to pick up some little something she'd forgot, and I run smack dab into her in the hallway before either one of us knowed the other one was on the place.

I handled myself pretty cool, which is a wonder. I said, "Well, how do you do? How's married life treating you?"

She sure was frosty. "Very well, I reckon. How have you been?"

"Fine and dandy. Even my head's might near well where your good friend Mother Goose conked me."

"Me and Wert feel awful bad about that."

It was a kind of a half-hearted excuse, but her eyes looked so full of pain I couldn't snap out at her. But I didn't want to stay around her neither, so I just turned and headed up the stairs.

All I said was, "Well, goodbye. You got your own row to hoe, and I got mine."

Upstairs I did watch out of the window till she come out, just for old times' sake. She was walking firm enough when she did come out, but it taken her so long to show up, I knowed in reason she must've put in some time bawling down there in her old room.

So, anyway, now then I didn't hardly know what to do next. If that town had been ugly one time, and then better looking, as of now it was uglier and seedier'n ever, and ever day that passed I felt like I couldn't force myself to spend another one in such a hole. I taken to sticking to my room most of the time, trying to read first one book and another that I'd checked out of the library. But I couldn't keep my mind on them to do no good. I'd read a few pages and then wonder what I'd read—doing the same thing miserable as I'd done happy. I'd doze off a good deal too, even up in the day.

And all the time it'd keep running through my head: something like, I've got to get out of here. I've got to leave this place. I've got to push on from here.

And while I set around, and laid around, about half-dead, the cussed weather turned prettier and prettier. You take if the weather's real bad, and you're in misery, you can stand it a whole lot better, I find. Because no matter if you actually think it out loud or not, you feel like the world out of doors is agreeing with you. But on pretty days you just know you've been left behind to suffer all alone, and everthing else is going glad on its way.

Out of the window I'd see a sky cleaned bright by the wind of the northers that picked the yellow leaves off of the trees as it passed. A cloud or two, little but shaggy, like their coats'd been thickened for winter, would skim along past the window. In less than a week we had two whistling northers, and a right smart of rain fell with the second one. And the night after it faired off from that one, it come the first frost of the year.

I started in to dropping by the post office again. Not that I really had any expectation of hearing from Ellen, but just because it give me one more thing to do to add to the little I had. A letter had come from Ma, been laying there for some time while I was flying too hot and heavy at Dilly to go after it. It sure was good to get the news from home, though they wasn't nothing special about it, just that Ma and Pap both was getting along all right. Some questions—did I think I'd be able to come home anyways soon? If I wasn't going to, did I reckon they ought to write and tell Reed and the rest of them about what had taken place? Ma said she herself didn't know what to think about it.

Well, that letter picked me up some, if it didn't do nothing more'n give me something to worry about. It made me see I'd have to come to some decision before long, or everthing'd go to pot worse'n it already was.

So, finally, after ten days or so had gone by from the time Dilly throwed me over, I jumped up out of my chair one evening about a hour by sun with my mind made up I'd had enough. I'd march myself right down to that phone booth in the bus station and see if I couldn't get in touch with Reed in Chicago, kind of explain things to him a little bit, pack up and head out the next day to where he was, at least visit him for a while, and then see.

But when I made it to the bus station and was in the phone booth, I got it in my head I wanted to hear a voice from home, just about any voice, before I undertaken to plan on going any futher away. So, in the place of Reed in Chicago, I telephoned W. D. Clagg in Milcourt.

Before I could ask him any questions about stuff down there in my part of the country, he got right down to business. Ike, he said, wanted to talk to me, had come by the office that very day, seemed to be pretty anxious about it. I said I wasn't anyways sure I cared about talking to Ike, the way he'd acted. But W. D. Clagg convinced me I ought to, said it was real important, he thought.

Ike's got one of the few phones out in the country there. I waited right next to the booth till W. D. Clagg called Ike and told him where to reach me.

Well, old Ike's voice sounded kind of good, I had to admit, when we finally got on the line. He commenced to apologizing all over hisself, said he didn't know what had got into him and the rest of them around the community when they turned again me. He made it sound like everbody and their dog'd be out to welcome me back if I just wanted to come home.

I stayed pretty leery about it all.

Then the subject got around to Haley, and there Ike switched on me. He blurts out, "Say, why don't you let me run over there and pick up Mr. and Mrs. Lamb and bring them over here and call you back and talk to you. I can sure pay for the call if you're in a tight for money."

I'd've loved to talk to them, but I thought it would be too hard on all of us right then. Besides, I wanted to get to the bottom of this Haley business. So I said, "Looky here, is Haley Blair up to something new?"

Then I knowed for sure he was, because Ike hummed and hawed around bigger'n ever, and all I could prize out of him was, "Well, in a way yes, and in a way no."

"Tell me the yes part of it."

"Well, Amon, Haley's as much again you as he ever was, and he'd do all he could to have you run off again if you was to come back. But the thing is, me and some more people are for you now, and...."

"While ago you made it sound like the whole community had their hands out to greet me, and now it's just 'you and some more.' I ain't so certain, anyhow, that I'd want to come back to a place where your neighbors're ready to ride you out of town on a rail the first time something don't go to suit them."

"I know it, Amon. You got a right to be mad. We done wrong, and I for one know it. And I ain't the only one, neither."

"Y'all must've decided on looking for the lost sheep pretty sudden. I just had a letter from Ma the other day, and she didn't say nothing about it. I think you better go ahead and give me the lowdown on what old Assface is up to before this phone bill gets so high you can't pay it."

I thought maybe a little cussing and a reference to the Bible at the same time might shake old Ike up some, loosen his tongue.

It did help too: "Well, I can't tell you all of it, Amon. I just can't. Because they ain't said I could. But I'll say this much. Haley and Mr. Gray come might near having a fight the other day, all of it over you. I taken it on myself to try and call you without consulting nobody, but I just couldn't stand it not to warn you. What Haley wants to do is try to have you declared mentally off—incompetent's what I mean. He thinks it could be worked so you wouldn't be allowed to come back here and live and control your own property, and yet money could be got out of you for the family. And Mr. Gray thinks Haley has got ahold of a lawyer that can pull it off, if they can just get the family's consent."

"You mean Ma and Pap's?"

"No. Well, yes, them too."

"What're you talking about, Ike? See if you can't speak a little plainer. Dammit! be straight with me."

"Amon, listen. I tell you, you've just got to come on back home. They's things here you have to tend to. What I want you to know is, I'll stand behind you. And so will Mr. Gray. And so will a bunch more, like Hap Carr for one, and even Gil Blair...."

I cut him off: "Hold on a minute, Ike. If you think I'm going to be chased out of a place like a scolded dog, and then come back wagging my tail when I'm called, you're mighty mistaken. You ain't told me about Haley Blair trying to do anything he ain't been trying all along. If they's something new in the situation, and you want to be on the level with me about it, why do it. But if you ain't, why just dry up, and I'll let you go. I'm about to take off out of this town anyhow, and I doubt if any of you down there will ever see nor hear from me *again*!"

He sure did sound anxious now: "Amon, you can't! I swear you just can't! Let me tell you something....Wait a minute. Listen, now listen, Amon. Will you please do this much? Will you just...will you just wait at that phone. I've just got to do some consulting, and then I'll call you back. If you don't...if you don't, Amon, you'll always be sorry. Believe me, you will."

Well, what with all that, I said I would. So I set down mad and worried in that old dingy bus sation, and waited, and waited.

It was close on to a hour before the phone rung again. I picked it up. This voice said, "Amon?"

I couldn't hardly believe my ears. It was Ellen.

"Ellen! What in the world!"

"I been hoping to hear from you, Amon."

I wasn't going to stand for that. I said, "You're the one that told *me* to go. It was your place to let me hear from *you*!"

"All right. You're hearing from me right now. I want you to come on home."

Her voice sounded awful dry and brittle, but that couldn't hide the misery in it. Nor it couldn't cover up how close she was to breaking out in tears.

That voice got me. I didn't hesitate. I said, "I'll do it. Just as soon as I can get there."

She didn't say no more, just hung up right straight.

As for me, a kind of a daze seemed to lead me wandering around over to the ticket counter, but I straightened up enough when I reached there to find out about when they was a bus leaving for Milcourt—I reckon the first time I'd mentioned the name of my hometown to anybody since I'd hit this burg.

They was a bus due to pull out about a hour from then. They wouldn't be another one, after that, till five-something the next morning. I bought me a ticket right then and there. I'd go to my room and get ready and leave on that early morning bus.

It taken me such a little time to bundle up, when I went back to the rooming house, that I could've made the first bus. But still I did want to give myself just a little time to consider things. I'd done made up my mind I wasn't going to tell Bee I was moving out. My rent was paid up till the end of the week, and she could just keep anything I might have coming back. Her being so talkative and all, she might spread it all over town I was leaving, before I even got started.

The one person I did decide to tell was Mrs. A. Going up there to see her was what held me up from catching that first bus.

I hadn't seen Mrs. A. since me and Dilly broke up. I'd avoided her so I wouldn't have to tell her about the bust-up nor the fight nor nothing. But she'd found out all about it, naturally, as I guess everbody else in town had.

Soon as I walked in the door of the cabstand, Mrs. A. commenced to apologizing, said how sorry she was she ever had encouraged me to stay mixed up with Dilly, and that whole bunch of drags, as she called them.

I tried to pass it off, said I didn't blame her for none of it, as of course I didn't. But she kep on acting like she was about halfway responsible, wouldn't let the subject drop, and nothing would do, finally, but for me to tell her all about what had occurred at the beerjoint, little as I wanted to do it.

But once I begun talking, I seen that the matter was a whole lot like going over something that'd happened to me away back years ago. All during the time I told her about it, I was deep in that feeling that in a few months there, from summer to fall, I'd lived through a lifetime or two. That feeling was to stay with me into the winter, too, and into everthing else that happened.

I done with Mrs. A. what I never had with nobody else there, not even Dilly. I said exactly where I was from, and made Mrs. A. swear she wouldn't tell nobody, and I didn't think she would. I didn't want people from around there to know where to get in touch with me, but somehow or another I just couldn't stand the notion of disappearing from a place altogether and not leaving a single track behind.

That night I didn't get much sleep, not having no alarm clock, for one thing, and being afraid I'd oversleep and miss the bus. And of course, I thought and thought. I kep a light on, dozed off ever now and then, got so pop-eyed about three in the morning they wasn't a chance of sleeping another wink. So I put on my clothes, turned out the light, and set there in the dark by the window. The night was still. The tree limbs, mostly bare of any leaves, stood out as a tangle of gray twigs in the streetlamp down there. I shut my eyes a good deal. I thought I'd feel better if I didn't have to give the town too many goodbye looks.

At long last the courthouse clock struck five. Feeling my way down the stairs and edging out of the front door, I creeped along the sidewalk till I was far enough away from the house for my footsteps not to echo back.

Lo and behold, the bus, I found out, would be about a hour late coming in from the north. And that really floored me. If I hung out around the station any time at all, somebody would see me waiting to leave and tell it around. So I just hiked out afoot. Out on the highway, if I didn't catch a ride, I could flag the bus down when it did come along.

It was still night, and when I left the last streetlamp behind me, I had to watch my step to keep from walking off of the shoulder of the road into the bar ditch. A dog or two barked at me from houses along the highway, but none of them come out enough to give me any trouble.

They wasn't no need to look back at the town. I knowed the life I'd lived there was drawing away from me faster'n I could leave the place, even by walking.

I was still plowing along the highway when the sun come up, hadn't even tried to catch a ride, and didn't try to now. They wasn't over a car ever twenty minutes anyhow. That sun was beginning to pour down hot for that time of the year when I walked up to a filling station away out in the country to itself. The owner was just opening up when I come by, so I stopped and bought me a soda pop and made out a poor snack on that and a package of old stale crackers. Setting there in the shade of that place, I like to went to sleep and missed the bus. But the filling-station man flagged it for me, and once I got on I went right off to sleep in my seat and didn't come out of it till away along in the evening after we'd done crossed the state line and was in a few miles of Milcourt.

Now the thought of actually coming in home hit me as soon as I woke up. Fear and excitement and joy all together taken possession of me. I wondered what I'd face, and still why I'd waited so many months to face it. If Haley Blair and ever law in the county had been waiting for me at the bus station, I wouldn't've felt no different. And I begun aching so much to see Ellen it was all I could do to keep from crying.

So now here was the old hometown, and I stepped down light with my suitcase, not hardly looking around me, partly because I expected, and I guess with some reason, to be nabbed any minute, and partly because I was afraid home wasn't real nomore, afraid it would crumble up right before my eyes if I looked at it too close.

The cabstand in Milcourt is straight across the street from the bus station. I went over there and crawled in the back seat of a empty cab and stayed half slumped down there till they finally noticed me from inside. I didn't want to run the risk of going in.

A driver come out, then. It was old Joe Morris, who don't say much. In a minute me and him was rolling down East Lamar Street. We'd spoke to one another, I'd told him to drive me out home, and that's all that was said.

4

Now I sure do wish I could put all the meaning I feel into what happened during the next few months. But I'm so far from being able to do it that I have my doubts about trying to set down anything at all. When it was all over with, and I'd decided to jump in and write down this second part, I didn't have no trouble at all to start out with. I just went aflying, seem like, till I come up again this very last bunch of happenings. I set and studied about these for a good long while, but then I still don't know how to go about saying what I'd like to say. Maybe I never will. But if I ever expect to write anything down at all, why it's time I commenced.

So I will. For even if I decide to burn up these tablets when I'm done writing, which I may well do, I'm still bound and determined to add on the wind-up of the story....

Before me and old Joe Morris had pulled up to the house good, Pap seen who it was and showed up in the door. The poor old fellow was stiffer in the joints than I remembered, I seen as he come hobbling down the steps hollering out over his shoulder it was Amon, Amon was home! And then Ma she come out on the porch right in behind him.

The next hour or so was quite a hullaballoo, you might know, with all three of us talking at once, and Ma and Pap aswarming around me getting in my way while I tried to put up some of my stuff and wash and shave. Ma had to fix me a bite to eat, of course, and I was good and ready for it. All that time they stumbled all over theirselves trying to catch me up on what'd happened right after I left home, a whole lot of what they said being confused and contradicting itself. But anyhow I learned that nobody had made much effort to track me down. A delegation of neighbors had come over to get me the next day after the meeting at the church-house, and not right straight that night—but led when they did come, as you might know, by Haley Blair. The law come around once too, later on. But the sheriff had balked at doing what Haley wanted, which was to send out a big alarm about a dangerous madman being on the loose in the country. Pap said then Haley had the dam nerve to come over to the house twice more after that, you might say forced his way into the house, he was so bold about it. But the last time Pap met him at the door with his shotgun—and that, Pap set up and crowed, was the last time he'd seen the sonofabitch.

"Here!" said Ma. "You better learn to hold on to your tongue."

"Well, that's what he is and that's what I'll call him," Pap growls out. "And the next time you marry a man you better inquire into his plain-talking qualities."

Ma had a sharp answer for that, and so they was off again.

Home was about the same, after all, looked like.

As yet I hadn't made no mention of Ellen, nor of Ike's phone call, kind of wanting to see what they knowed and what they'd say. But they didn't bring up a word about any of that, nor about what I taken to be Haley Blair's latest shenanigans, up to the time when I was done eating and all spruced up and fixing to leave out for Ellen's.

Now they'd been so much juning around since I got home that I hadn't taken account altogether of just how nervous Ma and Pap was. Like really they knowed a whole lot I didn't know, stuff they wanted to tell me and yet at the same time didn't want to tell me.

But even when I thought of that I was too anxious to see Ellen to tarry around long enough to go into the situation.

When I left the house they stood on the front porch watching me like

I was plumb leaving the country again. Even Ma, though, didn't make no remarks about where I was heading for.

When I first laid eyes on Ellen, and her on me, she was setting on the front porch, not of her little house, I mean, but on the lower porch of the big house. Nobody else was around but her. When I had parked the car by the front gate and was heading towards her, she stood up.

'Godamighty, good Godamighty!' I thought.

She had on a kind of a long smock a little bulged out in front.

Pregnant!

What I liked of falling over wasn't much. I didn't think. I couldn't. My head just swum around in circles like and carried me on towards her. When I got to her I wanted to squeeze her as tight as anything, and still I was afraid of hurting her or the baby. But then she right away put my mind to rest about that. She grabbed onto me like she'd suffocate me, and I wasn't long in doing her the same way. We just stood there all wound up together, me so addled I still couldn't even think. The Ellen I knowed and loved and had held so many times in my arms wasn't only hugging me back, she was pressing me into the round knot of the baby in her womb, like it couldn't grow without her doing that.

The next day we went right straight to town to the county judge and got married.

And so, it was all straightened out now as far as me and Ellen was concerned, and my folks and hers.

But they was still Haley Blair to deal with. That was another matter, and one I sure dreaded. Oh, from what I heard around he'd have a hard time getting a sizeable bunch on his side anymore. I mean like Hap Carr and of course Ike and first one and another come around to kind of welcome me home, Haley's brother Gilbert in the bunch. And all of them as friendly as you could ask for. But still I was uneasy about Haley. It wasn't like him to ever let a thing drop. My first idey was to see if I couldn't get a sort of a delegation together myself, maybe with Ike's help, and call old Haley to taw, make him say right out in the presence of witnesses what he still had again me. They wouldn't be much he could say without making a plumb dam fool of hisself. Let him squirm and worm and fess up, was my thought, and he'd have to be bound by it if he said it in the presence of other folks. But Ellen and all our folks on both sides was dead set again that. To their way of thinking, that might bring things to a boil again and make Haley think he had to get back at me in some way, no matter how outlandish.

Well, I could see their point, all right. But then again I couldn't be in favor of just doing nothing at all. For one thing, I just felt cussed enough that I wasn't going to pass up the chance to rub it in a little.

So what I done was have a long talk with W. D. Clagg again, and we come up with putting that piece in the paper, like I'd originally planned on doing. So we changed it up a little and stuck it in there, right next to the legal notices, and I ain't denying it sure did make me feel good to know how old Haley's blood'd boil when he read it. No need to repeat the whole thing. What it amounted to, in the main, was to sum up under three or four headings the things Haley'd done to defame my character. Then it went on to say that if any futher instances of that sort occurred, my intention was to bring legal action again him.

Well now, after that move it didn't look like they was anything at all Haley could do. He kep quiet for a long time, all right, and whenever we'd chance to meet around the community or in Milcourt, we'd just ignore one another. I hadn't spoke a word to him, nor him to me, since I come home. It was easy enough to stay out of his way nearly all the time, except at preaching, and that did put a little bit of a bind on things.

As for going to preaching, you know how women are when they get pregnant. They commence to thinking about the generations yet unborn and everthing along with it that might make for a stronger family tie. Religion's always one of the first things they light on. So now Ellen wanted to go to preaching might near ever Sunday, and go we did. So of course it was a hard matter to ignore old Haley altogether, with him setting up there on his usual bench putting on that pious business as much as he ever had. Ike, he made me sort of uncomfortable sometimes too, not that he ever made any direct references in the pulpit to mine and Haley's being at outs. But you could tell from the way he acted, looking down from one to the other of us, that he was just dying to make peace between us.

Things rocked along like that for a right smart while. It was away down in the fall, you see, when I come home. I'd got Ellen pregnant, as near as we could figure out, might near two months before I left—because she missed her second monthly before she knowed for sure what was the matter with her. So the baby was due to happen along, then, during the following March.

It was a peaceful life again now, the weather included. Fall didn't really end, and winter begin, till after Christmas. The days stayed clear and pretty a good deal of the time. Light northers would come and rain their little bit, and after a morning or two of chill the wind would shift into the south and the weather turn off warm again. During one of these times the sunshiney days lasted long enough and it got still enough to give us a spell of Indian summer. The haze and the drowse that went with it made a lull in our blood and turned our voices calm and tender. Then, after that, misty days begun to come along, low cloudy days brushing little currents of mist again your face when you walked out of doors. As the year moved on ahead into December the fog taken the place, right often, of the mist. The last day or two before Christmas was wrapped up in soft white air like the swaddling clothes they bundled the Christ Child in. Christmas Eve morning the fog was so thick that Ma's voice sounded muffled when she went around chirping out to everbody before breakfast, "Christmas Eve gift! Christmas Eve gift!"

But then, late in the night on Christmas Day, the cold weather hit in earnest, and it set in to snowing, although I didn't know nothing about the snowing till the next morning. I did hear some wind along in the night, and it woke me plumb up to where I was afraid I couldn't get back to sleep. As I laid there the lonesomeness from my life far off from home come back with the wind. But it couldn't get at me much, because all I had to do was scoot over close to Ellen, put one hand on her breast and lay the other one on her full womb, and feel all of the warmth and stillness of her body and our child.

Then when I got out of bed, a little after daylight, why there sure enough was the snow. It was falling quiet and thick in great big flakes. The postoak outside the front gate stood there reaching up with dark and naked limbs into the million motions of the white settling down.

I thought of a covered earth and the new life swelling underneath, of Ellen's womb and of the ground storing up to raise all the green things in the spring.

Over a month passed, taking us into a blustery January. Then, right out of nowhere, seem like, happenings all of a sudden took on a different turn.

First off, Mrs. A. wrote me a letter. Good thing I went to the mailbox myself that day and didn't have to let the rest of the family know nothing about it. I kep that letter around for a good while and read it several times. Just the other day here, I was looking for that letter, intended to copy it out in these tablets as a part of the record. But somehow or another I lost it in all the scramble that come about a little while after I got it.

What it said in a nutshell was this: Mrs. A. was fine, and so was everbody else around town, as far as she knowed. Then come a lot of particulars about her boy—he'd run off and joined the Merchant Marine, but he did write her ever now and again. Then she talked some about Bee and Boggs, and even old Bick. Finally she got down to business, that is to Dilly and Wert, and there she surprised me. They'd moved out to California, she said. Why? Well, this Orville, Dilly's first man, he showed up there in town, just come in there one day and got him a job at a service station down the street from the cabstand. Wert discovered he was there before he made hisself known. Still, nothing out of the ordinary happened. Dilly and Wert seen him around town first one place and another. Sometimes he'd even come by the cabstand. But he was civil to everbody, and so was Dilly and Wert to him. But Mrs. A. said it made Dilly and Wert nervous having him around, and I can't say I much blame them. So they hit on the idey of moving out to California, not to the place where Dilly and Orville had lived but to some other place futher on north, Mrs. A. didn't say exactly where. Their reasoning was, if they tried to have Orville pulled for molesting Dilly in the town where they was, he could always claim, which was the truth, that he'd done no more'n move back to his original hometown. But if he tried to follow them to a strange place, then they could get the law on him easier if they had to. They'd been gone for some time now, Dilly and Wert had, and Mrs. A. just wished Orville would stop hanging around the cabstand. He made her nervous too, so much so she didn't know what to do. Oh, he acted just fine, but the thing was, he asked everbody he could corner all about everthing Dilly had done while she lived there. He was always trying to pump her, Mrs. A. said, and if some way wasn't found to stop him she was going to have to find herself another job to get rid of him.

Well, in a way I was glad to hear all this stuff, and in a way I wasn't. A person's always curious, I guess, but really that life all seemed so long ago, now, that I just couldn't work up much interest in what happened to any of them—except I did feel sorry for Mrs. A.

That was all that happened, then, for a while, just that letter. But around a month or such a matter before the baby was due to be born, when I'd already planted Irish potatoes and was busy getting my ground ready for crops, things begun to break all at once. First I knowed of anything, here come W. D. Clagg, one evening late, down in the field where I was plowing, telling me that a Mrs. Armbruster wanted to talk to me long distance, and said it was right urgent.

Now we'd decided to put us in a phone out here at home, so we could get in touch with the doctor fast when it was time for the baby to come, but the company had held us up some trying to get another subscriber or two out on our road. We was now expecting them to install it just any day, but right then I was glad we still hadn't got it. For then Mrs. A. could've called me direct and I might've had to do some tall explaining to Ellen. As it was, she'd called the operator, who of course knowed me, and who my lawyer was, and had sense enough to put the call through to him.

I went on back to Milcourt with W. D. Clagg and called Mrs. A. back from his office.

"Amon? How in the world are you?"

"Finest kind, Mrs. Armbruster. And how're you?"

"Not any too good, Amon. I'm terrible worried, and it concerns you."

"If it's about Dilly and Wert, you can forget it. You know good and well I don't care nothing about what happens to them."

"Why, that hussy! After the way she done you, you think I'd turn to you with anything concerning her! No, that ain't it, Amon. It's about this Orville I wrote you about. I found out this evening he's gone, left town."

"Well? So? Sounds to me like he taken off after Wert and Dilly, in spite of it all. So the thing for you to do's to warn them, not me."

"Well now, this'll sound funny to you, Amon. And it's mighty peculiar, I'll admit. But I'm just certain of it or I wouldn't've bothered you about it. I don't know exactly how to say this so's to convince you, but...well, Orville's out to get you, as sure as I'm alive."

"Me! In God's name, why would he be out to get me? What've I done to him? We never seen each other in our lives."

"Well, let me try to tell you why, and then see if you don't agree with me. You see, he kep on asking me a lot of questions about you, and when I wouldn't tell him much he took to questioning everbody else that knowed you while you was here. Which looks funny, don't it? And then, after Dilly left, he asked a lot about Dilly all the time still, but he didn't say nothing about Wert. On the other hand, he harped on the subject of you, on and on, and he talked like he was plumb off, seemed to me like. One time, for sure, in my presence, he let it slip about what a terrible evil man you must be, being run off from home and then causing trouble in this place where you went to. You see, one person he talked to a right smart was that old blister that runs the beer joint across the creek, and no telling what she filled his ear with.

"Another thing, Amon, he stayed after me for I don't know how long wanting to know where you live now. And when I still wouldn't tell him nothing, he found out from I reckon the only other person in town that knows—the man you got the bus ticket from when you pulled out of here. I know this for a fact, because I know the ticket man, and I called him a little while ago and asked him.

"Now Amon, I've heard of crazy people fixing their mind on a person they don't even know and blaming them for all their troubles. I'm just mighty afraid that's what's happened here. Orville's gone, I know that. He didn't leave on the bus. I guess he hitchhiked, so I don't know for sure which-away he went. But I'm might near certain, I just feel it, that he headed for Milcourt."

And so, after that and quite a lot more, Mrs. A. made me see that they was a good chance she was right, and I had the right man right there—W. D. Clagg—to consult about it.

The thing to do, we decided, was to alert the laws, and we done that the same day, with me passing on to them a description of Orville that W. D. Clagg had done had me to get from Mrs. A. We wanted to try as hard as anything to keep the matter quiet, outside of letting the laws know, but we knowed they wasn't much chance of doing it. I told Ellen and Ma and Pap, naturally—had to, for a crazy man was liable to walk up on them just any time. They didn't spill it nowhere, of course, but somebody did. Maybe the telephone operator, maybe one of the laws around the county. God knows who. Anyhow, inside of a day or two it was all over the country that a dangerous man was after me. And since the belief I was a dangerous man myself hadn't plumb died out of people's minds yet, the two of them got mixed up. It looked for a while there like the worst kind of suspicion yet was going to come down on me. Like I was about to turn the whole community into a lunatic asylum. One story even got around that I'd taken the man's wife away from him, and that drove him crazy.

And of course, as you might know, that sort of excitement was all that shitass Haley Blair was looking for. I have to piece together here what I heard from several, but the gist of it was that Haley taken bold steps sure enough now. He run onto everbody he knowed, he marched hisself right back to the county laws—and though I don't reckon they was very glad to see him they couldn't afford to run him off again, because he just might have a point. His tale was that I was turning a law-abiding community into a savage evil place, bringing my feuds into it from someplace else, and no telling what kind of a place that was. But he had changed his tune in one way, all right. He was as sure as anything now that I wasn't crazy at all, no matter what other people said. I was just mean, I was dangerous, and if something wasn't done to head me off I'd ruin the community and get half the people killed by the outlaws that such as me attracted to a place. And so on....

Might near a week passed by after I'd talked to Mrs. A. and still nothing was seen of Orville. I taken to carrying a gun on my own place though, a six-shooter I hadn't even had a shell in for a long time. I felt plumb foolish with that thing ahanging around my waist or slung on my tractor. It just got in my way all the time. And I couldn't keep from thinking how this was like some Western show or something, or else maybe the days had come back from long ago when you had to go around armed and watch out for Indians and frontier desperadoes.

Ellen and Ma and Pap, they stayed pretty close around the house, and Pap kep his shotgun handy all the time.

The March winds meant to come on early, it appeared like. Because one day there the south wind blowed up like a storm, but the sky stayed fair and deep blue. That day I was laying out lister beds in that field—what Pap called the Shin Patch—not far off from the graveyard and in sight of the house too. It was well up in the day when I pulled up on the north end of a row, killed the engine on my tractor and walked out in the woods a little piece to take a shit. Because in the field I would've been in plain sight of the house and the county road both. About fifty yards, I guess, was as far as I ever got from the tractor, but I was out of sight of it because the timber was pretty thick between me and it.

When I started back, one little open space in the timber come up, as luck'd have it, to where I could see straight out into the field. Standing out there by my tractor, holding my pistol in one hand and looking it over, with a rifle in his other hand, was a big black-headed man that couldn't be nobody but Orville.

I just halted right in my tracks. He hadn't heard me. He couldn't see me, I didn't believe, having to look into the dimness of the windy woods, the way everthing was tossing and blowing. So I give myself a few seconds to calm down some, then I sneaked real slow and quiet right up to the edge of the woods. At that the dead leaves seemed to rustle terrible loud under my shoesoles. I was oh so glad the wind was strong.

I got in close to a bush and down on my knees and tried to think. Orville was between me and the house, and they wasn't no woods I could swing around through that led up close enough to the house for me to make it there before he shot me down, if he was any kind of a shot at all.

That's all I could think about, at the start, that he had me cut off from the house, and what if he started walking towards it any minute, with Ellen and Ma and Pap not knowing a thing about him being on the place?

But I couldn't just stay where I was. I was too close to him. He might walk my way any second too, might see my tracks....

That brought me out of it. I backed off a little deeper in the woods on my knees, got up and headed out the only way they was to go, towards the graveyard, come up to the fence of it before I still had any plan about what to do....

That big old monument rose up there above the dead grass that the wind was tossing around. Behind the monument the bare limbs of the trees was shaking in the wind. The sun gleamed along the still, polished walls of granite.

I thought, 'The wind can't move it. It's like death. Soon enough I may be down there where the wind can't reach me.'

And all of a sudden I loved the wind so much I wanted to cry. March wind, March wind. And that wasn't the only wind neither. There come drifting back over me in a flash the wind that used to blow lonesome on me when I was far from home. And I loved that too.

Then a fear hit me. What hit me was, 'Oh for the mercy of God, the minute Ellen finds out Orville's after me, she'll have a miscarriage. She'll die, the baby'll die. We'll all be in that grave.' And already, I happened to think, that was the grave of a woman who died in childbirth.

But I had to get ahold of myself, and I had to do it right at once. I peered around out of the edge of the timber into the open. Orville was out in the pasture a little northeast of the field, a little bit closer to the house and still between me and it. He was just standing there looking around, with his rifle ready and my pistol buckled on him. He stood there like he wasn't in no hurry.

The nearest help, the nearest house in any direction I could run to, was Haley Blair's place, and even that was a good ways off.

But Haley! Everthing, it looked like, had turned again me. Still, if I worked it right I could stay in the woods all the way to Haley's. It was my only bet. At least I didn't know that Haley Blair would shoot me down on sight, and I was sure Orville would.

But Ellen and Ma and Pap, what about them? They might or might not've seen Orville, but what could Pap and his old shotgun do again him, even so? I don't know why I didn't think of it before. My head just wasn't working, couldn't work, seem like, the way it ought to. It was just a glimpse of a thought, and I was already saying, 'Of course, that's what I'll do' before I hardly realized I'd thought of it at all.

The simplest thing in the world it was, to show myself and then run to lead Orville away from the house. I wasn't at all sure I could outrun him, but I did have some headstart, and what else could I do anyhow?

And so I stepped out of the wood's edge, with the wind awhipping around me, to where he was bound to see me.

He did. He fired a shot. He didn't miss me by much.

I darted back into the woods and lit out for Haley Blair's at a dead run. I'd seen him tearing out after me, and in its way that taken a load off of my mind. He wouldn't be heading for the house now.

I soon remembered I was running along the same way I'd coursed the bees when I'd ended up at the old house-place. I could call up to mind nearly ever hill and hollow along the route, and knowing them so well would be a big help to me in dodging Orville. In the wind he couldn't hear me far, neither, so I could tear out just as fast as my legs'd carry me.

I reckon he must've come straight to the place where he'd seen me and followed me the best he could from there. Or it could be he thought I'd circle and try to make a run for the house. So he may've stopped or turned around and figured he'd head me off. Somewhere, anyhow, he must've wasted a right smart of time, because he wasn't anyways close behind me there at first. I couldn't get rid of the idey, though, that he was right on my heels, and the bare thought of them two guns he had kep me running faster'n I ought to've been. If I'd just've gone at it a little slower I could still've run clear off and left him and been to Haley Blair's away out in front of him.

It was around two miles to Haley's place, the way I went, and I soon realized even if I didn't have sense enough to slow down much, that I couldn't keep up a stiff pace all the way. I was puffing and blowing and might near give out when I come to the woods road where me and Yas parked the night of our scrape, and where I'd left my car too the day when I give Haley the slip. So I just had to rest. I run on a little futher and flung myself out flat on the stomach behind the same rick of firewood where me and Yas had picked up the chunks to set on that night. I laid there gasping for breath and holding it ever few seconds to listen for Orville crashing through the woods. But the wind was too loud. It swept over my head and through the rick of wood. A loose splinter on one of the sticks buzzed in the wind. For several minutes there I was too tuckered to move a muscle, and all the time I kep thinking, 'He'll walk up and shoot me, he'll walk up and shoot me.'

I reckon I must have passed out, for that matter. And the wind seemed to be taking my breath away, and it seemed like forever before I could get my gasping kind of quieted down. I come out of it quick, though, once I did finally get ahold, with a mighty strong jolt of a thought that Orville was bearing down on me.

I had to make a choice now, when I staggered up to my feet: either stick to the woods, and that meant winding around some, or strike out right straight across the pasture. Because they would be timber, yes, that I could stay in all the way to Haley's, even if some of it was pretty scattering, so that a sharp-eyed person might see you dodging through it. In a couple of places it was just little thin stretches of trees between fields, and in another a copse on a knoll that'd had a lot of the timber cut out of it.

By this time I'd caught my breath good and I'd also decided plumb again taking out across the pasture. Orville couldn't be so far behind me but what he'd catch up this far by the time I'd cover the ground down to the simmon thicket and over the branch and up past the old house-place and the well, and then on into the next woods. And he'd have me out in the open where he couldn't hardly miss, with his rifle.

So I set off east towards the county road, turned then and kep to a little narrow band of timber along the road edge, crossed one of the stretches between fields, and pulled up then for a minute just inside the copse on the knoll. Still no sign of Orville. With the copse behind me, I could figure on coming next to the scattered timber on both sides of the branch, a small arm of that reaching up to the thicker woods on the slope across from me. These thicker woods stayed closed in as they angled off over a hill till they come mighty close to Haley Blair's house.

And all the time around me these woods was alive with the March wind.

But then, as I started out running again, one thing come up to fool me. The timber wasn't like it'd always been before. I hadn't been around there since I'd come back home, so I couldn't know it, but that arm of timber from the branchbed up the slope, it wasn't there nomore. Haley'd had about fifty yards of it bulldozed off, either to make a better pasture or put in cultivation.

So I had open space before me to cross after all.

I waited for a little at the edge of the opening, I looked back close in ever direction I'd come from. I couldn't swear to it, but I did think I seen a movement. Was it white? Wasn't Orville wearing a white shirt? Whatever it was was away back there above the edge of the simmon thicket. Then for a second I got worried all over again he'd gone to the house instead of trailing me, and that thought was so terrible I might near passed out. I tried to put that out of my mind and tell myself that all they was to do now was to make a dash for it. So I didn't wait no longer. I tore out....

The first shot come when I wasn't more'n ten yards from my taking-off place. I couldn't tell how close he come to me. The wind was so high in my ears I wasn't even altogether sure it *was* a shot, maybe just a crash of a sudden gust of wind in some trees. But now I wove around as I run, pounding on for ever ounce I had. The second shot, and no mistake about it this time, come as I jumped the branch. I hadn't much more'n landed and commenced to run again when I stubbed my toe on something and come might near afalling. The third shot, and that one did come close, went awhistling by just as I barged into the woods and found me a tree to duck behind.

Orville was a whole lot closer than I'd figured. He was already down in the simmon thicket and shooting from there. So I couldn't tarry but a second behind the tree where I was. Already he was running towards me as fast as he could go. It was a long chance, now, that I could even stay ahead of him till I made it to Haley's.

So I decided to throw him off again if I could. I wasn't sure if he knowed the whereabouts of the nearest house. I was just hoping he didn't. You still couldn't see Haley's from here. So I decided I'd run along the edge of the timber, showing myself up there about that blackjack south of the old well, the tree where I'd hid from Haley the day I found the tomahawk. By the time I got there, I figured, Orville would be close to where I'd jumped the branch. He'd take it for granted—or I hoped he would—that I'd decided to stay ahead of him, skirt my way around, and head back home, seeing as how he wouldn't be between me and home anymore. What I really would do, after letting him see me, would be disappear in the timber, tear out up the draw that leads to the top of the hill, cross the hill, and in a few minutes of sprinting I'd be at Haley Blair's.

Then, in a car, we could beat Orville back to my house.

Well, that scheme went all right at the start. Up by the blackjack I showed myself, bolting out like I meant to make a beeline across the pasture in the direction of home, like I didn't quite know what I was at. I was a little bolder about being seen now, because I could tell Orville wasn't no first-class marksman. He shot at me one time, and when he did I whirled around like I was plumb panicked now, dodged here and there, and then dived back into the woods.

And Orville, he fell for my little trick all right. He took off running up the branch past the old house-place, awful intent on getting someplace or another in a hurry and at first I couldn't dope out where. He was might near there before I seen what he was up to. He was headed for what was left of that little dam where Yas had held onto the bush to try and save hisself from drownding. He thought he might get there before I seen where he'd went to, I guess. Laying down behind the dam he could keep out of sight and maybe pick me off if I ever showed myself at the border of the woods, which come down pretty close to the dam over on that side of the pasture.

I give him time to get there, and myself time to rest for a breath or two. It looked like I'd be able, now, to reach Haley's place before Orville even knowed he'd been fooled.

Now he was right at the dam. In a second I could go. I sucked in the wind, feeling wonderful. My head was plumb light from just knowing I could get away easy enough now.

Right then I heard a voice. A yell. A yell loud and mad.

Orville?

No. In the other direction.

Great God in Heaven! Haley Blair hisself!

Yes, there he was. And doing what? Why, busting along afoot through that bulldozed strip with the wind flapping his straw hat, swinging a rifle in his hand. And ever little bit he'd holler out, "Hey, up there! Hey!"

He'd seen Orville running, for sure, but I guess he didn't have no idey who it was. I didn't of course know whe'er he'd seen me or not. He never did look in my direction. But I just had a notion, from the way he strode along there, and from the way he yelled, like he wasn't only feeling sure and firm on his own land and dead certain of his rights over trespassers, but like this was something Amon Lamb had stirred up, and now, at long last, like he had Amon Lamb right where he wanted him and just couldn't wait to hang the hooks to him. Looked like he was so cockeyed sure of it that he never even stopped to consider the danger he might be running into. And he must've heard the shots before. I didn't see how he could've failed to.

Orville had already charged up to the top of the dam when he first heard Haley. He whirled around, seen him, throwed hisself stretched on the ground and taken his time about aiming, with Haley coming on ahead like nothing was happening.

I had time to yell out twice, at the top of my voice, "Watch out, Haley! Watch out!"

But I'm satisfied Haley never did hear me at all, with the wind so high at that minute and blowing across the distance between us.

It wasn't but a couple of seconds anyway before Orville got a bead drawed on him and in that couple of seconds Haley hadn't let up nor turned aside one step.

The rifle went off loud. Haley kind of half spun around, like you'd batted him one good and hard on the right shoulder, and then flopped out on the ground.

Silence, even down to the wind, seemed to fall all at once. There was Haley still as death on the ground. There I was alone in easy reach of a crazy killer who'd probably heard me yell. And now they wasn't even my enemy's house to run to. Gil Blair's place wasn't too far off, but it was too much in the open for me to ever hope to make it.

I just froze, the worst possible thing I could've done, behind that blackjack tree. I felt like everthing in the world had turned inside out. This was some crazy dream of that very day months ago—might near a year ago—when I'd hid behind this same tree thinking Haley couldn't see me, when he really did. And there was Haley out there again, just like then, only dead probably. And that meant they was no way out of it. Soon I'd be dead too. And maybe his ghost would be out there in the pasture looking up this way at my ghost.

But I seen worse than ghosts. I seen bloody death and bloody abortion in front of my eyes. I seen Ellen still and cold and drained of all her blood in pools around her. I seen what would've been our child all mangled up and blood-covered because crime had reached in and tore it out of the womb. I seen myself dead in my own blood. I remembered the tomahawk and the blood it had shed right here in the Indian massacre. I remembered the blood I'd imagined that day when I was down in the well trying to save Ike's boy, the blood I'd pictured running down the dark walls of the well and into the water around the snake that was maybe swimming there. My heart and my hands all of a sudden just ached for that tomahawk. Like if I had it I could save us all. But it was at the bottom of the well and gone forever.

But I'll swear if Orville wasn't acting crazy sure enough now. He didn't bother to go towards Haley, was sure he'd killed him, I guess. But he didn't give hisself time to think, neither, that I was likely running for help in the direction Haley had come from and how easy it might be now to cut me off before I could get there. He still thought I'd taken off for home, hadn't heard me yell, I suppose, or got my yell mixed up with Haley's.

Anyway what he done was jump up and take off for the edge of the woods away across from me! Then he commenced to stalking along the first trees there. I think he must've felt so certain of hitting anything he shot at now, after Haley was such a easy mark, that he never took no thought at all. Because the way he was going about it I would've seen him long before he seen me if I'd been over there, and all I'd've had to do was step out of his way.

With him never looking behind him, that give me time to sneak back down to where Haley was laying. He was sprawled out, dead-still, kind of on one side. I wanted bad to do something, check at least to see if he was alive. But they wasn't no time right then. I just made a grab for Haley's rifle, never so glad to get my hands on a gun in all my life, snatched it up and skipped off a few yards and flung myself down behind a pile of bulldozed timber. It wasn't nothing, that gun, only a little old twenty-two target, but at least it was something.

Lucky for me, I never did have to make no use of that gun in that spot. While I watched him, Orville pussyfooted on around the edge of the woods for a ways, still never looking back. Then finally he went out of sight in the woods going in the general direction of my house.

Again the thought of Ellen and Ma and Pap taken charge of me in the wildest way. And there was Haley Blair laying dead or at death's door just a little ways from me. I had to make a run for home. I had to, but my legs went so weak at the very idey of another two-mile run that I didn't think I could hardly even get started, let along ever make it there in time.

But what was I thinking about! Of course. It wasn't no long way to Gil Blair's. They'd be help there. Some of them could tend to Haley while the rest of us struck out in their car for my house, sure to get there long before Orville could ever make it afoot.

So I made a run for Gil's, but even before I was halfway down through his orchard I seen him and some of his boys coming towards me, all of them carrying guns: they'd heard the shots, it turned out, and was coming over to see what was the matter. When I come up and told them what was up, they went to scurrying around sure enough. Gil and one of his boys went down to take care of Haley. Me and the two oldest ones run back and got their car and we lit out around the road towards home. We might have ever advantage now, but they wasn't no time to waste....

But then, as it all turned out, our big hurry to rescue Ellen and Ma and Pap was all for nothing. Orville was done taken care of by the time we got there. Pap, you see, had heard the first shot Orville fired at me, over there by the graveyard. That telephone I mentioned a while back, we'd finally got it installed in the house just the day before. Boy and howdy, it sure did come in handy! Ellen didn't do nothing, right before she fainted, but to call the law. Pap he run out with his shotgun. But he just seen Orville as he taken off to chase me, and they wasn't nothing he could do but stay there and do the best he could to defend the womenfolks. One good thing for their peace of mind, if you could call it that: they thought I must've had my pistol.

And the laws come, all right, just as soon as they could make it out from town, a whole bunch of them. They commenced to staking out little groups up and down the road and they sent a couple of parties off into the woods. Besides that, they put two or three police cars to running up and down the road between my house and Haley's, inspecting everthing that moved. But still Orville missed running into any of them, on his way back through the woods. He come out in the county road right below our house before he knowed they was after him. He lit in to shooting at the laws, and got one of them in the foot before they brought him down—and they brought him down dead....

Later on that day the south wind got up even higher. You could hear a big gust of it rushing through the timber a half a mile off before it come whirling in singing around your ears and filling your nose with the sweet dry springtime. I had the hope, right then, that the wind'd blow high for days on end. I feel like, still, that whatever born days I've got left on this earth I'll never have enough of a welcome for the blowing of the wind.

Now like I say, Ellen passed out the minute after she called the law. Ma stayed right over her, brought her to, kep her as quiet as she could. Ellen did have a few labor pains, but they dwindled right off without any miscarriage.

And then, Haley wasn't dead, after all. He was hit in the shoulder and lost a lot of blood. But he wasn't awful bad hurt, as it turned out. Inside of a day or two he was out of danger and on his way to recovering....

Well! So! That's about the wind-up of it.

Only not quite.

The day before I begun writing this second part the baby was born: our strong and wonderful son, William Amon Lamb. Him being born, well that's the crowning touch on all that's taken place in just over a year. When I seen him and picked him up for the first time, it was a funny thing, but I knowed for certain then I ought to set down and finish telling my story.

So I reckon I have.

Or not quite yet, at that. I guess I ought to put in that things have about got back to normal here in the community. Most of my neighbors appear to look on me now about like they used to before all this blowed up. Even old Haley Blair, I catch him looking at me kind of hang-dog ever once in a while. Why, we even nodded and spoke at preaching the other Sunday, but not like we was long-lost brothers by quite a bit.

So yes, back to normal, I say. But then really, no matter how anybody looks on me, I ain't the same as I was and never will be. I've landed somewhere I never could've gone to if I hadn't've been through what begun a long time ago and come to a head during this past year. Anytime I shut my eyes I can still see it all rise up before me. I can drift away back yonder to the baptizings by Parson in the young green grass, to that thicket below the swimming-hole, to Mary or Sherry in the dusty sunlight, to the coursing of the bees just last spring that led me to the old house-place and the tomahawk and the old well. And in there somewhere beside it all is that great big gravestone reaching up into the windy sky as high as any temple.

When it's all said and done, how glad I am I tempted God by leaping....

But just how can you ever finish up your own story anyhow? I suppose that's why the idey still comes to me, now that I've wrote it all out, that maybe I should just throw all these tablets in the fire and live life as it comes and forget telling any story about it, even to myself. It's done served its purpose, what I've wrote, and as far as that goes, I'm satisfied I'll never even read it over again.

But they's one matter that stops me. I just now finished doing what I always said I'd do: I dug Grandpa's old tablets out of my trunk and I read them, dim and fleeked up as they are. As I went I naturally compared them to mine. I figure he must've been a whole lot like me. I think of him deep when I hold his tablets out before me. And when I stand by the cradle I think of him being near.

So no. What I'll do with these tablets is what he done with his. I'll stick them in the bottom of a trunk and let them age according to their own fashion. If my son or some of my grandchildren ever come across them and put a value on them, well and good. If they don't, if all these pages still end up in the fire someday when folks're cleaning out all the musty old trash left by generations dead and gone, also well and good. It don't concern me. My life concerns me. What started out to be the worst year of my life, so far, has come out to be the finest. Writing about it as I went helped me to make it the finest. But the writing's turned into a record now, and the record don't belong to me. Just my life belongs to me. If anybody else ever happens to pick up the record and read it, why it belongs to them.

ABOUT THE AUTHOR

L. D. Clark was born and raised in Cooke County in the Cross Timbers country of north Texas that provides the setting for his fiction. After Clark published his first novel, *The Dove Tree,* in 1961, his longtime interest in the works of D. H. Lawrence prompted him to produce two volumes of criticism: *Dark Night of the Body* (1964), and *The Minoan Distance* (1980). L. D. Clark has also edited the *Civil War Recollections of James Lemuel Clark* (1984), and his definitive edition of Lawrence's *The Plumed Serpent* is forthcoming from Cambridge University Press. Among L. D. Clark's many honors and awards are a William Bayard Cutting Traveling Fellowship (1960-61), a Ford Foundation Publication Grant (1964), a Fulbright (1973-74), and a PEN/NEA Syndicated Fiction Award (1983). L. D. Clark is married to the author/photographer LaVerne Harrell Clark. They live in Tucson, Arizona.

Cover Photo by the Author
Book Design by Andrew Caldwell
Typesetting and Production by Marilyn Heath and Radford Parsons
Set in English Times Roman type by Confluence Typesetting